CASTLE BREACH

CASTLE BREACH

A SGT. DUNN NOVEL

RONN MUNSTERMAN

CASTLE BREACH– A SGT. DUNN NOVEL

Copyright © 2017 by Ronn Munsterman
www.ronnmunsterman.com

Published in the United States

Cover Design by David M. Jones
www.beloeil-jones.com

Printed in the United States of America
10 8 6 4 2 1 3 5 7 9

ISBN-13: 978-1544046181
ISBN-10: 1544046189

BISAC: Fiction / War & Military

Acknowledgments

To you, Dear Reader, thanks for going along with me on Tom Dunn's journey. I love hearing from you. My email address is in the Author's Notes.

This past December, on the 75th anniversary of the deadly Pearl Harbor sneak attack, we honored and remembered those who died there. January 25, 2017 was the 72nd anniversary of the conclusion of the Battle of the Bulge. The history of war is filled with great battles, tragedies, heroism, and sacrifice. Thank you to the men and women who have served, past and present, so others can live free.

I write these books because of my love for WWII history. Every book I read about WWII teaches me new things. The more I do read, the more I realize how much I *don't* know. Nevertheless, I continue to read in the quest of a more complete understanding of the war. I confess, too, that I'm always on the lookout for a nugget of information that might turn into a Sgt. Dunn book.

Thank you to David M. Jones (Jonesy's namesake), who, *again*, took an image right out of my head and created an awesome cover. His addition of the full moon enhances it beautifully. This is his sixth cover for the Sgt. Dunn Novels. His website is on the copyright page.

Thank you to my FIRST READERS. I gave them a seemingly impossible deadline and they came through with super flying colors so I could get this book into your hands sooner.

Zander Jones (Jonesy II)
Steven D. White
Steven B. Barltrop
Robert (Bob) A. Schneider II
Nathan Munsterman
John Skelton
David M. Jones (Jonesy)

Thank you to my friends Dave J. Cross and Derek Williams for their encouragement and friendship over the years. Thank you to my wife for her terrific help with the manuscript. My Author's Notes are at the end of the book. Please don't read ahead because it contains spoilers.

To those who left,
but
never came home.

CASTLE BREACH

Chapter 1

SS Headquarters
Former residence of the Mayor
Preveza, Greece
29 September 1944, 0137 Hours

Hauptsturmführer, SS Captain, Bertram Deichmann seated himself in a beautiful, scrolled wood chair behind an ornate table. Across from him was a Greek man in his thirties. A gold-trimmed white phone was positioned between them. Incongruously, next to the white phone sat an old black one with scratch marks, evidence of age and rough treatment. Its black wire exited from the rear like a bizarre mouse tail and snaked across the floor and into another room for the connection. It was not the usual occupant of the table.

The captain pushed a piece of paper across the table in front of the Greek.

In better than passable Greek, the captain said, "Word for word, that's all you have to do."

Stelios Pavlou's black hair fell over his forehead. He was sweating heavily, his shirt was soaked through. His dark eyes darted furtively at the piece of paper, then back at the captain.

"Take it and read it out loud. For practice."

Pavlou reached a trembling hand toward the paper.

Also in the spacious living room of the former mayor's house were a half dozen black-uniformed SS men, one lieutenant and the rest, sergeants. They were all armed with the MP40 submachine gun, which they each held rather haphazardly. Where was the Greek to run?

Curious, thought Pavlou, *the captain has not drawn his handgun.*

He picked up the sheet of paper and it flapped as his hand shook. He grabbed it with his other hand to try and steady it, but that just made it worse as both hands were shaking the paper. Both of his wrists bore the unmistakable signs of being bound tightly together for an extended period of time, red lines and chaffed skin.

He read the message silently and groaned.

"Out loud now," commanded the captain. He also was wearing the SS black uniform, but unlike Pavlou, he was not sweating profusely.

Pavlou read the message, halting every so often when his voice involuntarily hitched in his throat.

"That's not going to do, *Herr* Pavlou. Colonel Doukas must believe you are telling the truth. Completely. Otherwise, our agreement will be null and void."

Pavlou's eyes widened in a deep rooted panic. "Please, don't hurt my family!"

The captain shrugged. His blue eyes looked down his thin, aquiline nose at a terrified Pavlou. "Then do your duty."

Pavlou had been captured by the SS nearly eight hours ago, before dinner. They'd grabbed him before he made it home for the night. He had to assume someone had informed on him. What else could it be? He'd resigned himself to his fate. He believed he would never see the coming sunrise, but if he could save his three teenaged girls and wife, so be it. But the cost. Oh, the cost to the Greek Resistance on Greece's west coast, off the Ionian Sea. He was privy to basic information that an attack was in the works, and he was supposed to provide intelligence to the leader of the unit which would be making the attack, Colonel Doukas. He quickly reread the paper silently again, forming the words with his lips as if whispering them. He'd always gotten into trouble in primary school when he would read like this. He'd finally broken the habit at age eight. It seemed oddly comforting to know that at the end of his life he had reverted to such a younger version of himself.

He took a deep breath and read the message out loud. This time it was perfect, or at least the SS captain seemed to think so.

The captain checked his watch: 1:45 a.m. "It's time. Dial the number."

Pavlou picked up the white handset, putting it next to his ear and mouth. He heard the dial tone and dialed a number using the rotary dial.

The captain picked up the black phone's handset and put the earpiece next to his left ear. He covered the mouthpiece with the palm of his other hand.

The phone call was answered on the other end after just two rings.

"Yes?"

"I have information for my friend," Pavlou said, and he gave the proper code words. He wished they had created a duress code word. Too late.

"One moment."

A few seconds passed and another voice said pleasantly, "It's nice to hear from you, my friend."

"Good to hear your voice. I have something to tell you."

"By all means, I'm all ears."

Pavlou read the message, trying to not sound like he was reading it. After the last sentence, he said, "That's all I have."

"This is very good, thanks. It was nice to hear from you. Best of luck."

"Best of luck to you, too."

Pavlou hung up the phone as did the captain.

Pavlou looked at the captain forlornly.

"Don't look so glum. You did well. Your family is safe. I'm a man of my word."

Pavlou closed his eyes as tears of relief began to roll down his cheeks.

The captain flipped open his holster with his right hand and drew his Luger. "Open your eyes," he demanded.

Pavlou opened his eyes and found the enormous black hole of the gun's barrel staring at him from a meter's distance. He swallowed reflexively and thought he was about to urinate. Was it true that men vacated their bowels and bladder after dying?

"I'm a practical man, too. Pragmatism is my personal philosophy. I prefer making the most with what I have available." He waved his other hand around to include the SS men around them. "I use these men to the best of their abilities and select them for certain tasks depending on what skills they have to offer me. I think *you* have much to offer me, *Herr* Pavlou."

Pavlou blinked a couple of times, trying to come to grips with the possibility of living.

"I would expect you to make yourself available to me or my men at a moment's notice and to follow our instructions to the letter." He returned his pistol to its holster.

"You're letting me live?" Pavlou's voice was barely a croak, but the captain understood the words.

"For as long as you obey."

"But I just gave Colonel Doukas false information. When the . . . the event happens, he'll know I lied. He'll kill me to make an example of me."

The captain smiled. "Not at all. I will arrange for your supposedly trusted source to be killed. You simply explain that it was you who were betrayed first. That you took the information at face value."

Pavlou nodded, anxious to find a solution. He looked away thinking. Could he be a traitor to the cause? If it kept his family alive, yes. Or perhaps there would be a way to play the Germans at their own game. Maybe feed them useless information from time to time. Yes, perhaps that would work.

Pavlou looked back at the captain and was rewarded with a chilling smile. One that made the hair on his neck stand up.

"I know what you're thinking. You could work against us in little ways. Perhaps you could and you might even deceive us for a long time." He shrugged. "Or perhaps not. Are you willing to risk your daughters' future for the cause?" He smirked and said, "They are such pretty teenaged girls, aren't they? Your wife, too."

Pavlou's heart seemed to stop. He began shaking his head and moaned, "No, no, no . . ."

Deichmann slapped the Greek to shut him up.

"You see, I am right. One attempt to deceive us will ruin your family. Everyone. And afterward we'll kill you. This I promise you." The captain gave another chilling smile. Pavlou believed every word he said.

"I'll do it."

"Of course you will."

The captain stood up.

Pavlou rose slowly on shaking, unsteady legs.

Hauptsturmführer Deichmann stuck out his gloved hand. Pavlou hesitated, but shook it briefly.

"Two of my men will take you close to home and let you out so you can walk the rest of the way. This will allow you ample time to mull over your . . . predicament."

"Yes, sir," Pavlou said. He turned and walked toward the door, one SS soldier in front and one behind him.

Just as they reached the door and the lead soldier opened it, the captain called after them.

"*Herr* Pavlou?"

Pavlou stopped and turned around, sure he was about to be killed after all.

"A word of advice. I always keep my promises."

Pavlou nodded and stepped through the door picturing his family.

A half hour later he opened the door to his small home in the hills of Preveza. The house was completely silent, as it should be a little after two in the morning. He removed his shoes and walked quietly to the bedroom where his three daughters slept. He pushed the door open and stood in the doorway staring at the loves of his life.

His eyes filled with tears and he quickly closed the door.

He practically ran into the living room so his sobs would wake no one.

RONN MUNSTERMAN

Chapter 2

Hohenstein Castle
24 kilometers South-southeast of Salzburg,
Austria
29 September, 1330 Hours, Salzburg time

The castle was so high up the mountain, it could be seen from thirty kilometers away on a clear day, like today. It was situated on a very large outcropping on the mountain's eastern slope, so there were three sides going down to the bottom of the valley, and the west end met the upslope rising toward the mountain peak a thousand meters above.

Standartenführer Frederick Neubart, an SS colonel, was in charge of the castle and the SS garrison stationed there. It was normally a stress-free assignment, being in western Austria, far from any actual fighting. Most often, Neubart concerned himself with what he was going to have for dinner on any given night, or who he might invite to dinner from amongst the top echelons of Austrian society. On occasion, all-day meetings were held and the attendees typically included those from the Austrian Nazi Party, and the Austrian government, which amounted to the same thing. The castle's cooking staff was considered to be among the best in the country, most stolen away from the finest restaurants in Salzburg.

Sometimes, *Reichsführer* Heinrich Himmler would arrive for a few days to conduct meetings for his favorite SS members. Thus the stress of the day. Himmler was arriving in a few days—at least he'd given some advance warning—and Neubart was busy working out the details. Himmler's news also said two other guests of note were coming: Martin Bormann, Hitler's private secretary and the man who controlled access to the *Führer*, was also to arrive, and the *Führer* himself. Hitler had never been to the castle, even though his vacation home, the Berghof, was only seven miles away in southeastern Germany. Neubart was extremely worried that nothing would meet with the great man's approval.

Neubart practically ran through the main entrance hall, which was thirty meters in length by ten wide. The ceiling was ten meters above his head and four gold chandeliers hung equidistant from each other along the center line of the room. They were unlit and sunlight for the beautiful room shone through the windows on the south side of the room. The walls were vertical planks of ancient walnut. Paintings by various eighteenth century masters were hung with precision on the walls as were colorful tapestries.

Neubart typically paused to admire the art when moving through the hall, but today, he was focused on the job, the monstrous job, of preparing for the arrival of the German State's top officials. No time to enjoy much of anything. He was searching for someone, his very able and efficient aide.

He reached the end of the massive room and burst through the three-meter-tall double doors, also walnut, and entered a small hallway, only three meters wide, which led to the inner workings, the hidden work areas of the castle, his office, the kitchens, maintenance, housekeeping, billets for the SS guards, and other offices for those whose jobs entitled them to large work spaces. About half way down the hallway, he stepped through an open office door and said, "Seiler, I need you."

SS Major Obert Seiler looked up from the papers he was reading on his desk and examined his new boss. The overweight

Neubart's face was flushed from the exertion of running more in the last five minutes than in the last year.

"How may I assist you, my Colonel?"

Major Obert Seiler had neatly trimmed blond hair, blue eyes, and a strong jawline. Tall and strong, he had all of the attributes needed to be the perfect Aryan poster boy. He spoke German like someone from Berlin. Except he was not. Neil Marston was from London's West End and had been recruited from his English linguistics professorship at Oxford by MI5 in 1939. He'd spent nearly four years in Berlin as a British spy. His current assignment began a month ago when he'd been returned to Germany as a member of the SS with papers and a solid legend.

A local man from the nearest village, who hated the Nazis, had been reporting the goings on at the castle to a handler. London had decided it would be worth inserting an agent into the castle just to see what, if any, information could be gleaned from the people who moved in and out of it all the time.

According to his legend, Marston was single, both parents dead, the father killed in action at the Battle of the Somme, in late summer 1916. The mother died of typhoid in 1919, leaving a twelve year old boy to fend for himself. Marston's story said he'd been adopted by a German officer and his wife. The officer had been wounded in such a way as to prevent ever fathering a child. The boy attended school in Berlin and went on to college. During his senior year, both adoptive parents had been killed in a car wreck. After graduating from college with a degree in business, he'd gone to work for a small company in Berlin. Things had supposedly gone well for him, but when 1939 came, he decided to try for the SS, even though the entrance requirements were more stringent than for any other military services in the Wehrmacht. His papers said he'd been an excellent cadet and throughout his career had done well in his administrative duties, earning promotions along the way.

He ended up at the castle when he arrived with papers saying he'd been recommended by his current boss in Berlin as a replacement for Neubart's aide. The previous aide had the misfortune of dying on his annual vacation trip. His sailing boat capsized in high winds and he drowned in Lake Neusiedl located forty-five kilometers southeast of Vienna. His boating partner survived, but then disappeared before the police could question him. By now, he would be back in London.

Marston's legend background included that he was a student of history particularly of the Aryan Race. His interest in the castle was purely in the sense of how it related to modern Germans. Marston had done some research while in Berlin and had indeed located a family line that extended back to Austria and to the castle, the Bierschbachs. He planned to continue his research while there. He was sure the work would satisfy the commandant, but Marston was becoming more and more interested just out of plain old fashioned curiosity. He was developing a need to know who these people were.

Marston was unaware of the murder of his predecessor, and only knew what everyone else knew, a tragic boating accident cut short the life of a good young German.

His timely arrival was met with immediate approval by Neubart and they hit it off. Marston excelled at anticipating what Neubart would want done and many times, when his boss asked for something to be done, Marston could report it was already done.

"I've just found out that Hitler, Himmler, and Bormann are coming in just two days' time! Two days! We have so much to do."

In a very calm voice, Marston replied, "Sir, why not have a seat? I'll get us some coffee and we can work through an initial plan." Marston waved his hand toward a 17th century wooden high-backed chair in front of his desk.

Marston got to his feet quickly and moved around the desk to stand behind Neubart. "Your jacket, sir?"

Marston didn't want to give Neubart extra time to go off in a panic.

Neubart nodded and unbuttoned the black SS jacket, and allowed Marston to remove it. While Neubart sat down, Marston walked over to a coat rack and hung up the jacket carefully. He moved to a small serving table where a silver pot and several china cups and saucers sat. Pouring a cup for the colonel, he added some cream into the black, steaming liquid, and two cubes of sugar. He stirred gently for a minute until the cream and sugar were blended properly. He poured himself a cup, black, and took both with him.

He handed the colonel his cup and saucer, the spoon lying carefully on the saucer, and sat down at his desk, putting his cup and saucer off to the left. He opened a side drawer and removed a notepad, which he placed in front of him. He pulled a gold fountain pen from its gold holder.

He wrote a couple of words on the pad, and looked at the colonel. "Arrival date and time, sir?"

"Sunday evening, eight o'clock."

Marston wrote that down. "Very good, that gives us more than forty-eight hours."

Neubart frowned. "You seem terribly calm in all of this. I'm wondering if you understand the enormity of our task."

"I understand your concern, sir. I function best employing a systematic approach to problem solving. While I may appear to be very calm on the outside, I assure you, though, on the inside, I am running at a hundred kilometers an hour."

This elicited a small smile from the colonel. "Yes, good to know."

"And remember, sir, we do have the best staff in all of Austria. The Austrians even say so themselves."

"Yes, that is true."

Marston wrote "guests" on the pad, and below it, listed Hitler, Himmler, and Bormann in a column.

"What other important guests will we be receiving?"

Neubart pulled a piece of folded paper from his shirt pocket and handed it across the desk. He stirred his coffee and took a sip. His face broke into a wide grin. "Perfect, Seiler, just perfect."

Marston nodded as he unfolded the paper. He read the names. He recognized a few of the ten names, a couple of Himmler's staff who he never traveled without, and Bormann's assistant. Eva Braun, Hitler's mistress, was not on the list. Marston gave a sigh of relief.

Neubart raised an eyebrow. "What?"

"*Fraulein* Braun will not be joining us."

Neubart rolled his eyes. "No, thank *Gott*. She can be so demanding, I hear."

"Yes, I have heard the same."

"I see a General Glockner on the list. Do we know anything about him?"

"No. I will send inquiries to army administration in Berlin. Hopefully, we'll hear back soon."

"There's another name I don't recognize and he doesn't have any affiliation listed." All the other guests had their job title or military rank next to their names. "Wilbert Juhnke."

Marston shook his head. "No idea. I'll find out."

"Yes. Very well."

Marston wrote all of the names and their information on his notepad and handed back the colonel's note paper.

"I know the meal will be a big concern due to the *Führer's* preferences. I'll take care of coordinating the menu with our chef and the *Führer's*," Marston said.

"Oh, thank you. I know he loves *Leberknödl*."

Marston nodded and made a notation on his paper. "Liver dumplings. Not exactly vegetarian, sir. Is this an exception? Never mind, his chef will know."-

"Yes, good."

The men worked for another thirty minutes before agreeing they had a good start. They divided up the tasks and agreed to meet the next morning after breakfast.

Marston put his notepad away and slipped the pen back in the holder. He gathered his and the colonel's empty coffee cups, and saucers and laid them on the serving table. He removed the colonel's jacket from the coatrack and helped the man put it back on. They shook hands warmly and the colonel left, walking much slower, and apparently feeling much better about the next two days.

Marston sat back down at his desk and checked his watch: fifteen past two. Dinner would be at five p.m. He would work on the special event until then. After dinner, after dark, he would leave the castle for his evening walk in the countryside. A daily occurrence he'd started on his first day to get the guards used to his routine and to let them get to know him personally.

Cultivating friends.

Spies who made friends had a tendency to survive.

Chapter 3

Star & Garter Hotel Restaurant
Andover, England, 60 miles southwest of London
29 September, 1800 Hours, London time

The Star & Garter Hotel's restaurant was already packed with its Friday night crowd. Technical Sergeant Tom Dunn and his wife, Pamela, had decided to invite Dunn's seven squad members to their two-month anniversary dinner. Pamela had called ahead and requested a table for nine.

As the U.S. Army Rangers milled around the tables pushed together next to the windows, Pamela helped quickly arrange the men's seating. The soldiers, all wearing their American army uniforms, were behind their respective chairs, and Pamela behind hers. The soldier on her left, Al Martelli, pulled out Pamela's chair and helped her get closer to the table when she sat down.

Over her shoulder, she gave Martelli a radiant smile and said, "Thank you Al."

"You're welcome, Mrs. Dunn."

"Call me, Pamela."

"Of course, Mrs. Dunn," replied Martelli with a grin.

Martelli was an Italian Bronx boy through and through. He was wiry and tough, and had first joined the squad on a mission to Italy as a translator, borrowed from another squad. Events of that mission had cost Dunn three men killed and one who lost a leg. He had requested that Martelli be permanently assigned to his squad upon returning to England.

The men sat down and glanced around at each other.

Pamela was in the middle seat with the High Street window behind her. The setting sun shone through her blond hair, forming a halo effect. Tom Dunn was directly across from her and his mouth dropped open, as it was often wont to do at the sight of her. None of the men noticed his expression because they were all watching Pamela, mesmerized by her beauty, her hair, fair complexion, and killer blue eyes. She wore a light pink dress, which accented her skin color, and a thin silver necklace adorned her throat.

She looked at her husband and smiled. She gave him a little wink and he closed his mouth.

The men saw the wink and turned as one to look at Dunn. More than one of them thought he was the luckiest son of a bitch in the world.

Dunn winked back at Pamela.

"Gentlemen, thank you for joining Pamela and me for our two-month anniversary dinner. We wanted to share this moment, and give Pamela and you a chance to get to know each other."

Some of the men had attended the wedding, but didn't know Pamela well.

Sitting to Dunn's right, Dave Cross, who had been the best man, was smiling. Cross was originally from Maine where his father was a fisherman. Just prior to the war, he had moved to New York City in search of a life different from fishing on the Atlantic Ocean. His parents had been understanding and hadn't made an issue of it. Like Dunn, and many men his age at the time, he had gone down to the army recruiting office the day after Pearl Harbor. After nearly three years of war, all he dreamed about was returning to the Atlantic with his dad.

"Go ahead and open your menus. I know you're all starving."

"Too right, we are, Sarge," replied Stanley Wickham in his Brit-Tex accent. Growing up in east Texas had given him a good

Deep South drawl. Since his arrival in England, his speech pattern had slid into a blend of British and Texan. He'd discovered early on that the local girls loved how he talked and he was not stupid. The only time he turned it off was when under heavy stress. He was the second biggest man on the squad topping out at two hundred twenty pounds and six feet three.

Everyone laughed at Wickham's quip, but immediately opened their menus.

Two waiters—Pamela had arranged for this—came to take orders and the process went fast, always a good thing for hungry soldiers.

Sitting on Pamela's right was Bob Schneider, the only man bigger than Wickham at six four and two forty. He was the squad's radioman and also the German and French translator. Dunn had discovered on the squad's first mission into France back in June that he needed a translator. He'd asked his boss, Colonel Mark Kenton, to find one. Schneider was born in Texas but as an army brat had lived all over the country. His mother had taught him German and French starting at the age of four, thinking it would be good for his future someday. Although translating on a battlefield probably wasn't what she had in mind back then. He had unruly black hair, and brown eyes with sun or laugh crinkles in the corners. The biggest, but the youngest, he was only nineteen.

"Before we get too far along here, Pamela and I want to share some good news with you."

The men focused on Dunn as he spoke. All of the men trusted Dunn with their lives and would do anything for him, including die. Most had been with him about three months. Cross and Wickham were the only survivors of the original squad besides Dunn, proving that being an American Army Ranger was damn dangerous work.

Dunn reached across the table and took Pamela's hand. "We're expecting a baby," he said, with a grin that was part pride and part "golly."

The men jumped to their feet and cheered, which drew some startled glances from the other restaurant patrons. The men started clapping. Martelli shouted to the patrons, "They're having a baby! Give 'em a hand!"

The whole restaurant stood up and cheered and clapped. A baby was something special any time, but what with the war on, it was even more so. A cherished event to be celebrated.

After the applause dwindled to a stop, the men formed into a line. One by one they stepped next to Pamela and bent down to kiss her on the cheek. Pamela patted each man's arm as he passed by, tears of sudden emotion at their kindness rolling down her cheeks.

Next, the men shook hands with their boss and friend. Eventually, they all returned to their seats.

Pamela dabbed her cheeks with a handkerchief and she smiled at Dunn.

He had been completely surprised by the thoughtful behavior of his men and his face showed it. He looked around at his men, meeting each one's eyes. He found himself unable to speak.

Everyone at the table had ordered a brew, and Cross, sensing that his best friend was struggling with his emotions, stood up, raising his glass. "Gentlemen," a nod to Pamela, "and lady, a toast to Mr. and Mrs. Dunn and their coming bundle of joy."

Everyone touched glasses and said, "Mr. and Mrs. Dunn and their bundle of joy!"

Dunn had told Cross the news almost as soon as he found out, but had asked Cross to keep it quiet so he could make the announcement himself.

Rob Goerdt, sat at the end of the table between Cross and Martelli. When he joined the squad, he immediately became the bazooka expert. On the latest mission, he and his loader, the late Leonard Bailey, had destroyed seven Panzer IV tanks and captured three of the crews. He was the only other man on the squad from Dunn's home state of Iowa. While Dunn was from Cedar Rapids, Goerdt hailed from Dyersville, a small town just over forty miles northeast of Cedar Rapids. He wore his light brown hair close cropped and he viewed the world through blue eyes that indicated his German heritage. All of the men knew he was a third generation American, and thought nothing of his heritage, especially since he'd proven himself with the tanks and on other missions.

However, German heritage did pose a serious threat to the squad on their most recent mission. They parachuted into

Germany to steal a train loaded with V2 rocket engines. Unknown to them, their most recent addition, Konrad Griesbach, was a traitor who got them captured and nearly sabotaged the entire mission. Except for Dunn's quick thinking and reactions they might have been executed by the German *Sicherheitsdienst*, the SD, under Hitler's infamous Commando Order, or thrown into a German prisoner of war camp.

At the opposite end of the table, sitting across from each other were Dave Jones, known affectionately as Jonesy, and Eugene Lindstrom. Jonesy was the squad's sniper, using a 1903 Springfield with a Unertl eight-power sight. Jonesy's claim to fame was almost sniping Field Marshal Erwin Rommel as he drove back to his headquarters in France. An untimely attack by a British Spitfire had caused the staff car to crash just as Jonesy was squeezing the trigger. Dunn and everyone thought Rommel had been killed, and had been shocked to later learn he was recovering in a hospital. Jonesy was from the Southside of Chicago, a true White Sox fan, which often put him at odds with Dunn who loved the Cubs. Jonesy was a slender six-footer with dark brown hair. A widow's peak was centered over his sharp blue eyes. At twenty-three, he was a year younger than Dunn.

Lindstrom and Jonesy were inseparable. Lindstrom was the sniper's spotter and protector, always watching Jonesy's back when he was sighting on a target. Eugene Lindstrom had a sense of humor that may have started out as a childhood defensive shield because he was from Eugene, Oregon. He always told everyone his parents were either unimaginative or had a wicked sense of humor. When he turned eighteen in January, 1942, he'd enlisted the day after his birthday. He had missed Operation Torch by a few months, and had gone to North Africa several months after the invasion as a replacement.

The waiters brought out the meals and fresh pints of beer for everyone except Pamela who was drinking tea. Some of the men had chosen roast chicken and others a kind of Salisbury steak. Both entrees came with a few small potatoes. The group dug in and talk ceased for a few minutes.

Dunn swallowed a bite and said, "Jonesy, I saw a newspaper from two weeks ago. My Cubbies are only ten games under five hundred. Do you know how far the Sox are down?"

"Nope, Sarge. But I think you're about to tell me."

"I am. Twelve under. On the other hand, though, you're only thirteen and a half out of first place behind the Yankees. We are behind the damned Cardinals thirty-two games. Those bums are gonna win a hundred or more games again this year, mark my words."

Jonesy grinned and lifted his glass. "To everyone but the Cardinals!"

Everyone clinked glasses.

Pamela turned to Martelli and asked, "Al, what are you going to do after the war?"

"Probably work with my dad in the store. The grocery store. We live in an apartment above it. What are you and the Sarge going to do?"

"We'll go to the States. We think first to his hometown, Cedar Rapids. After that, maybe Chicago. I'm going to stay in nursing, although I'm pretty sure they'll make me take some classes to get my license over there."

"Wow, that's swell. My oldest sister is a nurse. Has been for five years. She works in surgery."

"Well that is quite something. It takes a very good nurse to get that assignment."

Martelli smiled at Pamela's compliment. He tipped his head toward Dunn and lowered his voice, "What's Sarge gonna do?"

"He hasn't decided. He might go back and finish his degree, but it might be different from the history degree he started with. We'll see."

Martelli looked off in the distance for a moment, then back at Pamela. "Mrs. Dunn, can I ask you for a piece of advice?"

"Pamela, please, Al."

"Hm."

"Sure, what's your question?"

"Uh, well, it's like this, you know? We were in Italy some time back. Am I allowed to say that? Oh, well," he laughed, "too late. Anyway. I met this woman there, Carlotta. She was," he paused as if at a loss for words.

"Beautiful?" Pamela coached.

Martelli nodded. "Yeah, beautiful, but something more. She had an aura about her. I could feel it when I was standing close to her. When we were about to leave, she came up and kissed me right here." He touched his lips. "She said to come back some day and visit."

"What's the problem?"

"I'm twenty-four, same as Sarge."

Pamela nodded. "I see. She's older. How much?"

Martelli nodded glumly and shrugged. "Ten years, maybe a little more."

"Al, if she kissed you and told you to come back, she meant it. I doubt your age difference matters to her."

"Hm," Martelli said, still not convinced.

A light bulb went off for Pamela. "She has children."

"A little girl, Marie, who's nine and a son, Damiano, who's seventeen."

"You're worried they won't accept you."

"Yes," he replied softly.

Pamela squeezed his arm gently. "Trust me when I say this. Carlotta wants you to come back. She's already thought through the age difference and what her children will do. You should trust her, too."

Martelli's face brightened. "Really?

Pamela smiled. "Really. Go back after the war. As soon as you can. Find out if there's really something there for you. If you don't go, you'll never know."

"Thank you, Mrs. Dunn."

"You're welcome. And please, it's Pamela."

"Of course, Mrs. Dunn." Martelli gave her a grin.

"I give up," Pamela replied. But she smiled.

The group finished their dinners and the waiters came to remove the plates. They returned a short while later with fresh brews for the men, and warmed up Pamela's tea.

Dunn stood up and looked around at his men. "I want to say a few things. Thank you for sharing your evening with Pamela and me. We're grateful.

"I am proud of all of you. Thank you for being so good at your jobs. I would like you to raise a glass in memory of our men who haven't come back."

The men rose and lifted their glasses. Pamela joined them and raised her tea cup.

"Timothy Oldham, age twenty, Eddie Fairbanks, age twenty-one, Patrick Ward, age twenty-four, Danny Morris, age nineteen, Clarence Waters, age twenty, Leonard Bailey, age twenty-two."

Everyone clinked glasses again and drank to the men lost.

"And to Squeaky Hanson, who lost a leg saving a teenaged boy in Italy. May he recover and find a way to work his dad's farm again. I miss him calling me 'Dunny.' "

The men chuckled at this memory and clinked and drank again.

"That's all. Thank you."

Everyone sat down.

Martelli leaned toward Pamela. "Squeaky saved Carlotta's son, Damiano. He took a grenade in the boy's place."

"Oh, my God. What a brave man."

Martelli nodded

Schneider asked, "Sarge, when are we going to get replacements for Bailey and Griesbach?"

Griesbach, the traitor, had murdered Bailey and thrown his body off a speeding train. Dunn later fought him on the top of the same train, like in a western, and had tossed *his* body off the train.

"I don't know yet, Bob. Colonel Kenton is working on it, but we might not get anyone before our next mission."

"Do you know what the mission is?" Lindstrom asked.

"I'm meeting with the colonel tomorrow morning. I'll let you know ASAP after that."

The men nodded. This was the way it always worked.

Pamela gave Dunn a look that conveyed her fear. He reached across the table again and gently rubbed her hand.

She mouthed the words, "You come back to me, Tom Dunn."

He nodded and mouthed, "I will."

The group settled into multiple conversations between two or three people. About fifteen minutes later, the waiter laid the sizable check on the table next to Dunn. Before he could pick it up to examine it, Cross's hand darted out and grabbed it.

Dunn stared at his friend. "I was planning to get that."

Cross grinned. "Did you really think we would let you pay when we got to have dinner with Pamela? Especially after hearing your wonderful news?"

Dunn glanced around the table at his men, who were all grinning at him. He shook his head slightly. "No. No, I guess not. You guys are the best."

Pamela said, "Thank you all. It was wonderful getting to know you. Please come back safe." She looked across the table and said, "Take me home, Tom."

Dunn gave her a sly grin. The men would assume that meant what it sounded like, just a request to go home. But it had a deeper meaning. Whenever Pamela said that, she was sending code for 'I want you to make love to me. Soon.'

Dunn, not being dumber than a rock, stood up and said, "Whenever you're ready, dear."

RONN MUNSTERMAN

Chapter 4

Hohenstein Castle
29 September, 1930 Hours, Salzburg time

Neil Marston, still wearing his black SS uniform, put his peaked black hat with the silver skull and crossbones SS symbol on his head and snugged it in place. He cringed mentally every time he put the uniform on, but even more so when he saw the hat. The SS history was just too horrific. He prayed he never got used to it.

He unlocked and opened the heavy, eight-inch-thick wooden door leading to the castle's exterior grounds. He had to turn around and push on the door to close it again. He could barely hear the metal latch fall back into place on the opposite side.

Two SS soldiers stood guard outside the door, facing out. Their MP40 submachine guns hung by a sling across their chests. As Marston passed, they raised their hands in a Hitler salute, which Marston returned crisply.

Marston stopped and turned around to face the two men. "Josef, Hans. Good evening. How are you both tonight?"

Josef, the elder of the two, replied, "Loving our job every day, sir."

Marston laughed. A running joke started on his first night. He had said that to the guards in response to the same question. As he always did, Marston offered a cigarette to each man, who, to play the game properly, first shook his head, gave in and took it, and placed it carefully in a jacket pocket.

"Thank you, Major. For later, of course," Josef said.

Marston nodded. "Of course."

"Enjoy your walk, sir."

"I will. See you in a few hours."

Marston walked off, heading down the steep gravel roadway toward the first gate. The castle had three concentric rings of defensive walls around it. The distance between each ring was perhaps forty yards. The interior ring, the final defense, surrounded the castle which sat on the only flat space on the mountain's outcropping. On the south side of the castle where he was, Marston saw a flower garden near the wall, and just beyond that was an opening in the wall where one could stand and view the expanse of the valley five hundred yards below. It was said you could see almost twenty miles on a clear day.

Marston ignored the garden and continued on his way to the gate. The two guards there greeted him in a friendly manner. Why wouldn't they? He treated them with respect and kindness, something not all that common in their world.

The driveway wound down the mountain using switchbacks on the steepest areas. It was guarded by another six gates interspersed roughly evenly down the hill.

Each gate had its own peculiarity, a method of defense used since the fifteenth century. The first that Marston would pass through was really a short tunnel, perhaps ten yards long by five wide. The guards raised the thick iron gate by turning a large wooden wheel, not unlike one found on a ship's bridge. Marston passed through into the first section of the tunnel. The guards lowered the gate, trapping Marston between gates. It was impossible to raise more than one gate at a time due to interlocking gears above the tunnel where all the machinery was located. This meant the most an enemy could hope for, was to crowd as many soldiers inside and open the gates one at a time. Far too slow to generate any speed on an attack. No one in the history of the castle had ever attacked the castle directly. Not once.

The second iron gate opened and Marston stepped through. Finally, he was outside the first gate, nodding to guards on that side of the entrance. Six more gates to go, each with its own oddity of passage.

It grew dark as he walked through the woods bordering the driveway, so Marston pulled a torch from his jacket pocket and turned it on. He played it across the driveway in front of himself. As he rounded a left hand curve the moon, full tonight, shone its light on his path.

He made it through the rest of the gates and reached the level of the valley floor. The driveway curved left and went off to the east becoming a wider road that would turn south and lead to the village of Lacher. To the east and south, the valley's land was flat and devoted to farming. To the west, a rich forest covered the mountain. There were no vehicles on the road, important knowledge for Marston's true purpose for the walk.

Marston strode along briskly a few hundred yards and he came upon a farmer's access road on his left. It went north and was also bordered by trees. Marston always assumed someone was watching him from the castle, which was why he took exactly the same path every night, no variation. A man who was just out for an evening walk.

He wanted to stop and just take in the beauty that surrounded him. The moonlit mountain peaks, the northern peaks of a few still carried last winter's snow, which glistened a sparkling white. The air was unlike any he had ever experienced. It was cool and clean, and wildflower and conifer tree fragrances filled the air.

After another hundred yards, he slipped off the road and entered the forest where he found a hiking trail that went uphill at an angle to reduce the steepness of the ascent. He turned on his light again and climbed about fifty yards until he was deep inside the trees. On the left of the trail he spotted his landmark tree, a gnarled oak nearly two yards thick at the base. He turned to his right and marked off five steps, and knelt beside a fallen birch, its bark still a radiant silver.

He swept away some leaves and uncovered his waterproofed radio. He quickly raised the antenna and switched on the set. He covered the lens of his torch with a hand. He moved his forefinger over the lens and a sliver of light struck the dial. He turned the dial to the correct frequency; he never left it on the frequency in case someone stumbled across the hidden radio. Turning off the light, he picked up the handset, confident that the Germans weren't driving around in a radio detection truck.

"Blue boy calling Mother," he said, speaking in German.

An answer in German came immediately. "Mother here, Blue boy."

"Uncle John and closest family arriving two days. Recommend sending favorite family members to say hello."

"Understood. Will pass along your thoughts to the family. All our best, Blue boy."

"Blue boy out."

"Mother out."

The whole transmission had taken less than twenty seconds. Marston turned off the radio, replaced the handset in its cradle, and lowered the antenna. Last, he turned the dial to the left and let it land on a useless frequency. He shoved the radio back under the fallen birch tree and swept the leaves haphazardly back over it.

Now that he'd started the wheels turning in London, probably at 10 Downing Street, Marston reflected on what he'd just done as he walked back out of the forest. It wasn't every day you requested a kill team to come in and assassinate a country's leader.

Such is the world we live in, he thought. He didn't debate the moral point of view, after all the Germans themselves had tried to kill the lunatic as recently as the 20th of July. They'd almost succeeded, too. If not for the hand of fate in the guise of a general at the table who moved the bomb to the other side of a massive oak table leg, Hitler would have been blown to bits and the war would probably be over.

He made it back to the castle near the time he told the guards he would. He carried some long stemmed wildflowers he'd picked along the way using his torch, which he always did. Some were blue, some were yellow, and a third type looked like a daisy with a white petals and a yellow center. This time, he would give them to the ladies on the kitchen staff. Next time, the housekeeping staff. Never a particular girl, lest people talk. Drawing unnecessary attention to oneself was not on the to-do list for spies.

RONN MUNSTERMAN

Chapter 5

Employee cafeteria
Rock Island Arsenal
Rock Island, Illinois
29 September, 1:12 P.M, U.S. Central Time

Construction on the Rock Island Arsenal started in 1863, and when it first opened it was a prison for Confederate prisoners of war. Years later, it was converted to a weapons production facility in time for the Spanish-American War. It produced everything from small arms to World War I tanks. It was located on a Mississippi River island, which was two and a half miles long by eight-tenths of a mile wide. Bridges connected the island to three cities: one in Iowa, Davenport, and two in Illinois, Rock Island and Moline.

Tom Dunn's youngest sister, Gertrude, had a folded newspaper in front of her, her uneaten lunch to the side. Her attention was focused solely on the paper. She rolled a fountain pen between her fingers as she read the crossword clue, forty-one across: "murder" four letters.

"Oh, give me a break," she muttered, as she carefully wrote in capital letters: KILL.

She filled in the last answer and laid down the pen. She checked her watch. Seven minutes. She shrugged her shoulders. Not her best time, but good enough.

"You going to eat your lunch, Gertie?"

Gertrude looked across the table at her best friend and roommate, Margie Williams. Both women worked at the arsenal in the M1 assembly department. They were the only two at the table built for eight because they were taking a late lunch. They'd both started working at the Arsenal in August.

Gertrude was eighteen and had graduated from high school the previous June. She had light brown, curly hair that tended toward being disobedient. Her brown eyes resembled her brother's and father's, as did her long slim nose.

She pushed the New York Times from the previous Saturday to the side and pulled her lunch tray closer. As she ate and chatted with her friend, a man walked toward her. He stopped at the end of the table, a polite two feet away.

Gertrude noticed him.

He was wearing a dark suit with a white shirt and a black tie. His haircut was neat, not military short, but not long either. He had a plain triangular face, with deep set dark eyes over a wide nose.

"Hello," she said.

"Hello, Miss Dunn." He gestured toward one of the empty chairs. "May I join you?"

Gertrude glanced at Margie, unsure of what was going on.

"What's this about, Mister . . . ?"

"I'm with the government, Miss Dunn. I do need a moment of your time." He looked straight at Margie. "In private, please."

Margie's eyes narrowed and she started to say something, but Gertrude spoke first. "This is my best friend. You can talk to me with her here."

The man smiled, perhaps a bit condescending, Gertrude thought. "No. I cannot. Perhaps we should go to the office instead."

"Am I in trouble or something?"

He held up his hands, placating her. "Oh, I'm sorry. No, not anything like that at all." He dipped his head. "Please."

Gertrude tapped the table with her fingers for a few seconds. "Okay." She looked at Margie. "I'll talk to you later, okay?"

"If you're sure."

"I'll be fine." Gertrude looked at the man. "Won't I?"

"Yes, you will be fine."

Margie grunted, but got up, grabbed her lunch tray, and started to walk off. She stopped and turned back around. "Make sure you finish your lunch, Gertie."

"I will."

Gertrude motioned for the man to sit down across from her.

"Thank you," he said as he sat down. He eyed the crossword and reached for it. "May I."

Gertrude shrugged.

He pulled it in front of himself and leaned over to examine the puzzle. He sat back and pulled a folded newspaper from his inside suit jacket pocket. He unfolded his paper and laid the solution grid next to the puzzle Gertrude had just solved.

Gertrude ate more of her lunch, watching the man as he dutifully and methodically checked every one of her answers. It only took him a few minutes.

He looked up at her and said, "Perfect!"

"Yes. It always is. Why are you here, Mister . . . ?"

"Thompson. Philip." He held out his hand and she shook it. "You must enjoy solving these puzzles. Are there other kinds of puzzles you like?"

"I like math, algebra, geometry, and calculus."

Thompson frowned. "When did you take calculus?"

"I taught myself my senior year."

"You taught yourself calculus. Interesting."

Gertrude sat back and crossed her arms over her chest. "You better start explaining why you're here or I'm leaving."

"Please don't. This is extremely important for the war effort."

"What I do here is important."

He nodded enthusiastically. "I agree. But your puzzle solving skills are, um, rather rare. Anyone can assemble a rifle."

"That's insulting."

"No, it's the truth. We need your unusual skills."

Gertrude let out an exasperated sigh. "Who's 'we' for heaven's sake?"

He reached into another pocket and pulled out an ID wallet. He held it so she could read it.

"What's the Office of Strategic Services?"

"The OSS. We solve puzzles and fix problems."

"You want me to come solve puzzles for you?"

"Yes. In a manner of speaking."

"What manner of speaking? What kind of puzzles?"

"I cannot tell you that unless you agree to join us."

"You're recruiting me to join your OSS bunch, but won't tell me anything about it until I *do* join?"

Thompson grinned. "That's about it."

"I need to think about this."

"Certainly."

"If I say yes, then what?"

"We send you to training."

"Where?"

"I cannot tell you yet."

"Good Lord, what can you tell me?"

"Not much, I'm afraid."

"How long would I work for you?"

"The duration."

"I see. I need to talk to my family about this. When do you need to have an answer?"

"Sunday night."

"I'll be at my parent's house for Sunday dinner."

"Give me the address. I'll come by to get your answer."

Gertrude smiled. "Are you inviting yourself to our family dinner?"

Thompson's face reddened. "No, no. Not at all. Just tell me what time to come afterwards."

"Two o'clock." She pulled the crossword paper closer and in the margin wrote down her parents' address in Cedar Rapids. She pushed it toward Thompson, who picked it up and read it before folding and sliding it into his pocket.

"Why me? How did you find out about me and the crosswords?"

"One of the managers we know very well noticed you a few weeks ago and noted how fast you completed the puzzle. Usually around seven minutes, he told us. He assumed they were accurately done. My colleague and I will need to administer and grade a battery of written tests when we come on Sunday."

"You want me to take some tests?"

"Yes."

"What kind of tests?"

"The interesting kind."

She thrummed her fingers on the table again.

"What's the pay like?"

He looked around the cafeteria, which was empty except for themselves. "Far better than here."

"Would there be travel?"

"For training. After that, very likely you'll travel to a few places."

"Like where?"

"All in good time, Miss Dunn, all in good time."

"Anywhere warm in the winter?"

He shrugged.

"Be there at two, Mr. Thompson." She got up, grabbed her tray and walked away without looking back.

Thompson pulled out a small leather bound notebook. He flipped it open to a particular page. Gertrude's name and basic information was written on it, including her home address. He'd asked her for it so as not to spook her. People tended to get wound up when they found out someone knew things about them. He jotted down a note: how did we miss her knowing calculus? And then he wrote: likelihood of a 'yes' answer: 90%. He snapped the notebook closed and smiled as he stood up.

RONN MUNSTERMAN

Chapter 6

Camp Barton Stacey
2 miles northeast of Andover
30 September, 1030 Hours, London time

Dunn drove his Willys jeep along the roads winding through the army base. Barton Stacey was a new military base for the American Army, as were all the rest in England. Bases were built in weeks, not months, during the buildup for D-Day. Barton Stacey rested in the countryside between Andover and Whitchurch, small cities a few miles apart. Several farmers had been given deals they couldn't pass up for their land. Some grumbled, some didn't, but being pragmatists at heart, as farmers tended to be, they all took the money.

Dunn passed a couple of men he knew and waved at them as he roared by in second gear. The soldiers grinned and waved back. In addition to knowing Dunn personally, they knew his reputation, as did most of the men in the camp. Secret missions or not, the rumor mill was pretty accurate. Dunn got the job done, no pun intended. He solved problems faster than everyone else and came up with some rather ingenious solutions. Word had it that he'd single handedly set off a nuclear explosion at the Nazis' atomic bomb laboratory near Stuttgart a few months ago. Dunn denied it, of course. He also didn't mention the Medal of Honor his boss had pushed for. It sat in a box in his dresser at the Hardwicke farm, where he lived with Pamela whenever possible.

Born in Cedar Rapids, Iowa in 1920, Dunn was twenty-four, nearly an old man by war standards. He'd signed up the day after Pearl Harbor along with his friends from college, the University of Iowa, where he was a semester shy of earning his degree in history. His path took him to basic training, then training for *Operation Torch*, the invasion of North Africa. It was in the Kasserine Pass that he showed his superiors what he was made of. When his squad leader was shot and killed, Dunn took charge of the squad and they wiped out a German machinegun nest that had been mowing down Americans. He was promoted to sergeant and earned the Bronze Star. Shortly after, he was sent to the British Commando School, Achnacarry House, in Scotland. Eventually he was promoted again to staff sergeant, and joined the school as a trainer.

He met his current commander, Colonel Mark Kenton, there. Kenton was a major at the time and commanded a brand new Ranger Battalion, which participated in what became known as the Anzio debacle. In spite of the many troubles, Kenton and his battalion, and Dunn, proved their mettle. Kenton flashed some tactical brilliance that Dunn grew to admire, partly because it rode the narrow line between recklessness and daring. Kenton, in return, saw a shining star in Dunn, who never let him down, not once.

Kenton and Dunn were reassigned to Barton Stacey and the colonel was tasked with pulling together squads of Rangers who would carry out special, and naturally secret, missions wherever circumstances and intelligence dictated the need. In the span of four months, Dunn and his squad had gone on eight top secret missions.

Dunn stopped the jeep in front of the camp's administrative building, where Kenton's office was located. He got out of the vehicle and stretched his six-two frame. He wore his standard uniform, trousers legs bloused into highly shined combat boots, a soft cap, and his brand new Colt .45 automatic. He'd lost his previous one while fighting the traitor on top of a speeding train in western Germany. He'd been forced to kill the man, who had infiltrated the squad and sabotaged the mission, getting Dunn and his men captured by the SS. Dunn had taken out his interrogator and the guards, and the squad escaped to complete their mission. They'd captured ten V2 rocket engines and delivered them by the same train to Belgium, and flown with them to England.

The traitor had been from New York City. As a boy, he had attended a summer camp conducted by the Bund. It was there he murdered his first victim, another teenaged camper who'd angered him, by pushing him over a cliff. He gotten away with it by claiming the boy had fallen while exploring.

A recent investigation into his family due to his actions with Dunn's squad had uncovered their membership in the American Bund Party, the Nazi organization, going back a decade. The FBI had wanted to arrest the man's parents, but could find no proof they were involved in the soldier's plans, though the agent in charge said unofficially that he was certain the father and son had cooked up the plan to together. The Bund Party pretty much disintegrated following Pearl Harbor, with only a few die-hard members still spouting Nazi propaganda. With nothing to charge the parents with, the agent did the only thing he could. He told the father what he thought had happened and that he was going to be watching the son of a bitch.

Dunn climbed the stairs and entered the building, walked down the hallway and knocked on the door frame to Kenton's office. The colonel looked up and saw Dunn through the open door. He smiled and waved Dunn in.

Already seated in front of the colonel's desk was Lieutenant Samuel Adams, Kenton's aide.

Dunn saluted Kenton, who returned it with a snap.

Adams and Kenton rose to their feet and shook hands with Dunn.

"Good morning, Colonel, Lieutenant."

"Morning," replied both officers.

Everyone sat down. Dunn crossed his legs, holding his hat in his lap.

Kenton was forty years old and his black hair was starting to show some gray along the temple. He told people they were his sergeant stripes because his sergeants caused them. This was funny the first couple of times. Now it elicited groans, but that didn't stop the colonel. A short man of five-nine, Kenton surprised people the first time they met him because his voice was a deep rumbling bass.

He was from Kansas City, Missouri, growing up in the Westport area and he'd attended the fairly new Westport High School. He'd earned a place at West Point, which he thought was swell because both schools had "west" in their names. His son, Robert—Bobby—who was eighteen, had also earned a coveted spot, and had started the fall semester just a few weeks ago.

Adams was a slender man, nearly Dunn's height, but forty pounds lighter. He had a narrow face and a disarming smile.

"How's Pamela doing?" Kenton asked.

Dunn smiled. "She's doing well. Some morning sickness going on, but other than that she's fine."

"When is the baby coming?"

"May."

Kenton nodded. "Bobby's is the fifteenth. Maybe that'll be the day."

"Could be, sir. How's your son doing at West Point?"

"Settling in. Starting to realize just how hard it's going to be."

Dunn could see the pride in Kenton's eyes. Bobby would graduate in 1948. Dunn prayed the war would be over long before that.

"Glad to hear it."

Kenton opened a desk drawer and removed a brown folder, which he put on the desk.

"This mission is a bit different from the others. You're going to Greece, the west coast. You'll fly to Leuca, Italy on the coast of the boot heel and take a British sub from there at night. You'll meet the Greek Resistance near Kanali, which is almost two hundred miles northwest of Athens."

Kenton opened the folder and pulled out a map of Greece. It had a red circle on a spot on the west coast. "Here you go."

Dunn examined the map. Kanali was north a few miles of Preveza, which guarded the narrow passageway entering the twenty-mile-long Ambracian Gulf. When he looked up, he said, "So what's in Kanali?"

"The Germans are preparing to move north because they're trying to consolidate their forces in northern Greece to get ready for the Russian onslaught that's steamrolling through the Balkans. Target's actually in another small city farther north on the coast road. Kastrosikia is home to a huge German armory that the brass want destroyed so the Germans can't take anything with them. You'll go in and advise on and participate in the attack."

"I take it aircraft bombing is out of the question?"

"The bastards put the damn thing in the center of the city. No one wants to kill Greek civilians, especially when the Germans are obviously leaving."

"Any particular reason the Brits aren't taking this one?"

The British Army was already in Greece and it was considered to be their area of concern, as Churchill often said.

"No one available in time. Colonel Jenkins has everyone out and Saunders is about to leave."

Jenkins was Kenton's British counterpart who ran British Commando squads across the European Theater.

Kenton was not upset by Dunn's questioning of the orders. Their relationship was one of mutual respect and trust built over time. While Dunn was perfectly aware of the difference between his five stripes and the colonel's silver eagle, he always spoke his mind. Dunn knew and appreciated the colonel's honesty and true concern for Dunn and his men. They both understood the mission came first, but Kenton always took care of his men, and made sure they were recognized for their successes.

"Okay. When are we due out?"

Kenton smiled. "Yesterday." Before Dunn could say something smart, Kenton said, "Lieutenant Adams has the particulars."

Adams turned slightly in his seat toward Dunn. "The flight is almost fifteen hundred miles, which is at the edge of a regular C-47's range, so you'll take one with extra fuel tanks from Hampstead tonight sometime after sunset. After an eight or so hour flight, that should put you in Italy before sunrise local time.

"Make your way to the British Navy's port at San Cataldo and see a Captain Holcomb. He'll get you to the submarine, whose name I don't have. You won't leave Italy until sundown so the sub can ride the surface most of the way to make better time.

I estimated the sub's transit to Greece to be almost nine hours. So, sorry about the length of the travel."

"Don't worry about it, sir. You know the guys will just sleep the whole time. When they aren't eating that is."

The three men laughed, comfortable in each other's presence.

When the chuckles died down, Dunn asked, "Are we taking anything for the Resistance?"

"Good question, but no, I understand that they are heavily armed already. Just take what you think you'll need," Kenton replied.

"Will do, sir."

Adams said, "When you conclude your mission, get back to the coast where you landed. A sub will be there, probably the one that took you there. They'll begin checking for you between the hours of midnight and four a.m. that same night. They'll be there for three nights in a row. After that, I'm afraid you'll be in trouble, so don't miss the boat." He didn't smile as he said this. Extracting the squad after that could become a logistical nightmare and the colonel might have to call in a number of favors from all over the place.

"Got it, sir. Don't be late." Dunn asked Kenton, "Any chance of a Greek translator?"

"According to our information, the leader of the resistance you'll be meeting, Colonel Kozma Doukas, speaks English well. Some of his men are said to speak it also."

Dunn nodded. "Okay. He's going to be okay with taking my guidance on the attack?"

"I sure the hell expect him to. He's the one who requested our help."

"Understood, sir. Since we're leaving tonight, I assume we're not getting replacements for Bailey and Griesbach?" He practically spat out the last name of the traitor who had murdered Bailey and thrown him from the train.

"No. No one's available. Plus, I didn't think you'd be very open to new men right now if you didn't have more time to get to know them."

"I'm afraid you're right on target there, sir. Gonna be tough trusting new men for some time, I'd say."

Kenton nodded his agreement with Dunn's assessment of the situation. All three of the men felt that they'd somehow missed something and Bailey's murder haunted them.

"Anything else for me?" Dunn asked.

"Nope, that's it. Please give my best to Pamela."

"I sure will, sir."

"I heard you took the men to dinner. Nice touch."

"Thanks. We wanted to tell them about the baby. It was a nice time. I think the men really needed it. I know I sure did."

The men rose to their feet and exchanged salutes and said farewell.

As Dunn reached the door, Kenton called his name and Dunn looked over his shoulder.

"Be careful, Tom."

Dunn nodded. "Will do, sir."

RONN MUNSTERMAN

Chapter 7

On the coastal road
1/2 kilometer East-southeast of Kastrosikia,
Greece
30 September, 1245 Hours, Athens time

A haggard looking Greek man checked his watch and grunted. The Germans were late. Odd.

Kozma Doukas, a slender six footer, knelt behind a tree as he kept an eye on the road from the south, from Kanali. A former school teacher, Doukas was forty-one and had been a Resistance fighter since late summer, 1941, when he joined the *Ethnikós Dimokratikós Ellinikós Sýndesmos*, the National Republican Greek League, known more simply as EDES. Its leader was a former army officer with the unlikely name of Napoleon Zervas.

Doukas's eyes were light brown and he had long black hair under a Greek hat, and a full black beard at least twelve centimeters long. He didn't realize it, but he would have fit right in with soldiers of the American Civil War.

"Where are they? Why aren't they here?"

This impatience came from Doukas's second in command, Stavros Georgoulakos. Georgoulakos was twenty-nine and where Doukas was tall and skinny, Georgoulakos was short and broad, a powerful man with arms that could crush a man. They'd known each other since the beginning, and had both risen in the ranks, although Doukas rose slightly faster, possibly due to him being a dozen years older or more than most of the men.

Doukas held the rank of colonel and commanded the equivalent of a British company. Georgoulakos was a captain. Their complement was understrength at 152 men, but Doukas kept his structure intact with four platoons of thirty-eight men each. He tended to attack with three platoons, holding the fourth back in reserve. When necessary he would throw the fourth into action to force the issue on the battlefield or to shore up a sudden weakness. However, today, all four would be needed in the initial assault.

Doukas's home village, Limiri, was only seventy-three kilometers due east from the spot where he currently knelt. His wife of ten years and seven-year-old son still lived there, so far untouched by the German war machine.

Georgoulakos was also married with two children and a pregnant wife at home. He often said it was for them he fought. Not an uncommon sentiment.

When Doukas first joined EDES, they worked together with the larger, more dominant group, *Ethnikó Apeleftherotikó Métopo*, the National Liberation Front, called the EAM, against the Germans, but it wasn't long before their political differences got in the way. Simply put, the EAM were communists, and well, the EDES were not. A civil war broke out and both groups spent an inordinate amount of effort killing each other while the Germans and Italians occupied their country. They still fought each other whenever it suited their needs.

With the surrender of Italy in September, 1943, and the eventual departure of Italian troops from Greece, the Germans had been forced to occupy the territory left unguarded, the west coast. The Germans themselves had been making noises of departing in an effort to meet the onslaught of the Red Army. Which is what brought Doukas and his 152 men to the coastal road.

They were better armed than they'd been six months ago having conducted numerous successful raids on the German truck convoys. They had gathered weapons ranging from the Mauser rifle to the fear-inspiring MG42 machinegun to potato masher grenades to panzerfaust rockets, and the ammunition required.

"They will come soon. Don't worry. Our intelligence is accurate. You know Stelios Pavlou always has it right."

Georgoulakos frowned, still upset, but he stopped complaining. He'd learned to trust Doukas in spite of having his own ideas. Doukas expected him to play devil's advocate while planning a mission, but once the decision was made he was to support it, at least in front of the men. Georgoulakos had brought up a concern that the ambush was much too close to Kastrosikia, which was where the next attack would be in a few days against the large German supply depot there. The Americans were sending in some special troops to help with the tactics against a stationary objective. This was because Doukas and his men excelled at hit and run attacks against convoys and small German units, but had little experience at defendable buildings. Doukas wanted to make sure he understood the best way to conduct the attack. He saw it as the penultimate final poke in the Germans' eyes, adding insult to injury.

The terrain was perfect for ambushing a German convoy. The steep, winding road rose almost eighty meters over a distance of just one kilometer. The heavily laden trucks would be forced to use first gear most of the way up, keeping their speed down as a result.

Looking south, Doukas could see the beautiful blue green of the Ionian Sea in the near distance, and the deeper blue at the horizon, thirty kilometers away, Mount Stavrota rose almost 1,200 meters above sea level. The mountain was located in the center of the Greek island, Lefkada. Doukas climbed the peak in his youth and it was easy to recall the joy of that success and the view that was gorgeous beyond anything he'd ever experienced before or since.

Finally, large engine sounds drifted with the southerly breeze and Doukas knew it was almost time. He changed his focus to the road and spotted the first vehicle in the German convoy.

Experience told him not to raise his binoculars. The noontime sun would reflect off the lenses and alert the Germans.

Unsurprisingly, the lead vehicle was an armored halftrack, the well-known Sd.Kfz.251. This version of the mainstay of the German army had two MG34 machineguns, one facing front and one to the rear, each with an armored plate to protect the gunner. Typically, the Germans loaded ten men in the open-air back. At the moment, only the forward MG34 was manned. The rest of the convoy vehicles came into view one by one as they rounded a curve at the bottom of the hill, about a hundred meters away.

Doukas's men were positioned along the east side of the road behind him. They were uphill from the road, so they would have the height advantage and would be able to fire down into the vehicles. Coming from the south, the road formed four sharp curves, left, right, left, and right again, before straightening out to head north to Kastrosikia. Each platoon was positioned on the outside of the curve for the left handers, and on the inside of the curve for the right handers. This gave each attacking unit a field of fire along the entire arc of the curve, a distance of about thirty meters each. They would overlap each other creating some deadly crossfire. There should be about three or four vehicles in each field of fire. There were a lot of bushes and trees that provided excellent cover for the men.

"Let's go ensure the platoon leaders are ready, Stavros."

"Yes, sir."

The men backed away from their position in the bush they were using for cover and ran in the bent over position so well known by combat veterans. Doukas found the four men quickly and each man reported that his platoon was set to go. As he left each man, Doukas patted him on the shoulder.

"Take your position," Doukas said to Georgoulakos.

The captain replied, "Yes, sir." He ran off toward the platoon stationed on the fourth and last curve.

Doukas joined the platoon on the inside of curve number two, staying behind them about ten meters. From here, he had a clear line of sight to all four platoons, although the reason he'd sent Georgoulakos to the last one was that it was seventy-five meters away.

Doukas kept his eyes on the convoy. The halftrack came closer and closer and truck after truck came into view around the curve at the bottom of the hill. All of the trucks had their canvas tops in the rolled down position, hiding the cargo bay, but Doukas knew there were at least ten to fifteen men in some of them and supplies in the others.

As the halftrack passed by him, he could feel the rumbling vibration through the ground. The view into the back of the halftrack was unimpaired. Nine German soldiers sat on the benches that ran the length of cargo area on each side and the tenth was the one manning the forward MG34.

The halftrack continued up the hill and around the third curve. The curved roadway was completely covered by German vehicles, a total of ten, nine of them trucks. Doukas watched the halftrack slow even more as it entered the last curve, a very sharp right hander. He shifted his gaze toward the trees where the farthest platoon was located.

The halftrack moved out of his view when it made it almost all the way through the last curve.

A sudden trail of smoke indicated the launch of a panzerfaust rocket. A split second later, the halftrack exploded in a great ball of fire as the fifteen-centimeter-wide warhead roared through tracks and the armor plating below and behind the driver. Flaming, red-hot pieces of metal shrieked skyward. Some German soldiers were tossed far into the air, their tunics on fire. No one survived the blast.

Doukas turned to his left and the last truck in the convoy erupted in flame, another victim of the deadly rocket weapon. The German trucks were penned in by burning vehicles.

The distinct sounds of his unit's MG42s, a buzzsaw sound, tore through the air, and then individual rifles began firing. More panzerfausts claimed additional targets.

Several truck drivers jumped from their stopped vehicles and ran to the cover of the ditch on the west side of the road. Some of them began firing, but their view was severely hampered by the smoke from all the weapons fire and the burning trucks.

The Greeks began lobbing potato mashers and more explosions rocked the area.

Doukas, from a habit that had kept him alive for three plus years of combat, constantly turned his head like a radar unit, looking for new threats. As his gaze found the road to the south, his heart nearly stopped. A Panzer Mark IV rounded the curve and smoke bellowed from its rear exhaust stacks as it accelerated to run up the hill to join the battle. Soon, another tank's snout showed itself.

Doukas made a decision and bolted for the platoon closest to him. As he ran, motion from the north caught his eye and he came to a stumbling halt. He lifted his binoculars and stared as ten halftracks, each full of German soldiers, barreled down the road from Kastrosikia toward his men.

Too late he realized the trucks his men were attacking were decoys and actually empty except for the drivers. He looked south and a fifth Panzer joined the attackers from that direction.

The lead Panzer raised its turret slightly.

It fired.

The 75mm high-explosive round screamed overhead and exploded just fifty meters beyond Doukas and his two center platoons.

The former schoolteacher said, *"Gamó!"* Fuck!

From the north, the halftracks' machineguns opened up, raking Doukas's men, killing many outright, and wounding many more.

Caught in the German's terrifying crossfire, Doukas had one chance to save his men.

Chapter 8

Colonel Rupert Jenkins' office
Camp Barton Stacey
30 September, 1055 Hours, London time

"It only took overnight for the powers that be to conclude this was actionable intelligence," Colonel Rupert Jenkins began. "The overall goal still has support from the highest levels of government. Even if some think it is the wrong thing to do."

Jenkins was a tall, thin man, with a face and nose that matched. He was forty-two and had missed the Great War, being only twelve when it started, but that fueled his desire, obsession, with the army. That led him directly to the doorsteps of the Royal Military College at Sandhurst, where infantry and cavalry officers were trained for both the British and Indian armies. He excelled at everything, a soldier's soldier, and was soon regarded as a leader among men who would be leaders. He finished second in his class of 1925. Second because no matter what he did, calculus continued to mystify him.

Army life took him all over the world, from Egypt to India, where he rose through the ranks as an infantry officer. A life-long bachelor, he had no time for a wife. He sometimes explained, to other officers, that the army was his wife and his men were his children. Although he never treated the men like kids. He was brusque, even unkind, but his goal was always the same: get the men to be the best soldiers possible.

Sergeant Major Malcolm Saunders and his second in command, Sergeant Steve Barltrop, and Jenkins' aide, Lieutenant Carleton Mallory, sat on wooden chairs in a semicircle around the colonel's desk.

At six feet tall, Saunders wasn't the tallest one in the room, but he was a wide body, built for power, and he seemed to take up a lot of space. At twenty-six, he had been recently promoted to Sergeant Major, after five years in the army. He wore his normal day-to-day Commando uniform, but had his red beret tucked in under his shirt's epaulets. The beret tended to clash with his red hair and handlebar mustache, but he wasn't worried about fashion.

He got his first taste of combat in North Africa with General Montgomery, going back and forth across the desert. That was where he and Barltrop met.

Barltrop was a little less than six feet tall, and built more compactly than Saunders. He had brown hair and blue eyes. He'd grown up in Cheshunt, which was located about fifteen miles north of London. The men were best friends and Barltrop had been the best man at Saunders' wedding just seven days ago. Saunders' bride, Sadie, was also from Cheshunt, although Barltrop never really knew her in school as he was several years ahead.

Both men had been assigned to the Commando School at Achnacarry House in Scotland, which was where they'd first met Jenkins, who was the school commandant at the time. Following that, they'd been tasked to join a new unit which Jenkins put together. A Commando Operations unit, which was made up of a number of special mission squads like Saunders'. Starting with his time at the school, Jenkins had expected nothing less than perfection from his men. That hadn't changed in the Commando Operations unit.

Mission meetings always took place in the colonel's office and today was no exception. The topic of the meeting, or to be

50   RONN MUNSTERMAN

more precise, the overall goal of the mission the colonel referred to, would have made the meeting something like TOP, TOP SECRET if there were such a thing.

Saunders nodded at the colonel's comment, but didn't say anything.

The colonel continued. "We have a trusted source at a castle in Austria, the Hohenstein Castle. It's located south of Salzburg. Intelligence from our source states that top leaders are expected to attend a dinner meeting, and spend the night at the castle before leaving early the next day. The dinner is tomorrow night."

"Oi. Tomorrow night, sir?" Saunders leaned forward. "That would give us little preparation time for something that's bound to be complex."

Jenkins shrugged. "I agree, but that's our timeline." He leaned forward himself and folded his hands on the desk. Speaking in a near whisper, he said, "The top leaders we're talking about are no less than Hitler and Himmler." He sat back.

Saunders' jaw clenched and unclenched a few times. Instead of answering Jenkins, he looked at Barltrop, whose expression mirrored his own. Deep concern. This would be a mission unlike any other in terms of risk to the men. Odds would heavily favor failure and probable capture or death.

"Our orders are clear. Kill Hitler and Himmler. Take photos as proof. Use your judgment on any other targets of opportunity. Extract the source, whoever he is, and bring him home. Let me be perfectly blunt. It may look like a suicide mission, but I expect you to complete the mission and return."

Saunders nodded slowly. "This castle. Do we have any information on it?"

Lieutenant Mallory spoke up. "We found a book on Austrian castles at Oxford, down the road. Hohenstein is listed and there are a few photos of both the exterior and interior, and it even has floor plans. I think someone earned their PhD with this." He lifted a massive book onto the colonel's desk in front of and facing the two commandos. It was nearly two feet tall and eight inches thick

"This is called an Elephant Folio, in case you're wondering. It was published in nineteen twenty-eight." He stood up and opened the book to a page he'd bookmarked with an index card, and then he sat back down.

Saunders and Barltrop leaned forward to examine the main photo of the castle, which sat part way up to the top of a monolithic mountain. It appeared to be several hundred yards higher than the valley. One face was a sheer cliff, the others in view were tree covered, but one had a more manageable slope.

Saunders looked up from the book to say, "Does our insider know where the armory is in the castle?"

Mallory replied, "We may be able to find out before you leave."

"Please."

Barltrop said to Saunders, "Ready?"

"Aye."

Barltrop turned the page.

The two men spent some time reading the text and closely examining the photos and the floor plans, which appeared to be quite thorough. Whether any changes had been made in the intervening sixteen years was just a guess. On the last page dedicated to the castle, they found a plan showing the grounds of the castle in its entirety.

"Bloody hell, there are three walls to breach," Barltrop said.

"Aye. Too bad we can't just drop right in there." Saunders pointed to a grassy area between the outermost wall and the middle one, a space perhaps fifty yards wide.

The two men glanced at each other, briefly considering exactly that.

"No, no chance," Saunders said. "We need somewhere to rehearse." He looked at Jenkins. "Got any friends who'd let us play 'breach the castle,' sir?"

"Funny you should ask. I have a place in mind. Arundel Castle is only seventy miles from here. I've already spoken to the owner and he has agreed to help the war effort. He's expecting you no later than two p.m. today. Lieutenant Mallory will accompany you to act as your liaison with the Duke of Norfolk, His Grace Fitzalan-Howard," Jenkins said.

"Can't be bothered by lowly sergeants, eh, sir?"

"Don't be snooty, Saunders."

Saunders grinned, the tips of his red mustache twitching. "Wouldn't dream of it, sir."

"He knows the military. He was a major in the Royal Sussex Regiment and was wounded in France in nineteen forty."

Saunders' eyebrows shot upward. That changed his opinion of the aristocrat. "Aye. Thank you for telling me, sir."

Jenkins nodded.

"Do we have anyone who can act as German soldiers for us?"

"What do you mean?" Mallory asked.

"We can practice a castle breach until we're blue in the face from the climbing, but we need someone to keep us honest so we're silent and unseen as long as necessary."

"I already have someone lined up," Jenkins said. "Just waiting for you to bring it up. As I knew you would. They'll be arriving there an hour before you." His lip curled into an uncharacteristic smile. "With their own officer."

Saunders and Barltrop chuckled.

Mallory lifted another, much smaller, book onto the desk next to the folio and opened it. "Here's information on Arundel. You'll see some similarities, but the Austrian castle and grounds are more compact making your distances shorter overall."

Saunders and Barltrop looked at the photo of Arundel. The main structure resembled a church, although perhaps the largest they'd ever seen, and the keep was probably over sixty feet tall. Another photo on the next page, an aerial shot, indicated the castle grounds were at least three hundred yards in length.

"Well, we've got our work cut out for us," Barltrop said.

"Aye."

Saunders looked at Mallory. "Can we keep these for a few hours?"

Mallory looked like Saunders just asked him for his first born. "Er, the librarian said I'm supposed to maintain possession."

Jenkins cleared his throat.

Mallory, who wasn't the colonel's aide for nothing, immediately said, "Certainly. You may have them for as long as necessary, Sergeant. What she doesn't know, won't hurt me."

The men laughed.

"Thanks, Lieutenant." Saunders looked at Jenkins. "We'll be on our way. Will you be going to Arundel yourself, sir?"

"I may."

"See you later, perhaps."

Saunders closed both books, stacked the smaller one on the folio, and picked them up. He and Barltrop rose, saluted and left the office.

As they walked down the hallway toward the building's front door, Saunders clapped Barltrop on the shoulder. "This ought to be an interesting one, Steve."

"Right. That's a euphemism, correct?"

"Ooh. A four syllable word, Steve. I'm telling Kathy."

Barltrop elbowed his boss in the ribs.

Chapter 9

Camp Barton Stacey Hospital
30 September, 1030 Hours

Nurse Pamela Dunn's duties while pregnant were extremely limited because she had experienced severe spotting a month ago at a field hospital in France. She had been on duty during a surgery when she'd fainted. The head nurse examined her and Pamela was relieved to learn it had not been a miscarriage. She'd been sent home straightaway and had a follow-up appointment with her family doctor, Dr. Swails. He pronounced mother and the baby safe and well, although she should avoid normal work duties until after the baby arrived in May.

Withstanding the boredom of staying home with her feet up every day lasted exactly three days. She asked her former boss, Sister Olive Cohn, at the Camp Barton Stacey Hospital if she could at least come in and read to the men who couldn't read for themselves due to an eye or hand injury. When the hospital became very busy with new patients, she would step up and do any work that would help out if she could be seated. Cohn had agreed only on the condition that Pamela didn't try to break their agreement and do too much.

Pamela pushed a small cart filled with books by British and American authors, magazines, and the latest available newspapers. The double doors to the ward were open and Pamela rolled her cart inside. She stopped briefly, examining the dozen men resting there. About half were asleep, but the others all turned their eyes toward her. They smiled at the sight of a beautiful blonde nurse.

Pamela recognized all but one of the alert men, a new patient. She selected him first and pushed her cart to the foot of his bed. She gave him a smile and he returned it. She picked up the patient's clipboard hanging from the frame at the foot of the bed. She read it carefully, making sure she understood what his problems were and perhaps more importantly, what his prognosis was. He was an American pilot and had crashed his flak-damaged aircraft on landing, breaking his right forearm and hand, and burning his left hand. The right hand and arm were in a cast, and the left hand was heavily wrapped. He probably couldn't even feed himself.

"My name is Mrs. Dunn. I'm here to read to you, Captain Burch, if you like."

Burch smiled. "I'd love it. I can't even hold a fork!"

Burch appeared to be in his late twenties. He had brown hair cut short and neat. His green eyes seemed to dance as if he was about to be ornery any second. He was sitting up against the metal backboard with a couple of pillows making it more comfortable for his back.

"What would you like me to read? I can bring the cart around so you can pick."

"Do you have a recent issue of *Stars and Stripes*?"

The *Stars & Stripes* was a resounding favorite amongst the Yanks.

"I do. It's the one from twenty-seventh September, so it's only three days old."

"Newer than I usually get! I'll go for that one."

"*Stars and Stripes* it is."

Pamela rustled through a stack of papers on the second shelf and pulled out the one she wanted. She walked around to the patient's right and sat down in a wooden chair. Also next to the bed was a wooden table containing a water pitcher and an empty glass with a straw.

"Would you like a drink of water, Captain?"

"Please call me Randy. And yes, please."

Pamela poured a half glass and lifted the straw to Burch's lips. He drank the entire amount.

"More?"

"No, thanks."

Pamela grabbed a tissue from a box and dabbed Burch's lips dry.

"Let me know if you need anything while I'm here."

"Will do," he said with a grin.

The two men on the beds next to Burch were awake. They rolled over onto their sides so they could face Pamela and listen in to the reading. They propped their heads up with a hand.

"Mind if we listen in?" asked one, another American.

"Please do."

She lifted the newspaper and asked, "Sports first?"

"Yes. How'd you know?" Burke said.

"My husband's constantly checking on the Cubbies."

"You married a Yank?"

"Yes. I did do."

The man on Burch's left muttered, "He's a lucky man."

Pamela nodded her thanks at him. "Okay, so first, the St. Louis Cards broke a ninth inning tie and won their hundred and second game." She looked at Burch. "That's really good, right?"

Burch frowned. "Yeah, I'm afraid so. My Pirates didn't stand a chance."

"Where are the Pirates from?"

"Same place as me, Pittsburgh."

Pamela looked at the ceiling for a moment. "That's western Pennsylvania? Close to Ohio?"

Burch grinned. "Yes, that's right. You're learning American geography?"

"Yes. Trying to, anyway. My husband's from Iowa."

Burch nodded.

Pamela went back to the paper, read the rest of the sports section, and started on the news. She read the lead paragraph to herself first, a way to decide what to say out loud. "Oh, dear," she said reflexively.

"What? Is it bad news?"

"The bridge at Arnhem. Things went badly for the British Army, the First Airborne Division. The three war correspondents with them haven't filed a report in thirty-six hours."

Burch glanced over at the man on his right and shook his head. "That's bad. They may have been captured." Burch's expression was glum.

Pamela quickly said, "Perhaps we could read some comic strips instead?"

"No, let's hear the rest of the news. Got to know what's happening out there. I have to get back as soon as I can" He lifted his left hand. "Doctor so and so smug face told me I might not be returned to flight status. I told him what he could do with his ideas."

Pamela covered her mouth with a hand to hide a smile. The doctor he meant was well known, and disliked by everyone for his Eeyore-like view of the world.

"Well, then. I'll go ahead and read the rest of the news."

Pamela read for another fifteen minutes and said, "Time for me to check on the others, Captain Burch. It was nice to meet you. Hope you get well soon." She turned to the other two men. "Same to you both."

All three men said 'thank you.'

She put the paper back on the second shelf and rolled her cart down the center aisle. She spotted a man at the end of the ward who was watching her. He beckoned a hand and she nodded. From habit, she glanced at each patient as she went by, on both sides of the ward. She passed by one patient, who was lying on his right side, his head swathed with a bandage around everything from the eyebrows up.

She paused and looked closer. His face had a terrible pallor. She stopped the cart and stepped over to him, bending down. His lips were blue. She grabbed a wrist and felt for a pulse. There was none. She gently rolled him onto his back. His eyes were closed. She raised each eyelid. There was no pupil response. She laid her head on his chest, but heard nothing.

She stood up and looked around. Only the man waiting for her to read was watching her. He raised his eyebrows. She shook her head. She gently pulled the man's covers up under his chin, not over his face. That would have to wait until a doctor declared time of death.

She walked briskly out of the ward and found the doctor on duty, not Doctor Eeyore, and gave him the news. He rounded up another nurse and they quickly examined the patient. The doctor whispered the time of death and the nurse dutifully recorded it on his chart.

Pamela retrieved her cart and pushed it to the man who was still waiting. She read his chart which said his reason for being in the hospital was a three-day-old bullet wound through the left thigh courtesy of an ME-109 pilot. She belatedly realized he could just read the book for himself because he had waved at her with his hand.

"Hello, I'm Mrs. Dunn. Can I get a book for you, Lieutenant Johnson?"

"Any new westerns?" Lieutenant Johnson was originally from southwestern Colorado and spoke with a southern drawl he'd picked up living a few years in Georgia.

Pamela checked the books on the top shelf. "Hm. Here's one. *Knights of the Range* by Zane Grey."

"That one! I love his books. When did that one come out?"

Pamela flipped open the book and checked the copyright page. "Nineteen thirty-nine. Fairly new."

Pamela held the book out for him, but he didn't take it.

"I was wondering if you would read it to me. I'd like to just lay back, close my eyes, and listen."

Pamela knew that as a pilot, it wasn't that he couldn't read, so she said, "I'd be glad to." She sat down. "Chapter one . . ."

A few pages in, the orderlies came to take the dead patient away. Pamela stopped reading to watch.

Lieutenant Johnson opened his eyes and when he saw what Pamela was looking at, sat up straight. A few others in the ward who were mobile, rose to their feet. Each lifted a hand in salute until the patient was wheeled out.

Johnson noticed Pamela had tears in her eyes. She sniffed and wiped her eyes.

"You okay, Mrs. Dunn?"

"Yes. I just . . . I was thinking that somewhere, sometime soon, a mother is going to get that horrible telegram."

Johnson closed his eyes for a moment, opened them and said, "I guess you don't really get used to it."

"No."

Pamela resumed reading.

Just as she was about to finish up with Johnson, the doors to the ward opened and Dunn strode in. His eyes zeroed in on Pamela right away and he grinned and waved at her. She waved back and held up a single finger: one minute. He nodded and stepped back out in the hallway.

"That Mr. Dunn?" Johnson asked.

"Yes. I'll see you tomorrow, Lieutenant Johnson."

"Yes, Ma'am."

Pamela rolled her cart away from Johnson's bed, parking it next to the wall nearby.

Dunn met her near the door with a hug and a kiss, carefully out of sight of the men in the ward.

"We're leaving tonight. Wanted to come over and say 'bye.' "

"How long?"

"A few days."

"You be careful, Mr. Dunn."

"Always am, Mrs. Dunn."

They kissed once more and then Dunn said, "See you soon."

"You better."

Pamela watched him walk down the hallway toward the front door. Just as he reached the exit, he looked over his shoulder and threw her a dazzling grin. Then he was gone. Her stomach immediately knotted up, a condition that would come and go until he returned. The price you paid for loving a soldier.

Chapter 10

On the coastal road
1/2 kilometer East-southeast of Kastrosikia,
Greece
30 September, 1305 Hours, Athens time

Doukas put a silver whistle between his lips and blew three times, waited a few seconds and repeated, and then once more. The third platoon leader reacted first and blew his whistle three times. Meanwhile, the men were still firing at anything resembling a target. After a few seconds the other three platoon leaders followed suit. Doukas's men began to withdraw from their positions, firing as they went. The terrain was typical Greece: mountainous with a few more or less flat areas thrown in just to give you hope. Therefore, the land went uphill from the road and was rocky creating a challenge to make a quick retreat.

The tanks were near the first curve in the road and they continued firing, now at point blank range. Doukas grabbed a couple of men with panzerfausts and pointed. They nodded and began to weave their way through the brush toward the tanks. After Doukas's men had crossed the dangerous open ground between the road and the woods directly to the east, he took off himself.

One man with a panzerfaust knelt beside a gnarled tree and lifted the weapon to his shoulder. The lead tank was only twenty meters away. It entered the first curve, slowing down as it did. The Greek soldier aimed at a spot in the center of the treads and fired. The round streaked the short distance and burned through the armor plate, exploding inside and killing the German crew, all in a split second. The second Greek was in position and he fired at the second tank with a similar result. Both tanks sat burning, blocking the road.

The two men dropped their empty tubes and ran to rejoin the rest of the company.

Doukas finally made it into the woods and he turned around to wait for the two men assigned to the tanks. He was relieved when he heard the explosions and then saw the two men making their way toward him.

Off to the west, he spotted movement amongst the trees. The German soldiers in the halftracks had disembarked and were giving chase, although they were clearly exercising caution. This was what he had counted on.

His first platoon had taken positions in the woods, including one of the MG42s.

The two men who'd destroyed the lead tanks ran into the woods. Doukas patted them on the shoulders as they ran past in search of their own platoon farther in the woods.

The Germans decided to send a squad toward the woods, perhaps to see what would happen. The men were moving along a tree line, but were periodically exposed to Doukas's men. At a range of fifty meters, the Greeks opened fire, the MG42 making its peculiar buzzsaw sound. Most of the German squad was cut down, but two men escaped through the trees, heading back where they came from.

The three surviving Panzers had no choice but to back up to retreat from further attacks by panzerfaust, their greatest fear.

Doukas kept an eye on the tanks, although he wasn't concerned that they would attempt to follow; the ground was just too difficult. He ran over to the position of his first platoon leader, who was firing at the Germans with his Mauser. Doukas touched the man on the shoulder.

"Hold here for two more minutes, then disappear."

"Yes, sir."

The rest of the company was already on the way to the road a little less than a kilometer away where trucks and cars awaited for a faster retreat into the Greek countryside.

Doukas took one last look at the Germans' position. A couple of the halftracks that had come from the north had driven a little farther on the road and stopped so the men could get out. They ran to Doukas's left and formed a line of two squads. Curiously, they held their fire. This caught his attention and he immediately wondered what they were up to. His gaze settled back on the other halftracks and his curiosity was satisfied, but not in a good way.

Exiting a halftrack were three mortar crews who ran to the opposite side of their vehicle to set up, leaving a spotter in the vehicle. The German 81mm mortar was deadly and a good crew could fire up to twenty-five three and a half kilogram rounds per minute. This was a far more dangerous threat than the Panzers.

Doukas jumped into action. He grabbed the platoon leader by the shoulder.

"Mortars. Get the men out now."

The man passed the word and the platoon began a fighting withdrawal. In the span of sixty seconds, the men moved a hundred meters farther into the woods. Doukas ran along with them. Just as they reached the bottom of another, larger, rocky hill, the land behind them lit up and shook as the mortar rounds found the area the men had just vacated. As the men began climbing, the mortar rounds started walking through the woods, getting closer. The hill was thirty meters higher than the land to the west. The men were tiring from the exertion, but the mortar rounds added an unparalleled impetus.

When Doukas reached the top of the hill, the last to arrive because he wanted to be certain everyone made it, he turned and looked back at the enemy. The mortars stopped firing and he could hear the halftrack engines wind up as they got ready to depart.

It had turned into a complete rout. He was unsure of his losses, and wouldn't know until later when the survivors were accounted for.

One thing he did know: someone was going to pay for the faulty intelligence.

Chapter 11

Neil Marston stood alone on the gravel driveway just outside the main entrance to the castle. He checked his watch. The general and his traveling companions, an aide, and a man who Marston had been able to find out was from the *Abwehr*, German Military Intelligence, were supposed to arrive at 12:30. A moment later, he heard the growl of a heavy staff car and the crunch of tires on gravel.

The sky was completely blue, no clouds in sight, and the fall air was cool and clear. He hadn't yet grown accustomed to how fresh it smelled every day, especially compared to Berlin or London. He could see miles and miles off in the distance across the valley. The green and brown patchwork of the farmland was as evident as if flying over it in a plane.

The black Mercedes stopped at the last security gate, forty yards from where Marston stood. As he watched, the SS guards carefully examined the driver and the three passengers, comparing their identification photos to their faces. When the two guards were done, they stepped back and gave a Nazi salute. Another guard raised the latticed iron gate and the car trundled through. The driver guided the vehicle up the last bit of the curving driveway and stopped precisely in front of the castle's entrance.

Marston glanced at his watch. His mouth twitched. Exactly on time. He stepped forward and opened the rear passenger door and the general climbed out. Marston gave a Nazi salute. "*Heil* Hitler, General Glockner. Welcome to Hohenstein Castle."

Glockner clicked his boot heels and returned a sharp salute. "*Heil* Hitler."

The general was much shorter than Marston expected. He appeared to be about five foot seven. He had a sharp narrow nose and greenish eyes that might have been hazel. He was fit and slender.

A colonel climbed out of the front passenger seat and stood next to Glockner.

"My aide, Colonel Berkner," Glockner said, tipping his head toward the colonel.

Marston dipped his chin, acknowledging the man, who also clicked his heels.

On the other side of the car, the driver got out and opened the rear passenger door on that side. A large, heavyset man struggled out of the Mercedes' deep backseat, and then the driver closed the door with a heavy *thunk*.

The man waddled around the rear of the car and stopped next to the general.

Marston looked at the man, who was wearing a rumpled brown suit. "Welcome to Hohenstein Castle, *Herr* Juhnke."

Juhnke's doughy face was offset by sharp, small blue eyes. He seemed to stare through Marston.

Marston repeated his salute and received one in return.

Marston turned toward the open door of the castle and beckoned with his fingers. Four SS soldiers, each armed only with a holstered Luger, strode out and went directly to the rear of the car where the driver had already opened the boot.

Juhnke scuttled back to the rear of the car and reached into the boot, pulling out a medium-sized square wooden case. "I'll take this one."

He rejoined the general and Marston.

The British spy said, "My name is Major Obert Seiler, and I'll be taking you to your sleeping quarters so you may freshen up if you so desire. I've arranged a luncheon for you at one p.m. where Colonel Neubart will join us. I hope that is satisfactory."

The general spoke up. "That will be perfectly fine."

Juhnke bobbed his head in agreement.

"Excellent. Following lunch, I would be happy to conduct a tour of the castle and the grounds, if you are so interested."

"Yes, that would be interesting," the general said.

Marston started to turn away, but Juhnke spoke up. "Are the sleeping quarters secure? I must be able to lock my room and have the only key."

Marston looked over his shoulder at the man, who was holding onto the square case for dear life. This immediately set off Marston's spy radar, although his face remained impassive. What in the world did the man have there?

"Absolutely, sir."

The man seemed to sigh in relief. "Thank you."

"Certainly, sir."

The driver pointed out which bags belonged to each man and the soldiers quickly emptied the boot.

Marston said to the visitors, "Gentlemen, please follow me." He led the way into the castle, and across the stone floor of the main hall. He turned right and began ascending a stone spiral staircase. Along the right side a two-inch-thick rope looped through brass rings for a handrail. The guests and the men carrying all the luggage followed.

At the top of the stairs Marston went down the long hallway. The walls were covered with paintings and medieval weaponry. He stopped at the second door on the left and opened it. He stepped out of the way and held up a hand indicating to the general to enter. "Your quarters, sir."

The general walked into the room and examined it briefly. A four-poster bed sat on the left across from a large dresser. A window was opposite the door. In the right corner by the window was a secretary's desk with the writing surface folded closed.

"Does this meet with the general's approval?" Marston asked after stepping in behind the man.

Without turning around, the general said, "It does." He went to the window and looked out at the valley.

The men with the general's luggage entered and placed the cases on a low table designed for that purpose situated next to the dresser.

Marston turned to the general's aide and said, "I can show you to your room, and you can return here afterwards. It's just next door."

The aide glanced at Glockner, who nodded. Again he didn't turn around, seemingly very interested in the view.

Marston got the aide into his room, and guided Juhnke two doors farther down the hall to a room on the opposite side of the hallway. When Juhnke walked into his room and looked around, he turned to face Marston. "No room with a view of the valley?"

"No, sir," Marston replied. "However, there is a particularly lovely view of one of the castle flower gardens."

Marston started to make his way to the window, but the man said, "No, this won't do. I want a better room. Arrange it for me."

Juhnke raised a hand as if to place it on Marston's arm for emphasis.

Marston glanced down at the hand as it neared his sleeve, and looked up at Juhnke. Marston's expression must have done the job because Juhnke withdrew his hand and looked away.

"Find another room for me."

"Regretfully, there are no others available."

"Move someone."

"Whom would you suggest, *Mein Herr*? The general? Perhaps *Reichsführer* Himmler? Or the *Führer* himself?"

Juhnke waved his hand, careful not to brush against Marston. "After further reflection, this room is more than adequate. Thank you."

"Entirely my pleasure, sir." Marston pulled a skeleton key from his pants pocket and held it out. "Your key."

Juhnke snatched the key away from Marston and looked at it briefly before putting it in his pocket.

"This is the only key to this room?"

"I assure you, it is so."

"Thank you." He turned away and laid his case on the top of the dresser, where it took up half the available space. An SS soldier carried in two suitcases and put them on the bed—there was no table in this room. The soldier left.

Marston said, "Please let me know if you need anything, sir."

Juhnke ignored him.

"Lunch will be served precisely at one p.m. I will be at the base of the stairs to direct you and the others to the dining hall."

"Thank you."

Marston left, pulling the door closed behind him. He waited outside the door for a few seconds. His curiosity was satisfied when he heard a key being inserted in the lock on the other side of the door and twisted to lock it. Marston shook his head at the mystery of it. Naturally, he would have to find out what the man was so worried about keeping secure.

Marston stopped by to tell General Glockner and Colonel Berkner about meeting at the bottom of the stairs for lunch. He received a 'thank you" from both men.

He walked down the spiral staircase, heading for the dining hall to ensure all was well there. Didn't want anyone to suffer disappointment.

Chapter 12

Arundel Castle
30 September, 1912 Hours, London time

The trip from Barton Stacey to Arundel Castle had taken Saunders almost an hour and a half. On arrival he and his men found a place outside the castle to connect what they saw in front of them with what they'd learned from the Oxford Library's book. Saunders and Barltrop decided on a particular approach, and that led them to the spot where the squad stood.

Lieutenant Mallory had gone inside the castle to meet the Duke as well as the other unit who would be playing the enemy. Saunders had also decided to wait until it was dark to match conditions for the real castle breach.

Saunders' men waited with him at the base of the castle's main keep. Christopher Dickinson often performed magic tricks for his squad mates and on occasions where he went to Andover, kids would flock to him and he would amaze them with sleight of hand tricks. Bernard Thurston and Francis Handford had joined the squad just prior to a mission to Belgium, and went on the more recent excursion to Poland. Timothy Chadwick was

Dickinson's best friend and where one went so did the other. Geoffrey Kopp was like Saunders, from London's East End, another true Cockney. The son of a pastor, Edward Redington grew up in Leeds. George Mills was the squad's singer and recently the men convinced him to sing at a pub, where he'd been well received. Arthur Garner, from Liverpool, was the demolitions master.

The stone was cold and damp, as it had often been, except when last a man touched it. About seven hundred years ago, a skilled workman had helped put the stone in place. It had been dry, and heavy then, fresh from the quarry. The hand resting on it belonged to Saunders. The stone was slippery from the rain falling from the night sky. Saunders would have been soaked through if not for the poncho covering him. His suppressed Sten was hanging from its sling which draped across one shoulder and his chest. The barrel was, of course, pointed down to prevent water from getting inside the barrel. The weapon was empty of rounds as were all the men's. Damage to the castle had been forbidden, which meant Saunders would have to find another way to force doors open. The byproduct of this would be the ability to strengthen the stealth aspects of the castle breach.

The curved stone was at the bottom of the castle's south corner tower, the primary keep. Saunders' goal was to make it to the parapet walk on the wall extending northeast from the tower, forty feet above, and then into the castle through the keep. Barltrop and he had studied the problem and prepared their men on the drive over in the back of the bouncing truck. They both thought getting inside was the easy part. Getting back out, not so much. That's what happens when you're dealing with Nazis. They tended to get grumpy when you just broke in and tried to kill them.

Saunders turned his attention to the parapet, and also noted the wind direction, which was from the west at perhaps ten miles an hour. Enough to affect the grappling hook's flight. He tapped Corporal Tim Chadwick on the shoulder.

Chadwick was standing about six feet from the wall. He raised his grappling hook launcher and he, too, noted the wind, adjusted his aim and fired. The steel, four-pronged hook flew into the dark sky, a three-eights-inch diameter knotted climbing rope trailing it, uncoiling from its place on the ground to Chadwick's right. His target was one of the square battlements in the wall, where men with bows and arrows would have been stationed during an attack on the castle.

The grappling hook sailed over the parapet's wall and landed on the stone walkway, bouncing once. Chadwick laid down the launcher and got a grip on the dangling rope. He pulled on it carefully. The hook was too far away to hear it scraping across the stones, but when he got some tension on the rope, he tugged harder, leaning back a bit to increase pressure on the hook. He was sure it had seated itself against the parapet's outer wall. He had hit his target and the rope hung from the lower portion of the square cutout.

"Good to go, Sarge," he said to Saunders.

Saunders pointed at Edward Redington.

Redington grabbed the rope and began climbing. It was slow, difficult and painful even through his leather gloves. Eventually, he topped the wall. He raised his head to look down the guard's walkway toward the northeast. It was clear. He pulled himself over the battlement and checked to be sure the hook was still seated properly, which it was. Leaning over the wall, he waved at the tiny men below. He pulled his Sten off his shoulder and knelt beside the grappling hook, keeping an eye on the walkway.

In fairly short order the remaining nine men of Saunders' squad arrived at the top. Saunders, the biggest of them all, was last. Chadwick carefully pulled the rope up, coiling it as he went. He slipped it back inside a large black pack along with the launcher. He tied the grappling hook onto the outside. Lifting the bulky pack, he snugged it in place on his back.

Saunders looked around. The walkway extended fifty feet to his right where it ended at a large wooden door built into another tower. Looking north, the parapet walkway ran from the corner tower to yet another one about a hundred feet away. He faced the corner tower on his left. The door was narrow and less than six feet tall, meant for the twelfth century's men of shorter stature.

On the right side of the door, halfway up was a metal latch, which stuck out perpendicular to the wooden door. It was a lift latch so that when you pulled up on the lever, the metal prong on the other side would rise above a metal slot on the wall next to the door, and the door could be opened.

Knowing better, he lifted the latch. It didn't budge. No big surprise there. That meant there was a metal plate dropped over the slot to lock the door. Barltrop and he had a simple plan for this event.

Saunders waved his men back and they retreated a few feet. He pulled a small torch out and while standing very close to the door to hide its light, turned it on. He examined the gap between the door and the tower wall. He found what he wanted and turned off the torch, slipping it into a pocket. Pulling his combat knife out, he slid the blade into the gap several inches until it struck the latch. He raised the point little by little while keeping forward pressure on the blade. After a few seconds, the knife tip rose an inch or so and Saunders thought he heard a tiny clink.

He grabbed the latch and lifted. The door opened. He ducked and peeked inside, but could see nothing. He got out the torch again and switched it on, shining it into the darkness ahead. The round space of the upper keep was empty, so he pulled the door all the way open and waved his men inside. There was plenty of room for everyone, plus the opening to the stairs that would lead them to a tunnel below and into the rest of the castle.

Saunders checked the walkway behind him and, finding it still clear, stepped through the door to join his men. He pulled it closed and locked it with the metal plate he'd jostled free. Giving the door a shove, he was pleased to see it stayed snugged tightly in place.

With the door closed, the space was in total darkness. Barltrop switched on his small torch and pointed it at the first step. In the dim light, Saunders nodded and took the lead. He started down the stone stairs. The rest of the men followed silently, Barltrop bringing up the rear.

Saunders couldn't help but admire the workmanship of the staircase as he descended. Even on the interior, where only the king's soldiers would see the work, the stones were laid with care and the mortar between the stones was smooth to the touch. It wasn't hard for him to imagine working on the stones in the sunshine, before the roof was erected. He loved architecture and the art of building things. If he came through the war, he wanted to start his own construction business.

He reached the bottom of the stairs. Straight ahead was a long tunnel under the south ramparts. There would be a right turn at about fifty feet. There were no lights anywhere. He raised his Sten with his right hand—his left held the torch—and began his silent sliding-step walk along the left wall of the tunnel. The floor and walls were dry, a bit of a surprise there. His men followed close behind, their Stens raised and pointed to the right so they weren't aiming at their mate's back, even if the weapons were unloaded. As they neared the intersection, Saunders made sure the beam of his torch didn't extend into the intersection where someone down the adjacent tunnel could spot it.

Saunders turned off the torch and leaned around the corner. It was nothing but a black hole. Flipping the light back on, he pointed it down the tunnel. The tunnel walls gleamed white, but beyond the range of the torch, it was completely dark. Saunders drew up his mental map. This tunnel ran for about a hundred feet and entered the castle main near the southwest corner.

Saunders took off. Instead of using the slide-step he was nearly running, his rubber-soled boots making a slight whisper as they brushed against the stone floor. He didn't need to look over his shoulder, he knew his men were keeping pace with him. The floor seemed to be perfectly level. Another tribute to the workmen of seven hundred years ago. The air suddenly turned stale when Saunders reached the end of the tunnel. Here it was a mixture of damp and mold. That meant they were approaching a part of the castle that had been experiencing water leakage for a few centuries.

The door in front of Saunders was practically identical to the first one. He played the light over the locking mechanism. As he expected, because the door was in proximity of excess moisture at different levels over time, the door and jam had expanded and contracted many, many times, leaving a quarter inch gap, wider than on the first door. Kneeling, he shone the light on the gap next to the lock. There was the metal tongue that held the door fast with the locking plate on top. He repeated his lock picking with his knife and when it clicked, pulled up the door latch, opening the door slowly, in case the hinges decided to make an inopportune squeak. Fortunately, the hinges were silent and the door opened all the way smoothly.

Saunders aimed the light through the door opening. Another tunnel went off to the right. He took off again, this time using the slide-step. About ten feet ahead, on the left, was a dark opening. He checked it quickly and moved on. Twenty feet ahead was the one they were interested in. It would lead upstairs to the castle's basement, or more accurately, the level below ground level.

When he reached the next tunnel, he stopped.

He leaned around the corner and a blinding light came on.

"Halt!"

Saunders started to raise his Sten, but way behind him he heard another "Halt!" and a second light shone on the British Commandos.

"Bloody fooking hell!" Saunders shouted.

From the other side of the light came, "Hello, mate. Looks like we got you."

"Shite. Nigel, is that you?"

A Commando walked around in front of the light, his hand extended. "Hiya, Mac. You buying?"

Saunders shook his friend's hand. "Aye."

Nigel Blevins led another Commando squad, but for the purposes of the exercise, he had three squads stationed at various points on the castle grounds, some inside some outside.

Saunders turned to his men. "All right, lads, first exercise is over. Let's get over to the conference room. We'll debrief and see where we fooked up. Nigel, we'll meet you there."

"Righto, mate."

Blevins turned and gathered his men and disappeared into the darkness of the tunnel.

Saunders followed, as did his men. As he walked he shone his light on his watch. He grimaced. In a little more than twenty-four hours, they would be doing this for real. He was not looking forward to explaining the failure to his boss, Colonel Jenkins.

No, not at all.

Chapter 13

Hohenstein Castle,
30 September, 2042 Hours, Salzburg time

Neil Marston, aka Major Obert Seiler, had the run of the castle, as one might expect of the aide to the garrison commander. Soon after his arrival, in addition to conditioning the outdoor guards to his evening walks, he'd wandered all over the castle interior at different times of the day to make his presence commonplace and accepted by the staff and other members of the garrison without a second thought. He was known by everyone as an unusually gregarious SS officer, a pleasant change for the staff. On various occasions, he had corrected people in public for minor errors just to make sure they wouldn't think he was a pushover. He wasn't cruel, but he didn't let anything slide by either.

General Glockner, his aide, and Wilbert Juhnke had enjoyed their lunch earlier in the day. Following lunch, Marston gave the men an hour-long tour of the beautiful castle inside and out. The men had been quite appreciative of everything they saw, especially the great dining hall, which was reserved for high level dinners such as was planned for the next evening with Hitler and

Himmler. The men knew who the guests were, but Marston had made a point of reminding them.

Later, after dinner, Marston had offered to conduct a second, more detailed tour, but the guests begged off, giving no particular reason. This suited Marston perfectly anyway because he had his own plans of touring the castle in some of the out of the way locations.

The castle dated back to 1460, when the King of Austria, Frederick V the Peaceful, decided he wanted a castle on the western boundaries of his kingdom. The castle, as it appeared now, was largely the same as it was at that time. Of course, over the centuries improvements had been made, both to the interior and exterior. The castle had passed to the Bierschbach family, a distant cousin in 1476, when the king had grown bored with it. Cousin Bierschbach married in 1490 to a lovely woman ten years his junior, Adelaide. The linage continued unbroken to modern times, and the castle was currently in the hands of Albert Bierschbach and his wife, Mathilda.

Marston had met the two, now in their elderly years, he eighty-one and she seventy-nine, soon after arriving. They lived in a cottage—which was four times bigger than Marston's family home in London—on the castle grounds. They rarely entered the castle proper and it was only on one of Marston's excursions on the grounds that he'd found them.

He had visited with them for a short time and they'd given him a brief history of the castle. He also learned they lost their only heir in 1915 to the Great War. They asked Marston if he could keep a secret. He'd agreed and they'd told him they hoped to leave the castle to the Austrian government, that is, after the Nazis left. They'd looked at him with fear in their eyes as they suddenly realized what they'd said to an SS officer. He comforted them and reasserted his promise to say nothing.

He started in the main hall, the one where the spiral staircase led to the second floor and the bed chambers for the guests. He crossed the stone floor to the side opposite the spiral staircase and opened a door to a room known simply as the Portrait Room. He stepped through and entered the wide and long room. The floor was the same sort of field stone as was found throughout the main floor. His boots clicked on the stone. Paintings of people from about the fifteenth century onward adorned both walls, with a lot of space between each portrait, each of which was lit by a single lamp just above the frame. A six-foot-wide dark blue carpet ran alongside each wall in front of the paintings.

Near the end of the room hanging on the right hand wall, one portrait in particular caught his eye and he stopped in front of it. A young woman, perhaps in her late twenties, sat on a chair in front of a willow tree. She wore a burgundy dress with a modest neckline. A single strand of pearls accented her fair skinned throat. Her hair was carefully wrapped in plaits and partially covered by a translucent veil which also covered her visible right ear. Marston thought the painter had captured the woman's beauty and the essence of her soul. Her blue eyes seemed to catch his gaze and not let go. The painting's light appeared to be late afternoon and there was a reflection of sunshine on a stream behind her. Marston wondered what had happened to her. Was this her wedding portrait? Had her life been happy? He felt completely taken by her. If she was a living, breathing woman in his view, say on the commons at Oxford, or the streets of London, he would have felt thunderstruck, he was sure. Perhaps he would have worked up enough courage to talk to her. Maybe.

He reluctantly pulled his gaze from her and turned away. He walked to the room's door and left, still thinking about her.

RONN MUNSTERMAN

Chapter 14

Dunn's barracks
Camp Barton Stacey
30 September, 2100 Hours, London time

Dunn and Cross sat across from each other over Dunn's tiny desk. A topographic map of western Greece lay between them, turned sideways, Dunn on the east and Cross on the west. The door to Dunn's quarters was closed.

"It looks a little like where we were in Italy to me," Cross muttered.

"Yeah, mountain peaks aren't as high as they were near Ville Di Murlo."

"No." Cross drummed his fingers on the desk before asking, "Do you have any worries about the Greeks? They're an unknown for us and I don't like unknowns."

Dunn picked up his black speckled Zippo lighter and a pack of Lucky Strikes. He flicked the package so a few cigarettes slid out. He offered them to Cross, who took one and tapped it against the desk to pack the tobacco tighter. Dunn did the same and flipped open the lighter and rolled the thumbwheel. He held out the flame for Cross and then lit his own, snapping the lighter shut when he was done. He stared at the lighter. The speckles seemed to dance in the light from his desk lamp.

He recalled reading somewhere that in 1941, Zippo had ceased all civilian production and from then on only manufactured for the military.

Dunn held up the lighter to Cross. "Do you realize how many of these there are? Do you know anyone who doesn't have one?"

Cross dug into a pocket and held his up. "Twins, huh? No, I don't know anyone without one."

The two men puffed silently for a few moments. Cross was content to wait for Dunn's answer to his question.

Finally Dunn said, "You're right about the unknown, but there's only eight of us. If we're walking into trouble with the Resistance there, we're fucked, just like back in June when we were near Calais and Luc turned out to be a traitor. No way to get ourselves out of it. So, yes, I'm concerned, but we'll tell the men to just stay alert. Don't want to worry them anymore than necessary."

"Of course not. We're not taking extra supplies for the Resistance?"

"No. They're well armed and also have plenty of explosives. Most of everything was probably stolen from the Germans at some point."

"I know Jonesy has a standing order on taking his oh-three, but for this mission?"

As always, Dunn and Cross discussed who was doing what on the mission, either confirming no change, or making new assignments.

Dave Jones was the sniper and the 'oh-three' was his 1903 Springfield with a Unertl scope. Jonesy had, on his arrival to the squad, put on a shooting exhibition at the firing range. When Dunn had discovered Jonesy was using the Springfield instead of his M1, he'd demanded that Jonesy prove his skill with the bolt-action sniper rifle. Jonesy had fired ten shots in under sixty seconds. When the range sergeant retrieved the target, he pulled out a measuring stick. Jonesy had grouped his shots within a diameter of seven and a half inches from six hundred yards out. No one on the squad had ever seen that kind of shooting.

"Yep. Never know if you're gonna need his skill on that."

"Ayup, that's the truth," Cross replied in his Nor'easter accent.

"Do you think we should move the radio around a bit? Is Schneider getting tired of it?"

Cross shook his head. "You saw how he was when that crazy bastard Griesbach shot up his last one on the train."

Dunn chuckled at the recollection. Schneider had practically cried when he saw the radio full of bullet holes. "Okay, we'll leave the radio in his capable hands."

"Jonesy and Lindstrom stay together?"

"Yep. And Goerdt will eventually need someone to replace Bailey, but this trip we're not taking the bazooka. I sure wish we had our own Greek translator. Too bad neither Schneider nor Martelli can help us there."

Cross nodded. It had often proved exceedingly helpful to have someone who spoke the local language.

"Weapons?" Cross asked.

Dunn frowned. "I'm a little iffy on this, but what about taking the Garands and the Thompsons? Do you think the men'll buck against that?"

"Buck against your decision? No, not happening, at least not out loud."

"Okay, just thought I'd ask. Maybe it won't be too bad."

"Nah. It'll be fine. We'll figure it out."

The men finished their smokes and stubbed them out in a metal ashtray that already had a half dozen butts in it. The air was turning blue. Dunn suddenly noticed and got up. He opened the single window behind his desk, a lever-style window that stuck out at an angle when pushed open. Some fresh air trickled in and the smoke swirled. For a moment he thought about asking Cross to crack the door an inch for better airflow, but remembered his next topic, which required privacy. He sat back down, and pulled some files from a drawer. He plopped the stack on the desk.

"Time to go over promotions to recommend to the colonel."

Cross nodded. Part of the job. Most of the time it was kind of fun knowing you were putting more money in a man's pocket. "Who's first?" he asked

"Wickham, to sergeant."

"That's a yes."

Dunn opened the top file and wrote his signature in the proper place as an endorsement of the promotion. Dunn could have handled the promotions by himself, and perhaps most squad leaders would have, but his relationship with Cross prevented that. If he depended on his friend's input on the battlefield, why wouldn't he do the same thing for paperwork?

"Schneider, to sergeant."

"Ayup."

They worked their way through four more files: Lindstrom to corporal, and Jonesy, Martelli, and Goerdt to staff sergeant. There was one more file.

Dunn flipped it open and signed the paper without asking Cross's opinion. He handed the paper to his friend.

"Me to technical sergeant." Cross looked up at Dunn. "I'm grateful, but that's a double jump, skipping staff sergeant. They won't go for it." He handed the paper back to Dunn.

Dunn grinned and shoved the paper back across the desk. "You big goof. Take a look at the bottom."

Cross read the signatures on the bottom. Signatures? Two of them. "You already got the colonel's. How'd you do that?"

"I just explained that you deserved it based on your work. I added that since I was promoting the others, you needed to be a step above them. I'm sorry I haven't thought of that before. Plus, there's something I want to tell you."

Cross looked a bit alarmed.

"No, it's all good."

Cross relaxed.

"The colonel and I have been talking about you taking your own squad. What do you think about that?"

"You think I'm ready for that?"

"Dave, come on. You know you are. Do I have to list the whys?"

Cross shook his head. "No, I guess not." He fidgeted in his seat, and finally ended up crossing his legs. "I know this is a big deal, and I'm grateful, but I would rather stay here. With you. And the guys."

Dunn said nothing.

"I mean, we've been together a long time, right?"

Dunn nodded.

"So . . . can I stay?"

Dunn smiled. "I told the colonel this would happen."

"Oh. What'd he say?"

"That it was up to us for the moment."

"What's that mean?"

"It means he's reserving the right to change our minds for us and move you out if he thinks it's the best thing for the outfit."

"Oh. I won't be able to say 'no' the next time?"

"That'd be correct."

"Damn. Maybe he'll forget." Cross looked hopeful.

Dunn didn't have the heart to dissuade him. "Maybe so. For now, we'll forget about it ourselves. Okay?"

"Ayup."

"Let's go tell the men they have more money coming."

Cross frowned. "You don't have the colonel's signature on their paperwork yet."

"I already talked to him about each one. He said yes. Besides I want to do this before the mission."

"Ah, okay, then. Let's go make some guys happy." Dunn stood up and grabbed a cigar box sitting on the corner of the desk.

Cross opened the door and led the way into the barracks area.

The men were sprawled out on their bunks. Some were writing letters and others were reading.

Lindstrom spotted Dunn first and jumped to his feet. No one called out 'Attention!' like you would for an officer, but the rest of the men followed suit as a sign of respect for Dunn.

"Relax, fellas. Got some stuff to take care of before we leave for Greece." Dunn went to a spot near the armory area, where the men's M1s, Thompsons, Stens, Colt .45s, and Jonesy's Springfield were stored. Cross took a spot to Dunn's left. Dunn handed the cigar box to Cross who flipped the lid open.

Dunn drew himself to attention and called out, "Private First Class Eugene Lindstrom, front and center!"

Lindstrom marched to a spot right in front of his squad leader.

Dunn grinned and said, "Congratulations, Corporal!" Dunn held out his left hand and Cross dropped a pair of corporal stripes into the palm.

Dunn handed the stripes to Lindstrom, who took them with his left hand. The men shook hands. Lindstrom was grinning.

"Thanks, Sarge!"

"You're welcome."

Lindstrom did a smart about face and went back to stand at the foot of his bunk.

Dunn and Cross promoted the rest of the men and then Dunn took the cigar box from his friend. Dunn did a left face and Cross a right face.

"Sergeant Cross, congratulations. You are hereby double promoted to Technical Sergeant." Dunn pulled the last pair of stripes, five with the letter T in the center, from the box and handed them over. When the two friends shook hands, the squad began applauding and whistling, perhaps not exactly military decorum, but Dunn wasn't about to stop the happiness the men were bestowing on Cross.

Dunn did a right face. "Congratulations to each one of you. You know I'm proud of you, and this is just a way for the colonel and me to recognize all the hard, incredible work you've done.

"We're departing for Hampstead Airbase at twenty-three hundred hours, so you have plenty of time to sew the new stripes on. Be sure you do more than just baste them in place. It'd be awfully embarrassing for them to fall off in front of the Greeks, don't you think?"

The room erupted in laughter as the men imagined that very thing happening.

"Goerdt, no bazooka."

Goerdt nodded. He hadn't expected to take the rocket weapon on the trip.

"Men, we're taking the Thompsons *and* the M1s."

The men simply glanced at Dunn and nodded, and they got busy with their new stripes.

Under his breath, Cross said, "Told ya so."

Dunn grinned. Good men, damn good men, each one of them.

Chapter 15

Conference room
Arundel Castle
30 September, 2130 Hours

Saunders and Barltrop stared at the book on the Austrian castle. They were seated on the same side of an enormous conference table. Across from them was Lieutenant Mallory. Colonel Jenkins sat at the end of the table.

Saunders sat back and ran both hands over his face, and rubbed his eyes with the heels of the palms hard enough to see bright shapes.

"Fook!"

Jenkins said, "My thoughts exactly." His expression was as glum as Saunders' and Barltrop's.

"Colonel, we had two failures today and one success. We're going to build on the success, the things we did right."

Jenkins nodded. He'd accepted the news of the failures with surprising patience and grace. He knew just how difficult the task was.

"I have every confidence in you and your men."

"Thank you, sir."

"I want to be clear on your objectives. First, with highest priority: Hitler. Then comes Himmler. If any other members of the top echelon are present like Göring, Ribbentrop, or Speer, kill them, too. After that, for any targets of opportunity, use your own judgment."

"You said we had a source inside?" Saunders asked.

Jenkins nodded. "Correct."

"And we are to bring him home with us?"

"Yes, assuming he makes himself known."

"Very good, sir."

"Let's review your plan."

Saunders leaned forward and said, "Yes, sir. We still have to go up the east side through the heavy forest there. That'll give us plenty of cover until we reach the first wall."

Barltrop looked at the ornate ceiling, twenty feet above him. "What if we used a couple of ropes for each wall? Spread out the load and speed up getting over? Reduce our exposure time."

Saunders nodded. "Aye, that would help a lot on the outer rings."

"Yeah. Five in each group."

"We should hit the castle wall about twenty-two hundred hours. Another fifteen minutes to get over the other two, and then we can breach the castle itself by twenty-two thirty. The dinner party should still be going strong," Saunders said. "Does that sound about right to you, Colonel?"

"It does. It's well known that Hitler is a true night owl and is often up until three or four a.m. Which means everyone else will still be there."

"Aye. Right, then. Moving on . . ." Saunders said.

After thirty minutes of discussion, Saunders looked at Colonel Jenkins. "That's what we have, sir."

"I concur with your plan. Lieutenant Mallory, would you lay out the extraction plan and back up?"

"Certainly, sir. Oh, and we now know where the armory is." He flipped a few pages in the Oxford book. He stopped when a floor plan appeared. He looked at a piece of note paper and then at the floor plan. He traced his finger across the page. "Here. It's near the main entrance on the south side, but one floor down. See this, that's a spiral staircase that goes to the upper floors of this part of the castle. Next to the stairs is a door that opens to a down staircase. That will take you right to the armory. The source says the door to the staircase is unlocked, but the door to the armory isn't. He reports no guards at the armory door."

Saunders and Barltrop examined the floor plan and burned the armory's location into their memory.

"Okay, good. Thanks."

"You're welcome. Here's your extraction plan."

Mallory pushed a large map toward the two Commandos. It showed the area around the castle, including a nearby village, Lacher. A black X was drawn at a point half a mile directly east of the castle. Two red circles were drawn much closer, perhaps an eighth of a mile from the castle, one east and one northeast.

"The X is where your C-47 will land to pick you up once your signal has been given."

"How will the pilot know to be on station?"

"We'll start a shuttle with three aircraft. With a travel time of two hours that means you'll never have to wait more than an hour."

"You make it sound like a train schedule, sir," Barltrop said.

Mallory smiled. "That's where I got the idea. They'll start flying at twenty-one hundred hours, so the first one will be overhead at twenty-three hundred hours. They will continue their flights until four a.m."

"Your back up plan, should you miss the planes for any reason, including a compromised landing zone, is to make your way to Hitler's Junkers 52. It will likely be parked in one of the areas denoted by the two red circles."

Saunders raised his eyebrows. "Our backup plan is to steal Hitler's plane?"

"Correct."

"I doubt the pilot will follow our instructions, sir."

"He won't, I'm sure you're right." Mallory shrugged. "We're sending two pilots with you who know the aircraft."

Saunders started to object, but Mallory held up a hand. "You can have them hide out where you can find them again afterwards. Just don't forget them, please." Mallory smiled again.

"Wouldn't think of it, sir."

Barltrop spoke up for the first time in a while. "Just one question, sir?"

Mallory nodded.

"Would there happen to be a third backup plan?"

Mallory glanced at Jenkins, and then back at Barltrop. "If you still have your radio, and you are safe, you can call for a pickup aircraft. If you must move to a safer position, call from that point. Repeat as necessary. All the while, you should be heading south-southwest."

"What's on that heading, sir?" Barltrop asked.

"At one hundred forty miles, you'll hit Venice. You can connect with an Italian Resistance group there for help."

Barltrop simply nodded, but said, "I do believe I prefer the first plan, sir."

Everyone chuckled.

But not for long.

Chapter 16

Aboard the HMS *Torbay*
Submerged, the Ionian Sea, 1,000 yards off the
Greek coast
1 October, 0503 Hours, Athens time

Over the submarine's intercom Dunn heard his name. "Sergeant Dunn to the bridge. Sergeant Dunn to the bridge."

Dunn and his men boarded the *Torbay* the night before in San Cataldo, Italy, which was located on the east coast of the Italian boot heel. They'd flown by C-47 to an airstrip seven miles southwest of the port city. The flight had taken a seemingly forever eight plus hours. Of course, the men had done what soldiers know to do whenever possible, sleep. A deuce-and-a-half-truck carted them to the tiny port village.

The sub had been moored against an ancient looking stone pier. She was a T-class, so called because all boat names started with a T. With a length of 275 feet, she carried a complement of fifty-nine men, plus the eight passengers. Commissioned on January 14, 1941, she'd patrolled the North Atlantic, the North

Sea, and the Mediterranean. The crew far preferred the consistent warmth of the southern patrols.

After almost nine hours of nighttime running on the surface, the sub reached its target with no problems. The captain had submerged the boat about thirty minutes ago.

Dunn climbed down from his top bunk, and left his temporary quarters. He'd been given a courtesy tour soon after boarding, and had been amazed by just how small the space was, although it wasn't his first time on board a sub. That had been a few months ago following a mission in France to seek and destroy a Nazi superweapon, an electromagnetic pulse weapon.

Dunn made his way along the narrow passageway to the control room, where he found the boat's captain, Lieutenant Commander Earl Reynolds. He was a slightly built man, with a David Niven mustache and dark wavy hair. He was at the periscope and pulled back from the view pad.

"Mr. Dunn, we're here. Would you care to take a look at the Greek coast?"

Dunn smiled. "I would like that, sir."

Reynolds stepped back and Dunn took his place. He put his hands on the silver handles and peered in. Early morning light reflected off the fairly calm surface of the water. In the distance was the coast line. "Are we about a half mile off?"

"Yep, a little more. A thousand yards."

Dunn noticed the reticles in the scope and wondered how you calculated a torpedo's course. Now wasn't the time to pester the captain. Perhaps he'd ask his brother-in-law, Danny Young, after the war. Young was Hazel's husband and he was aboard a sub in the Pacific, the executive officer, the last Dunn heard.

Dunn admired the view for another second, and stepped back. "Thank you, sir."

"Anytime, Mr. Dunn. I hope your trip was satisfactory."

"It was fine, sir. We appreciate the ride. Thank you."

Reynolds nodded. "You're welcome. You may as well get your men ready at the forward hatch. Charts show we can make it another five hundred yards before it gets too shallow for us. Think you can manage rowing ashore from there?"

Before Dunn could reply, a young sailor, no more than nineteen and wearing the sonar headset, said, "Captain. Picking up high speed screws. Light in sound, probably a fishing boat. Heading towards us."

"Mr. Dunn, hold on there," Reynolds said immediately. He stepped in front of the periscope and peered in. "You are correct, Mr. Blakeway, he is coming our way. Too far yet to ascertain weapons. XO, load tube one. Set for five hundred yards."

The executive officer, a man of thirty named Childs, responded, "Load tube one, set torpedo arming for five hundred yards, aye, aye, sir." He leaned over and repeated the order into a tube connected to the bulkhead. He received an acknowledgement from the forward torpedo room. Less than a minute passed before he heard over the same tube, "Tube one loaded, set for five hundred yards."

Childs repeated the reply for the captain, and placed his hand near a row of large black buttons above him.

The captain kept his eyes on the approaching boat. Suddenly, it swung to port, the captain's left, and slowed down. He examined the boat from bow to stern. There were no weapons on board, and no places where a cannon might be hidden. He zoomed in to make sure and was rewarded by seeing a man on the boat standing near the port railing. The man held up a small American flag. A moment later, the boat turned its bow toward the *Torbay*.

"Surface the boat," commanded the captain. "Gun crews prepare to man your weapons."

The sub had a four inch gun on the forward deck and mounts for the sailor-preferred .303 caliber machinegun. The big gun was made of waterproofed steel, but the machineguns were dismantled and carried below whenever submerging.

Off in the distance, Dunn heard running feet.

The men on the bridge worked in a choreographed way to raise the boat that Dunn found fascinating.

A sailor scrambled up the ladder in the conning tower and opened the hatch. Sea water poured over him and splashed onto the floor. Fresh sea air followed and Dunn took a grateful breath. You didn't realize the air in the sub was slightly pungent after the first few minutes, when your nose got used to it. With fresh air coming in, the odors became obvious and unpleasant again, until the fresh air moved them away.

The captain turned to Dunn. "Anyone with you speak Greek?"

"No, sir, afraid not."

"Right. Assemble your men at the forward hatch, but wait for my command to go on deck."

"Yes, sir."

Dunn took off. He went to various quarters along the passageway and got his men up and ready, although most were already on their feet due to all of the sudden activity on the sub. Dunn stood next to an uncharacteristically large sailor. He was about Malcolm Saunders' size, thought Dunn, wondering why he'd chosen submarines.

Dunn's men were lined up along the corridor behind him. The gun crews shimmied up the ladder to go man their weapons. With the hatch above him open, Dunn and his men received the benefit of more fresh air.

Sounds of a muted and distant conversation trickled down to Dunn's ears. After a couple of exchanges, he heard, "Mr. Dunn, come on deck."

Dunn squeezed past the big sailor and climbed the ladder to the deck. He squinted in the bright sunlight. He looked around and spotted the captain standing near the four inch gun. The barrel was lowered and aimed at the Greek fishing boat, which was about ten yards off the sub's right side, starboard, remembered Dunn. Two of the machineguns were pointed at the Greek vessel.

Dunn walked across the deck and said to the captain, "Dunn here, sir."

Reynolds raised a hand and pointed at a tall, slender man standing by himself on the other boat. "He speaks English and asked for you."

Dunn took a step forward and raised his hand. "I'm Dunn."

The man's face broke into a broad smile and he said in pretty good English with a heavy Greek accent, "Welcome to Greece! We thought we'd come out to greet you and save you from rowing in. Is that okay with you?"

Dunn eyed the man carefully and looked around the other boat. The only other person aboard was a man in the wheelhouse who was staring at him. The man raised a hand and grinned.

"What's the code word, my friend?"

The man raised his right arm, pointing somewhere in the sky and turned his head to his right. "It was the best of times, it was the worst of times." He left his arm up, but turned his face toward the sub. "Charles Dickens, yes?"

Dunn shook his head and smiled. "It was the age of wisdom, it was the age of foolishness. And yes, Dickens."

"Okay to bring the boat alongside?"

Dunn turned to the captain.

"Bring your boat alongside, sir."

The Greek lowered his arm, and gave a sharp salute. He said something to the pilot and the boat began to move toward the sub.

"Permission to bring the men on deck, sir?"

"Granted."

Dunn walked back to the hatch and called down to the men. Soon, all of them were on deck with their gear.

The Greek pilot was good and soon had the boat riding the light waves parallel to the sub. Several old truck tires were permanently lashed to boat's side to act as bumpers. The other man threw a rope across and a sailor grabbed it, and cinched it to a clasp. The fishing boat's deck was about five feet below the sub's, so the Rangers jumped down one by one, each one helping the one following.

Dunn said, "Thanks again for the ride, Captain Reynolds." He saluted.

The captain returned the salute. "Our pleasure. Good luck to you."

"Thank you, sir."

Dunn ran across the deck and leapt down into the Greek vessel.

The same sailor untied the rope and tossed it aboard the fishing boat.

The Greek who'd given the code words grabbed Dunn's hand and shook it vigorously. "Welcome to Greece. We're glad you're here." He turned to the pilot and gave an order. The man nodded and gently guided the boat away from the sub. When there was a gap of several yards, he gunned the engine and the stern dipped. He turned the wheel and headed for Greece.

"Stavros Georgoulakos. That's me." The man thumped his chest.

"Tom Dunn. Glad to meet you, Mr. Georgoulakos."

"Stavros out here, please."

"Certainly, Stavros. Where are we headed? And how safe are these waters from German patrol boats?"

"We are safe. The Germans are too lazy to get up this early. We're headed toward the beach south of a village called Kanali. From there, we drive to one of our command caves, where you'll meet our leader, Colonel Doukas. He is very grateful for your help."

"How'd you know where we were out there?"

Georgoulakos waved a hand. "It was nothing. I just looked through my binoculars for a flash of reflected light on the water. I knew your boat's periscope would do that against the rising sun."

"Hm." Dunn wondered whether the captain would be pleased to know this. Surely he already did.

"How long to the cave?"

Georgoulakos shrugged, "Half hour, maybe a bit more."

As they got closer to the beach, Dunn spotted a small jetty the boat seemed to be aiming for. At least they wouldn't get wet when they reached land. That'd be nice.

The boat pilot slid the vessel up gently against the jetty and Georgoulakos jumped onto it to tie the boat down. A large, covered farm truck that had been invisible from the water broke through a gap between some trees and headed toward them.

Dunn and his men jumped onto the jetty and organized themselves into a single file. Each man carried a pack, an M1 over one shoulder—or in Jonesy's case, his Springfield—and a Thompson over the other. Colt .45s were on the belt on the right hip.

Georgoulakos patted Dunn on the arm and swept a hand toward the truck.

Dunn marched off, followed by his men.

When the Americans reached the end of the jetty, six Greeks suddenly appeared from behind the truck, three on either side.

All had their submachine guns aimed at the Rangers.

Chapter 17

The Dunn family home
Cedar Rapids, Iowa
1 October, 2:00 P.M., U.S. Central time

The Dunn family was seated in the living room having just finished Sunday dinner. Gertrude and her older sister, Hazel, sat on the sofa in front of the open window facing the street. Gertrude was turned sideways with her left arm over the back of the sofa so she could see the street and driveway. Henry Dunn and his wife, Elizabeth Ann, each occupied a plush armchair. Henry was reading the Sunday paper and Elizabeth Ann had a Hercule Poirot mystery, *Evil Under the Sun*, in her hands.

Henry looked like an older, fifty-one, version of his son, Tom, with the same brown hair, brown eyes and slim nose. He taught high school math and Gertrude and Hazel had inherited his skills. Tom had too, to a certain degree, but the girls earned better grades in the subject.

Elizabeth Ann was a year younger. On Saturday, she'd had her blond hair set for church, in small waves framing her face.

Her blue eyes had been passed on to Hazel, the oldest of the three Dunn children, as had the blond hair.

Hazel was twenty-seven and was married to Danny Young, who was on a submarine in the Pacific somewhere. Hazel hadn't seen her husband in two years, but she received regular letters from him, which helped in a small way.

Gertrude glanced at the clock for about the tenth time in one minute. "Maybe they aren't coming," she said for the second time.

"I'm sure if they said they would be here, they will be," Elizabeth Ann said in the mother's voice.

Gertrude sighed.

And then a black car pulled into the driveway and the engine shut off. Gertrude got up on her knees peering through the window over the back of the sofa. Mr. Thompson was in the driver's seat, and he had a passenger. Both men got out, looked around at their surroundings casually, and headed toward the porch. The passenger carried a black briefcase.

Gertrude flew off the sofa and ran to the door. She smoothed her hair first, then her green dress. She glanced at her mother and held her hands out as if saying, 'well?'

Elizabeth Ann gave her the OK sign and a smile.

Gertrude gave a nervous smile. The doorbell rang and she jumped a foot in the air. When she recovered, she put a hand over her heart and gave her family a sheepish grin. She pulled herself together with a few deep breaths and opened the heavy front door.

"Hello, Mr. Thompson. Please, come in."

She pushed the screen door open a little and he pulled it open the rest of the way.

"Thank you, Miss Dunn. This is my colleague, Andrew Johnson."

Johnson doffed his black hat and said, "Pleasure to make your acquaintance, Miss Dunn."

"Andrew Johnson?" Gertrude asked, smiling. She was thinking of the seventeenth president.

Johnson tipped his head and shrugged.

She nodded and stepped aside to allow the men into the living room.

She introduced her family, her mother and sister first. The men said the polite words and turned to Gertrude.

"Where might we three sit?"

"We can sit here in the living room."

"No, we need to have a table and privacy for your tests and any questions we might ask you to help determine your suitability for the position. Just the three of us."

Henry didn't like the sound of that and stood up. He walked over to the trio and said, "We're her parents. We have a right to hear what it is you're going to talk about."

Thompson, who was clearly the one in charge said, "Sir, no. Your daughter is eighteen and we don't require a parent's presence due to the nature of the work, which is classified."

"Well, I'm sure your work is important, but frankly I think you just lied to me. You can't share classified information with my daughter. She doesn't work for you yet."

"Nevertheless," Thompson continued with no intentions of replying to being called a liar, "you cannot sit in on the interview we have with Miss Dunn. That is regulations. Go sit down, sir." He raised a hand and pointed at Henry's chair. "Now!"

Before Henry could even react, Gertrude turned on Thompson, her face red and her jaw set in defiance. "You want me to help you but you treat my dad with disrespect? Get out of our house!"

Thompson turned to face her and held up his hands. "There's no need to be angry, Miss Dunn. I'm just following protocol."

Behind Thompson, Hazel and Elizabeth Ann both got to their feet and stepped closer.

Johnson saw that Thompson was about to be surrounded by an angry family. He stepped forward to try and sooth things down.

Gertrude saw what he was up to and shouted, "You stop right there, Mr. Johnson. Don't you dare touch my family."

Amazingly, he stopped moving and turned to stare at the young woman. He tapped Thompson on the shoulder and leaned in to try to whisper, but it came out loud enough for everyone to hear, "Wow. She's really got something, Phil. We need her. Bad."

Thompson raised his hands and covered his face, shaking his head. A second later he was laughing. He lowered his hands and got himself under control. "Okay, folks. Why don't we do this? Can we all just sit down at the dining room table?" He pointed to the dining room.

Most of the others were smiling, and had chuckled along with Thompson. Everyone except Gertrude.

"No one move." She put a hand on Thompson's shoulder and as she leaned closer, her brown eyes focused intently on his, she said, "Not until you apologize to my dad." She backed up and folded her arms across her chest. She tipped her head in her dad's direction and raised an eyebrow for emphasis.

Henry said, "There's really no—" He stopped when Gertrude gave him a look.

Thompson's lip curled into a half smile. It turned out he agreed with his colleague. They did need her. She was exhibiting an interesting zero tolerance for bullshit. Thompson took a small step toward Henry and extended his hand. "I do apologize, sir. I was overzealous and I'm sorry. It's just that your daughter has already shown how well she can handle some of the work we do."

"That's quite all right. Why don't you and Mr. Johnson go on with Gertrude into the dining room? We'll stay in here. I think she's shown she can handle the situation, don't you?"

Thompson grinned. "Yes, I do think that. We'll require an hour of Miss Dunn's time."

The two groups separated. When Gertrude and the men from the OSS entered the dining room, Thompson said, "Would you please sit at the end of the table?"

"Surely." Gertrude took the seat normally reserved for her dad, with her back to the front window. Each man took the seat nearest her on the sides of the table, like they were playing a game of three-handed gin rummy.

Johnson laid his briefcase on the table, which was covered by a white table cloth. He opened it and removed several manila folders, which he laid on the table in front of him. He reached back inside the case and pulled out a box of sharpened pencils

Gertrude looked from one man to the other. They looked remarkably similar. Not just their black suit and shoes and hats, but their faces. Nondescript was the word that came to mind. Everyone's image of a thirty-year-old man getting on the bus to go to work every morning. Seen and forgotten. She thought perhaps that was a trait that would be useful as an agent.

"May I see your IDs, please?"

"You've already seen mine," objected Thompson.

Gertrude just held out her hand.

Both men reached into the same inside breast pocket of their suit and handed a black ID holder to her. She read each one carefully. Except for the names, they were identical. The front showed "Office of Strategic Services" below which was "Washington, D.C." Then came "The Bearer of this pass" and a line with the men's name typed in. Next came "Whose photograph appears hereon is a duly authorized representative of the Office of Strategic Services." It was signed by William J. Donovan. Gertrude didn't know who that was, but obviously he was a boss. She flipped the cards over and each man's picture was there in black and white. Above, it said "OSS" and below were red numbers. Thompson's was 1424 and Johnson's was 5903. Gertrude inferred that meant Thompson had more time in than his partner. She handed the IDs back.

"Thank you. Will I get one of those?"

"Yes, Miss," replied Thompson. "Are you ready to begin?"

"Yes."

Johnson slid the box of pencils toward Gertrude, who picked it up and pulled out a half dozen. She laid five of them down to her right in a neat row, their tips lined up, and kept one in her right hand.

Thompson glanced at the pencils and then at Johnson, giving him a slight nod. Preciseness was an attribute not an irritant.

Johnson opened a folder and removed one page of paper. He handed it upside down to Gertrude.

"When I say 'go,' turn the paper over and solve the puzzles."

Gertrude took the paper and waited. "How long do I have?"

"Five minutes."

"Okay."

He pulled a stopwatch from the case. He held it up and pressed the silver knob. "Go."

Gertrude turned over the paper. It was filled with word puzzles, grouped in fives. Not crosswords, but with one or two letters of each word filled in, like the word game hangman. Under each puzzle was a line. She figured it was a sentence made up of the words she had to determine.

She licked her pencil tip and set to work.

The two men watched her scratch the paper entering the missing letters at an alarming speed. They glanced at each other trying to stifle their excitement. Neither had seen a recruit work this fast.

Johnson eyed the watch's second hand. Just as he was about to say 'two minutes to go,' Gertrude handed the paper to him and put her pencil down, next to the others. He pressed the stopwatch button. He looked at the dial and then at Gertrude, and then at Thompson.

"Three minutes."

Johnson scanned the answers and nodded. "One hundred percent."

Thompson nodded. "Next one, please."

By the time Gertrude had used all six pencils, each one fresh for a new set of puzzles, twenty-five minutes had passed, well under the expected thirty. As she neared the last test paper, the puzzles were taking her a little longer, but still under the five minute limit.

Thompson said, "We have six more to do, which are math related. Are you up for them?"

"Sure."

When Gertrude looked at the first one, she said, "I'm bit rusty. The last time I did this level of math was last May, you know, in high school."

Thompson said, "Your time is running."

Gertrude smiled. "So it is."

A half hour later and six papers done, she sat back. "I'm rather thirsty. Would you gentlemen care for some lemonade?"

Thompson immediately said, "Yes, please."

Gertrude disappeared into the kitchen.

Thompson whispered carefully, "Holy shit, Johnson. She's got to be in the top five percent."

Johnson nodded his head. "She's gifted."

"Okay, pack up the stuff. Let's make the offer now."

"Don't we have to wait for approval?"

"I already talked with Mr. Smith. He said to go ahead if we're satisfied."

Johnson shrugged. "Okay." He began putting the tests and pencils away, along with the stopwatch.

Gertrude returned with a silver tray on which three glasses of lemonade sat. She put the tray down and handed each man a glass. They drank gratefully. Thompson drained his glass and stood up. "Miss Dunn, could we rejoin your family?"

"Sure."

When they walked into the living room, the Dunn family rose to their feet, expectant looks on their faces. Hazel walked over to another plush armchair and waved at the sofa. "Why don't you gentlemen sit there?"

After everyone found a place, Thompson began.

"Miss Dunn, we're both satisfied that you have the skills we're looking for. We're pleased to be able to offer you a job with the OSS. Interested?"

"Yes. But I have some questions."

"Please, by all means."

"Er, what's the pay?" She put her hand over her mouth. "Oh, can I ask that?"

"You can ask whatever you wish." He told her the monthly salary.

Her eyebrows jumped up.

Henry said, "Wow."

"That much?" she asked.

"Yes, Miss."

"I would need to give notice at the arsenal."

Thompson waved it away. "No, not necessary. We'll take care of it with your supervisor. You won't need to report for work tomorrow. Instead, we'll arrange for your train travel to the training center. You'll leave on the noon train."

"That soon?"

"Lot's to do, Miss."

"Where's the training center?"

"St. Louis."

Elizabeth Ann said, "Oh, good that's not too far away."

"Actually, after training, Miss Dunn will be transferred to Washington, D.C."

"How long is training?" Gertrude asked.

"Two months, six days a week. At the end of the two months, you'll have a seven-day furlough so you can come home to be with your family."

Gertrude looked at each of her family members. They all nodded. "Okay, I accept your offer."

Thompson stood up. "Excellent. Someone will call you later today and give you the details for your travel, as well as what you should pack."

Johnson pulled a camera from his briefcase and rose to his feet. "I need to take your picture, Miss Dunn."

"Oh, why?"

"Someone will meet you at St. Louis Union Station. The picture will help confirm your identity. You have a driver's license?"

"Oh, I see. Yes, I do have a license."

"Be sure to bring that with you." He raised the camera. "Look here, please." He tapped a spot just over the lens.

Before Gertrude could smile, he snapped it.

"I didn't smile."

Johnson gave her a wry grin. "It's unlikely you'll be smiling by the time you get off the train."

"I bet I am!"

"How much?"

"Two bits!"

"You're on." Johnson tipped his head. "Okay. Smile!"

Gertrude gave him a beaming smile, white teeth gleaming, and he snapped the photo.

"I'll give them both."

"Well, there you go, then."

The Dunns stood up. Thompson stepped over and shook hands with them, one by one, Henry last.

"Sir. If I may." He glanced at Gertrude. "Don't let this go to your head, young lady."

Gertrude vigorously shook her head.

"Miss Dunn is the highest scoring recruit I, personally, have ever seen. You can be very proud of her."

"Thank you, Mr. Thompson," Henry said, pride on his face and in his voice.

"One more, very important thing, Miss Dunn. You can't tell anyone what your new job is. No family outside this group can know, and definitely no friends."

Gertrude's mouth dropped open. "No one?"

"Absolutely no one. You can say you've taken a job with the U.S. Government, but that is all. This is for security reasons."

"Well, yes, I figured that out."

Thompson smiled. He was growing to really like the young, but forthright, Gertrude. To the family he said, "The same applies to you as well. You can't discuss this with anyone."

He received nods from the parents and Hazel.

"We'll leave you now. It was a pleasure to meet you all."

Gertrude saw the OSS men to the door and then ran back into the living room where she was surrounded and given a family hug.

"We're so proud of you, dear," Gertrude's mom said.

"Yes, we are," Henry and Hazel said in unison.

Elizabeth Ann disengaged from the hug and said, "Well, we better start packing!"

"We don't know what's on the list I'm supposed to get," Gertrude objected.

Elizabeth Ann patted her daughter on the shoulder. "There are some things that we don't need a list for."

RONN MUNSTERMAN

Chapter 18

**Entrance
Hohenstein Castle,
1 October, 2000 Hours, Salzburg time**

Neil Marston stood on the front drive, along with Colonel Neubart and an honor guard of SS soldiers, armed with rifles, as well as ten members of the castle's main floor staff. General Glockner and Wilbert Juhnke, and the other important guests, stood next to the colonel. Exterior lighting was on casting long shadows of those waiting.

Everyone's attention was focused on the gate forty yards away. A guard on the opposite side snapped to attention and raised his right arm in the Nazi salute. The sound of a heavy car swept across the distance to the men waiting for the *Führer*.

Headlights belonging to a large Mercedes from the castle's car pool came into view. The other guard raised the latticed iron gate. He shot a salute and clicked his heels. The Mercedes drove along the curving drive and stopped in front of the colonel and Marston. Several other cars from the castle's car pool followed, carrying Hitler's and Himmler's additional staff members.

Marston stepped forward, opened the door, and stepped back. He snapped his heels together and raised his arm in salute to the *Führer*. All the other people on the drive did the same. All were smiling and seemed star struck. Hitler stepped out of the car and gave a half wave, more of a wrist flap. He wore his officer's hat with a brown bill and a burgundy band. His long black leather great coat covered his uniform completely. The German eagle rested on the outside of the left bicep.

Colonel Neubart said, "Welcome to Hohenstein Castle, *Mein Führer*."

Hitler replied, "Thank you, Colonel." He looked up at the castle with an admiring eye. A self-professed student of art and architecture, he enjoyed the lines of the stones and the battlements. The Nazi flag waved from above, a light had been turned to make it visible for tonight only.

"If you'll follow me."

Hitler nodded and the colonel marched off toward the main entrance.

Marston stayed put with his arm raised, as did everyone else. A small man with wire-rimmed glasses climbed out of the car next. Heinrich Himmler saluted and nodded to Marston, and followed his hero into the castle. Last out of the car was a frumpy looking Martin Bormann. He saluted and hustled by without looking at anyone. A moment later, he was also inside the castle.

The great dining hall was illuminated by overhead electric chandeliers, and candelabras positioned in recesses in the walls designed for them. Red, white and black Nazi flags hung in the center of each of the four walls. A gold Nazi eagle with a two meter wing span sat on a tall table behind Hitler's empty chair. Red and white bunting draped the lower half of the walls. All in all, it reminded Marston of the nighttime marches the Nazis had been so fond of in the thirties.

The dining table was set for two dozen men. All of the SS officers were wearing their dress black uniforms and red armbands with a black swastika centered in a white circle. More than half of the men, whose ages ranged from the twenties to the forties wore an Iron Cross at their throat. Most also had one or two rows of ribbons above the breast pocket. Juhnke, the *Abwehr* man, wore a suit that was sharply pressed in contrast to the rumpled one he'd arrived in. Only the sides of the table were occupied.

Everyone was present except Hitler, who finally entered the room wearing his white uniform tunic and black trousers. His only medal—pinned on the breast pocket—was the Iron Cross earned in the Great War, when he was a corporal running messages from one area to another on the front line. Everyone, including the SS waiters, who stood in a line along the far wall near the kitchen door, rose to their feet and turned toward Hitler raising their arms in the Nazi salute. He walked steadily toward his seat on the far side of the table, in the center along the side, the power seat. A waiter already stationed by the chair drew it back for the *Führer*, who nodded and sat down.

The guests waited a few seconds and when Hitler nodded, seated themselves. Himmler sat to Hitler's right and General Glockner to Hitler's left. Colonel Neubart, the castle commandant, was directly across the table from the *Führer*. Marston was to Neubart's left. Juhnke, the only man not in uniform, was on the same side of the table as Marston and to his right at the end.

Hitler looked directly at Neubart, who quickly raised a hand. The six waiters burst into motion carefully picking up the appetizers from the holding tables set near the kitchen. Each table was covered with a white satin cloth. The appetizers rested on silver serving trays. Hitler was served first, followed immediately by Himmler, and then Glockner, who was the third highest ranking man present. The rest of the diners were served from the center of the table outward, since those toward the middle were of highest importance. No one spoke, or moved.

Hitler picked up a silver fork and stabbed a piece of fruit and took a bite. Only then did the rest begin eating.

Himmler was first to speak. "Events went very well at Arnhem, *Mein Führer*. You were brilliant."

"Yes, I was." Hitler put down his fork and leaned forward looking up and down the table. "By ordering General Bittrich to rest and replenish the ninth and tenth SS Panzer Divisions at Eindhoven and Arnhem, we were prepared for Montgomery's lunatic attack. Why he ever thought he could break through our superior forces is beyond understanding. He so often underestimates our power and ability to outmaneuver him. If he's the best the British can offer, it's only a matter of time before we send them all back to the sea, just like Dunkirk."

The men spontaneously burst into applause.

Marston joined in, smiling half crazy the way the others were. He was thinking, *Dear God, these people are such idiots.*

The applause died down and Hitler continued, "As soon as we drive the British off the continent, we can focus our attention on Bradley and his impetuous Patton. We'll retake France again."

More applause. Marston, who had been undercover for some time, and away from newspapers, still knew that Hitler was just throwing bloody bullshit out to these men, who believed every bloody word.

Finally, Hitler held up his hands and said, "Let's enjoy our main course and visit with each other. After dinner, I'll make a special announcement that I know you will welcome."

Dinner was served. Everyone received a chicken breast and roast potatoes, except Hitler who was carefully served his favorite Austrian dish, *Leberknödl*, liver dumplings. This was the only exception to his 'no meat' rule. Marston knew that Hitler was known to oftentimes make fun of the omnivores at his dinner table and tell graphic stories of slaughterhouses in order to convince them to avoid eating meat. This was sometimes met with unfortunate results, and more than a few dinner guests had embarrassed themselves by running from the room to find a bathroom. Marston wondered idly whether Hitler would do it here.

The men dug in, making small talk with their neighbors, all the while keeping one eye on the *Führer* in case he should either finish eating or begin talking.

The man to Marston's left, a captain from Berlin, said, "This is my first meal with the *Führer*. I feel so blessed to be here."

Marston glanced at the man, whose blue eyes seemed to shimmer with the inner light of fanaticism. "We are indeed fortunate. What announcement do you predict he will make?"

"Oh, I would never presume to predict what *he* might say." He leaned a bit closer to Marston, though, and said in a low voice, "But if I were to guess, I think it must have something to do with General Glockner's presence. Why else would he be here?"

Marston looked at the general, who was conversing quietly with Hitler. Marston noted that the men didn't look at each other, they just turned their heads slightly toward the other, faces aimed at the table.

Marston had had the exact same obviously logical thought, but said, "Why, you are a perceptive one, Captain. I believe you are on to something. We'll soon see, won't we?"

The captain nodded sagely, obviously pleased by Marston's compliment.

Marston turned back to his chicken, which was fabulous, as good as any he'd had in England or during his time in Berlin. Thinking of Berlin caused him to recall the time he'd been forced to kill for the first time. He'd just photographed top secret papers in a minister's office and was returning to his flat at three in the morning when a sentry spotted him. The soldier told him to empty his pockets, which of course he absolutely could not do because his mini-camera was there. He activated his spring-loaded wrist knife and the fight had begun. He'd won, but had been stabbed in the left arm by his own knife before forcing the weapon into the sentry's heart. He made his way home through the darkened streets, but had to stop and throw up once at the thought of what he'd done. Thinking about it now didn't affect him at all, which made him wonder whether his soul had been permanently damaged.

A ringing sound brought Marston back. Himmler was tapping his wine glass with a knife.

Marston groaned in his head. A bloody toast was coming.

Himmler rose to his feet, raising his glass. Everyone else stood up and lifted their glasses.

"To our beloved *Führer*, who has restored Germany to greatness and who is the righteous ruler of all of Europe. To Adolf Hitler!"

The entire room said, "To Adolf Hitler!" and everyone clinked glasses with their neighbors, including Marston, who felt sick.

Hitler beamed and nodded. He lifted his glass, which was partially filled with lemonade, to the room, and took a sip. Everyone else took one of their wine.

Hitler set his glass down and motioned for all to be seated. He swept hair from his forehead with his right hand, a well-known habit.

"We have here with us tonight a great leader, General Glockner. He has shown tremendous resourcefulness and skill in fighting the Russians. Effective today, I am promoting him to the rank of Field Marshal and awarding him command of Army Group B. As you are all aware, Field Marshal Rommel was seriously injured in a cowardly attack on his staff car in July and is still recovering from his wounds. Field Marshal Glockner will assume command tomorrow from Field Marshal Model, who I will reassign elsewhere." Hitler turned toward Glockner. "I have complete faith in you and trust that you will attack Bradley and Patton with a fervor they will be unable to match or stop."

He held out his hand and Glockner shook it. A photographer suddenly appeared behind Marston and Neubart captured the moment.

The men at the table rose and applauded.

Marston eyed the new field marshal, calculating how to include him in Saunders' attack.

Chapter 19

In flight over Austria
1 October, 2033 Hours

The British Commandos sat five to a side on the C-47's long benches. Most were dozing, their helmeted heads dipped toward their chins. Barltrop was closest to the door and would be first in the stick to jump. He was awake, a bit restless, as he thought about Kathy, the beautiful redhead he'd met at Saunders' wedding, just eight days ago. They'd hit it off and squeezed in a couple of dates in a matter of a few days, before he had to conduct some training for the squad. They'd agreed that something good was happening between them and they should continue to date whenever possible. He would go to London, where she worked for the Royal Navy's Staff Department, by train whenever he got a few days off.

Saunders was seated at the opposite end of the men. He would go last, making sure everyone got out okay, especially those with the heavier than usual bags. Half the men were carrying fifty feet of coiled rope, two were hauling the grappling hooks and launchers. On top of that were their weapons, the

Stens with the integrated suppressor, and their monstrous .455 caliber Webleys, plus the required extra ammunition.

The two additional pilots who would fly Hitler's Junkers 52 if need be sat directly opposite Saunders and were zonked out.

The jumpmaster sat near the door. He was watching the lights over the cargo door, waiting for the yellow lamp to flicker on telling him to get the men up and hooked onto the static line cable running the length of the aircraft's ceiling.

Saunders nodded to himself. One minute. Probably two minutes from jump time.

The first indication of trouble was when the men were startled awake by the sounds of a German night fighter's 20mm cannon shells tearing through the aircraft.

Everyone jumped into action. The jumpmaster was yelling to get hooked up as were Barltrop and Saunders. He opened the door.

As the men leapt to their feet and slapped their hooks on the cable, Saunders ran a few steps toward the cockpit.

An explosion sounded on the left side and he looked out one of the windows. Flames and smoke poured from the engine there.

Saunders made it to the cockpit where the pilot was struggling with the controls and the copilot was triggering the burning engine's fire extinguishers.

Saunders knew they were busy, but he needed to know. "How far?"

"We're one minute from your jump location!" shouted the copilot.

Just then, more cannon fire struck the right engine and it, too, burst into flames and stopped running.

Saunders turned around and leaned out the door. "Now! Now! Go Now!" He waved his arms above his head.

The jumpmaster saw him and shoved Barltrop out the door and grabbed Chadwick to go next.

Now on its third pass, the Me109G, outfitted with special radar, fired its cannons again.

Thuds and explosions rocked the aircraft's nose and shattered the cockpit windows. Rounds struck the pilot and copilot. When the pilot's lifeless hands let go of the wheel, the plane began a slow roll to the left.

Fire burst into the cargo area from the left engine. Saunders stared at the wall of flame just feet from him. He couldn't see through the fire and had no idea what was happening with his men.

He spun around and ran back into the blood-spattered and smoke-filled cockpit. He slammed the door behind him to cut off the heat and smoke, hopefully long enough.

He looked at the broken windows. Too small. He glanced up. Somewhere, sometime he'd learned about an escape hatch. There it was, just above his head.

The plane continued rolling and was now at a ninety degree angle to her original position. The nose began to dip.

Saunders fell to his knees against the bulkhead.

The escape hatch was now in the left hand wall to Saunders. He grabbed the lever and yanked on it hard. It slid easily and he pushed against the hatch. It popped open and the airstream took his breath away.

The plane jolted and bucked and continued to roll over with her nose dipping more and more toward the earth.

Saunders grabbed the sides of the hatchway with both hands and pulled himself through, almost going through upside down.

He cleared the aircraft and tumbled over so he was in a feet-down aspect. He yanked on the D-ring release praying he hadn't damaged his parachute popping through the hatchway.

The plane trailed flames and smoke. A moment later, it exploded and its charred remains fluttered earthward.

The parachute popped open and Saunders' body jerked when it fully deployed, much to his relief.

He was moving sideways along the original line of travel. He turned to look over his left shoulder. His eyes darted here and there in the night sky, searching for the half-round shapes of his men's chutes. There they were. They were much lower than he was and the chutes were easy to make out in the full moon.

But something was wrong. He couldn't believe his eyes. How many chutes were there? In a panic, he counted.

Four? Only four got out?

No, that can't be.

He forced himself to take a deep breath and he looked across the sky again. Maybe there were two groupings of chutes and he just missed the other one.

He swiveled his head and looked all around himself, even in directions that made no logical sense.

No other chutes were visible.

Four.

He had four men left.

Who?

Chapter 20

Cave
Somewhere on west coast of Greece
1 October, 2140 Hours, Athens time

Dunn and his men were in a cave and had been all day long. They were hungry and thirsty. Their captors had not been kind or good hosts.

"I bet this isn't the cave we're supposed to be in," Cross complained. He was sitting with his legs out in front of him, leaning against the cold rocky cave wall. His hands were tied and his ankles were roped together. He felt like a calf who'd been trussed up by a rodeo cowboy.

"I think not," replied Dunn, sitting in a similar position on Cross's left.

"I hate to say it, but I told you so about the Greek Resistance being a possible problem."

Dunn grunted. "So you did."

Two big Greeks stood guard twenty feet away at the dark entrance, facing inward. A table and a couple of chairs were along the right wall from Dunn's perspective. A lantern sat on top of the table, throwing soft, but helpful light around the cave. A second lantern was on a crate next to the wall on Dunn's left.

Before being forced into the truck, Dunn and his men had been frisked and everything of value was taken, including money, cigarettes and Zippos. When one of the Greeks attempted to take away Jonesy's Springfield, he fought them off and yelled, "No one takes my rifle."

Finally the leader, the man posing as Georgoulakos, walked over and pointed his pistol at Jonesy's head. "You fucking Americans think you're untouchable. You're in *my* country now. Give me your damn rifle!"

Jonesy gave it up, but gave the man a stare from hell.

Several times, Dunn had tried talking with the man who called himself Georgoulakos, but the Greek had ignored him.

Cross leaned closer to Dunn and whispered, "I don't suppose you have your little pocket gun?"

"Nope. Found it right away. They're better at frisking than the Germans in Blankenheim." Dunn had used a gun given to him by Colonel Kenton as a gift to extricate himself and then his men from the Germans' grasp on the last mission.

Dunn checked on his men. Everyone seemed to be as comfortable as possible.

Sounds of people moving through brush and grass came from outside the cave and Dunn looked at the entrance. Two men walked inside. One was the fake Georgoulakos. The other carried himself like a leader, expecting others to immediately do his bidding. They made their way over to Dunn and stopped. The leader examined Dunn for a moment then said something in Greek to the other man. He walked over to the table and sat down, crossing one leg over the other.

The fake Georgoulakos drew a knife and bent over. He sliced quickly through the ropes around Dunn's ankles. He sheathed his knife and said, "Get up."

He grabbed Dunn by the shirt and pulled, helping Dunn get to his feet. He shoved Dunn forward and the Ranger stumbled his way to the chair opposite the leader, grabbing it to steady himself. He straightened up and stared at the Greek leader.

The man smiled, and in heavily accented, but clear English, said, "Welcome to Greece, Sergeant Dunn."

"Who are you?" Dunn examined the man and his uniform in the lantern's glow. He had a dark complexion with hair and eyes to match. His nose was large and bent to one side, obviously a result of a fight. A long beard adorned his face, leaving little bare skin. The uniform's color was difficult to discern, but was probably black. His dark shirt was open at the neck, but he wore an ascot as an affectation the way some British officers did.

"I am Colonel Manos, commander of the forces of the *Ethnikó Apeleftherotikó Métopo*, the National Liberation Front, in this part of Greece. You and your men are my prisoners."

Dunn laughed. "Prisoners? I can see that. The question is why you think you can treat us this way. We came here to help."

Manos slapped his hand on the table, making the lantern almost topple over. "Help? You aren't here to help. You're here to deny the communist party its place as the righteous leader of my country."

"Oh, bullshit. Where is Colonel Doukas?"

"So you admit you were in cahoots with the EDES?"

Dunn laughed again at the sound of cahoots in accented English.

The colonel drew his handgun, a revolver that Dunn didn't recognize. He pointed it at him and pulled back the hammer. He realized it was probably a 7.62 mm weapon, which was a little smaller than a .38, but deadly, nevertheless.

"Laugh once more and it's your last."

Dunn said nothing.

Manos released the hammer and set the gun on the table. "Tell me what you were planning to do with Doukas."

Dunn nodded, as if agreeing, and said, "Might I sit down?"

Manos waved a magnanimous hand and Dunn sat down, but not before glancing quickly around the cave to get the positions of the two guards and the fake Georgoulakos. The guards were still at the cave entrance, but now they were facing outward. Georgoulakos stood a few feet away from his commander, to Dunn's right.

Dunn sat down keeping his feet flat on the cave floor.

"Aren't the Nazis your enemy, too?" Dunn asked.

"Internal enemies are more important to the future of Greece."

"You obviously mean the other Resistance groups. The ones who think communism is the second worst thing to happen to Greece."

"We will win the battle, Sergeant."

"Not if you don't defeat the Germans first."

"You are not here to debate the future of Greece with me."

Dunn shrugged. "Then why the hell am I here? In this cave with you?"

"Tell me what you were planning to do with Doukas."

Dunn shook his head and lied, "I have no idea. We were just told to show up and provide guidance."

"And arms?" Manos pointed over Dunn's shoulder. Dunn glanced that way and was relieved to see his men's weapons stacked behind him. That changed things. He eyed the revolver on the table and began a mental calculation.

"Answer me!"

"Those are just our personal weapons. Besides, really? You're worried about eight weapons?"

"No soldier goes into battle with two long guns."

"We're not regular soldiers."

"Yes, I know. You are *Rangers*." He said it with disdain as if it tasted bad to say it.

Dunn shrugged. He replayed his calculation. The first one hadn't worked out right. He glanced at the pistol without meaning to.

Manos grinned and picked up the weapon. "I think not, *Ranger*." He slid it back into his holster.

Chapter 21

Somewhere south of Salzburg, Austria
1 October, 2050 Hours, Salzburg time

Saunders ran in the direction of his men, to the south of where he'd touched down. He'd nearly hurt himself by landing badly because he wasn't paying close enough attention. He was too busy trying to keep his men in sight.

The man he reached first was Geoffrey Kopp, who was rolling his chute into a ball. Saunders suddenly realized he'd forgotten to do that.

"Kopp, are you all right?"

Kopp looked up. It took a moment for him to realize Saunders was really there. His eyebrows shot up and his mouth dropped open.

He finally blurted, "Crikey! Sarge! I thought you were a goner."

"I'm fine, lad. Got lucky." Saunders took a quick look at Kopp's back, where both his pack and the squad's only radio rested. Relief surged through him even as he realized how hopeless the mission was now. Five men against a castle's worth of potentially armed SS guards. He shook his head, but got back in focus.

"Go take care of my chute, will ya? I'm gonna check on the rest of the men."

Kopp patted Saunders on the arm, perhaps to make sure he was real. "Sure will."

Saunders took off again. As he ran over the top of a rise, he saw the other three survivors just ahead. They were running together toward him, but were too far away for him to tell who any of them were. He kept on running.

Soon, the gap closed enough for him to see who had gotten out of the doomed aircraft. The four men practically crashed into each other out of sheer joy at seeing each other.

"Mac! I thought you . . ." Barltrop started, but couldn't finish. He grabbed Saunders and gave him a hug.

"Steve!"

Saunders hugged back and looked over his friend's shoulder at Tim Chadwick and Christopher Dickinson. He let go of Barltrop and embraced each of the two men.

The four men stood in a circle for a moment, saying nothing. They were the last survivors of the original squad coming out of Achnacarry House.

"Geoff made it out, too," Saunders said. "He's back over the hill." He tilted his head. "Let's go join him." Saunders took off at a run.

The men turned and followed, keeping pace.

They found Kopp kneeling near the west side of the open field. The men greeted him warmly, patting him on the back and shoulders.

Saunders took a look at their surroundings. They were in a valley and mountain peaks rose on either side, far off in the distance. Their target landing zone was a point two miles south of the castle's location. The copilot had said one minute. He figured the plane would travel a mile in about thirty seconds, so if he added that to the target point, they should be only three miles from the castle.

He knew the valley ran north to south, but he checked the heavens anyway, and found the North Star easily. He followed the valley's line north and after a few moments found the shape in the terrain that represented the mountain outcropping on which the castle sat.

He turned his attention to the western edge of the valley field where the pine trees began growing thick and tall.

"Come on lads, let's get ourselves out of sight and think this through."

He led the way into the trees and found a bare spot large enough for the five of them. As the men entered the area, they removed their packs and put them down. They sat down and looked at each other in the moonlight that filtered through the trees.

"First things first, lads. A moment for our friends: Arthur Garner, Francis Handford, our old friend from Achnacarry, George Mills, Eddie Redington, and Bernie Thurston. I also want to remember the four pilots and the jumpmaster."

The men removed their helmets and bowed their heads.

Saunders allowed a minute to pass, thinking, *this one might seem to be a dead duck, but we're never going to get another chance at Hitler like this.*

"I'm open to ideas on how the five of us can pull off the mission," Saunders said. "Any ideas at all."

No one said anything for a time, evidence of the shock they were feeling.

Dickinson cleared his throat, and said, "I have a couple of things to say." He looked down at his boots, not wanting to meet anyone's eyes. "This is the biggest cockup we've ever had." He raised his head and saw the other men nodding in agreement. "But I say we go ahead. We were planning on a near-midnight attack anyway. Most of the people at the dinner will be drunk or close enough to it."

"That is probably very true," Barltrop said. He looked at Saunders. "Sarge, we can still breach the castle walls. We can breach the main castle, although now it will have to be at a single point, instead of the planned two."

Saunders thought through what Barltrop and Dickinson said. "Our biggest problem is that we don't know who our source is on the inside and we can't contact him." He remembered Madeleine from the French Resistance, who had done some incredible things to help Dunn and himself, and added, "Or her. Our exit plan may be buggered because we won't be able to leave men on post to keep the way out open.

"On the plus side, like Christopher said, most will be drunk. The guards, however, won't be. We'd have to push the timetable back, and attack around two a.m., when the number of guards should be reduced."

A sudden thought came to him and his heart seemed to seize up. He looked around quickly. He unexpectedly couldn't recall who had the climbing equipment. "Ah, fook! Does anyone have a grappling hook and launcher?"

Everyone came to the same realization and their faces showed it.

"Garner and Redington had them, right?" Saunders asked, when his memory caught up.

"Yes," Barltrop replied, his voice sounding defeated, the way everyone felt.

The men became silent once again as everything seemed to be getting worse, the problems piling on.

Saunders reviewed what he knew, which seemed to be all bad, and was getting worse by the moment. What else could go wrong? His head snapped up and he said quickly to Kopp, "Try the radio. Right now." Saunders had to fight some panic rising in his throat.

Kopp grabbed the radio and turned it on. To everyone's relief, it powered up right away.

"Everything seem all right?" Saunders asked, now able to keep his voice calm.

Kopp moved the radio so it received some moonlight directly. He rotated the critical piece of equipment and examined the casing, looking for any damage. He looked up and said, "Seems to be okay, Sarge. No damage I can see. Plus, I had a good landing."

"Good man," Saunders said as he reached out and patted Kopp on the shoulder.

"I'm going to repeat myself: anyone have a single idea on how the five of us can pull off the mission? Under the new circumstances?"

The men looked at each other, and each one shook his head.

"Sorry, Sarge," Barltrop said. The other three men said the same thing. No one wanted to let Saunders down.

Saunders agreed with them, but the one thing that kept nagging at him was what he'd thought of earlier: this was still the best, probably the only, chance to get Hitler. He wasn't interested in the politics or ethics of the order to kill the dictator. Only in the order itself. Although he did think the war would end sooner if Hitler was dead.

"Kopp, tune in and get ready for a transmission."

Kopp turned the dial to the required frequency. "Sarge, are you calling for a pick up?"

Sarge managed a smile. "No. I'm hoping a friend can drop in and join us."

Barltrop sat bolt upright and looked at his friend. Of course, that would work. They'd be able to depend on Dunn. They always could. He was a top notch soldier.

Saunders took the handset when Kopp said all was ready, and he began his transmission.

RONN MUNSTERMAN

Chapter 22

Cave
Somewhere on west coast of Greece
1 October, 2155 Hours, Athens time

Dunn's hands were in his lap, still tied together. He leaned forward, a plan in mind, his muscles tensed.

However, rifle fire erupted from somewhere near the cave entrance. From the corner of his eye, Dunn saw the two guards run out of the cave. The colonel made a mistake and looked at the entrance.

Dunn was also surprised, but since he'd already had an idea, he just implemented it. He grabbed the underside of the table and upended it, pushing it like a battering ram against the colonel, who fell over backwards.

Dunn landed partially on the upside down table lying on top of the colonel.

He got to his knees and flipped the table out of the way. He rolled the Greek onto his left side.

His hands darted forward like a snake on the attack. He jerked the revolver from its holster and thumbed the hammer back.

Fake Georgoulakos was fumbling with his holster flap, trying to draw his pistol, but Dunn aimed his at the man's heart. The man raised his hands.

Rifle fire increased outside, and some automatic fire joined in.

The colonel made a grab for the gun, but Dunn elbowed him in the nose. As the colonel fell back, his hands grasping his broken nose, Dunn scrabbled to his feet and said to the fake Georgoulakos, "Toss your gun."

The man complied.

Weapons fire seemed to be right outside the cave.

"Both of you lie down face first."

After the men were on the ground, Dunn knelt beside the colonel, who was still trying to cradle his nose while lying down. Dunn found what he was looking for and slid the knife from its scabbard with his left hand. He stood up and awkwardly tossed the knife toward Cross, hoping he hadn't overthrown it. The knife clunked on the floor two feet from Cross.

Cross scooted himself forward and grabbed the knife and set to work on the rope binding his hands.

Dunn kept an eye on the two Greeks on the ground.

There was a lull in the weapons fire.

"Hurry up, Dave!"

Cross sliced through the last bit of rope, and set to work on his feet. That was done quickly and he freed Schneider, who was sitting nearby. Leaving the knife with the big man, Cross ran across the cave to the stash of weapons. He plucked up a Thompson, the best choice in this particular firefight, and yanked the charging bolt back.

Weapons fire began hitting rocks just outside the cave entrance. Dunn prayed some rounds didn't make their way inside.

As each Ranger was cut free, he ran over and grabbed a Thompson.

Dunn told the fake Georgoulakos to get to his feet and to help the colonel stand. "Over there and sit down cross-legged," he said, pointing with the gun. The men followed directions, although the colonel's eyes seemed to burn with hatred. That and a bit of tears from the broken nose. He breathed through his mouth, which was covered in blood.

Jonesy, who was last to get free, came over and cut off Dunn's ropes.

"Ah, thanks, Jonesy."

"Welcome, Sarge. Want me to watch these two?"

"Yep." Dunn handed off the pistol and Jonesy aimed it rock steady at the colonel's heart.

Gunfire ceased outside, but a commotion ensued at the entrance and a single shot was fired. A body thumped to the ground and a half dozen Greeks ran into the cave, weapons at the ready.

The Rangers aimed their Thompsons at the Greeks.

No one fired.

A tall, slender Greek pushed his way through and held up his hands.

"Are you the American Rangers?"

Dunn stepped forward. "Dunn here. Who are you?"

"Colonel Doukas."

"I suppose it's a little too late to exchange passwords."

Doukas stepped closer. "Alas, you are right. Someone impersonated one of my most trusted men."

"Yeah, let me guess: Stavros Georgoulakos."

"Correct. Is the imposter here?"

Dunn tipped his head.

Doukas's eyes followed. He strode over to the two Greeks on the ground.

Jonesy wasn't sure what to do and looked at Dunn. Dunn shook his head and Jonesy stepped aside.

Doukas stopped in front of the two men. He was breathing hard. He raised his submachine gun and aimed it at the fake Georgoulakos, who glared back.

In English for the benefit of the Americans, Doukas said, "You murdered my friend." His finger tightened on the trigger.

"It's war, Colonel, as you well know." This came from Colonel Manos.

Doukas pulled the trigger and the fake Georgoulakos fell over with three red holes in his chest. He altered his aim and said, "As I do well know, you bastard." The weapon jumped again and Manos collapsed.

Chapter 23

Great Dining Hall
Hohenstein Castle,
1 October, 2303 Hours, Salzburg time

Marston had never experienced a more terrifying, yet boring dinner in his life. It was breaking into its fifth hour, dessert consumed and forgotten long ago. After the announcement of Rommel's permanent successor, General, now Field Marshal, Glockner, Himmler had risen from his seat. He'd talked for over an hour on the great and marvelous things the SS was doing and would be doing on behalf of the Fatherland and, of course, by extension, for Hitler. The German people received no accolades in this tribute, but were instead told they would have to continue to sacrifice in many ways to help support the Third Reich's front lines, factory work must double, and food must be shared among all equally.

It was all Marston could do to not stand up and shout, "You bloody buggers! The war is lost. Surrender so I can bloody well go home!" At one point in Himmler's pronouncements, he evidently went off script when he said something complimentary about one of the generals on the Russian Front, and how he had recently made a brave stand against the Red Menace. Hitler had said nothing, but cleared his throat loud enough for the men at the far ends of the table to hear. Himmler smoothly continued saying that, of course, the general had been inspired by the *Führer's* wonderful and powerful leadership. Hitler promptly nodded as the men all applauded.

Marston's left hand rested on the table. He rotated the wrist toward himself. He checked Hitler and the other men directly across the table from him to make sure they were not looking at him. He stole a quick look at the time, and looked at Himmler who had raised his hand to emphasize some point or other. *Dear God in Heaven, please just let this end*, he thought, not for the first time this evening.

Himmler finally finished and concluded with yet another *Heil* Hitler. Arms shot up in salute.

Martin Bormann stood up and Marston stifled a groan. Bormann was shorter than Hitler by a few inches, but had at least thirty pounds on the dictator. His brown hair was combed straight back with a wide widow's peak. It was pretty well known that he fancied himself a lady's man, and evidently certain ladies thought so, too, even though he had a wife and ten children at home.

He began by thanking Hitler for his leadership of the great nation of Germany. This evoked yet another round of applause. He said, "I wish to congratulate a member of the *Abwehr*, who joined us here tonight. *Herr* Juhnke." He lifted a hand indicating he wanted Juhnke to stand.

Marston noticed a sudden stillness in the room as all eyes turned toward the man wearing a suit. The relationship between the SS and the *Abwehr* was poor at best. The SS regarded the *Abwehr* as untrustworthy, ironic, since they were the Military Intelligence arm of the services. The SS also thought it was a pit of anti-Nazi traitors, and had members involved in anti-Hitler plots. Some thought these plots and intrigues went all the way to the top, to Admiral Wilhelm Canaris. The admiral had once been seized by the lapels by Hitler during a briefing because Hitler thought the admiral was spouting defeatism, the one true great sin of a German.

Hitler glanced over at Bormann and a signal must have passed between them that Marston couldn't discern, because Bormann started clapping. Grudgingly, the SS men joined in, although it was mechanical and unenthusiastic. Marston wondered why someone had decided Juhnke should be here in the first place among what amounted to political enemies.

Bormann seemed to thrive on the feelings of animosity circulating the room. He dramatically held his hands out, palms down to stop the applause. It died off immediately. You didn't have to tell these officers twice to stop clapping for the *Abwehr*.

Juhnke got to his feet, Marston thought a bit shakily, and the worst thing possible happened for him. Bormann smiled and waved for Juhnke to come stand beside him. Marston thought he actually saw the man's face pale and he gave a slight shake of the head. Bormann ignored all of it and waved even more energetically.

"Come, *Herr* Juhnke, you have a great gift for the *Führer*. Bring it here so he can examine it himself."

Defeated in his attempt to stay put, Juhnke reached down and picked up the odd square box Marston had noted on the man's arrival the day before. He trundled around the table, as if walking on wooden legs. When he reached Bormann, the secretary stepped back and gestured for Juhnke to place the box on the table. Marston eyed the box carefully, looking for anything that might indicate what it was used for.

Juhnke put the box on the table, but looked decidedly uncomfortable. Marston attributed his reaction to the cold reception by the SS officers, but soon discovered that wasn't it.

Juhnke drew himself up and seemed to suddenly find some courage. He looked at Hitler and said, "*Mein Führer*, this box represents an intelligence breakthrough and Admiral Canaris himself has directed me to present the fact that we have obtained it to you." He swallowed heavily. "The admiral requested that I make the presentation to you in a more," he looked around the table at all of the SS officers staring at him with barely concealed anger on their faces, "private setting."

Instead of Hitler, it was Himmler who reacted to Juhnke's words. He jumped to his feet, his face red, and he practically spat out his words, "How dare you cast aspersions on the loyalty of my SS officers! These are men who have promised to die for the *Führer*! Apologize to them right now!"

Juhnke's courage stayed with him. "*Reichsführer*, I recognize that your men are dedicated to the *Führer* and Germany, but critical intelligence during wartime, by its very nature, must have a restricted audience. I mean no disrespect, but these were Admiral Canaris's own instructions to me."

"You are forgetting who Admiral Canaris reports to, *Herr* Juhnke," Himmler shot back.

"Not in the least, sir. I'm merely doing my job as instructed."

Himmler's jaw muscles were working overtime and Marston thought he was about to go apoplectic. "I could have you—"

"Investigated, arrested, and probably shot. Yes, sir."

Hitler apparently tired of the exchange and Marston assumed his curiosity was getting the better of him. "*Herr* Juhnke. I hereby grant you permission to present your information to me, here in this highly secure location in front of my most trusted men."

Juhnke immediately nodded and said, "Certainly, *Mein Führer*."

Himmler sat down, but he was still fuming at having been talked back to. Marston decided he was already scheming how best to obtain retribution on the poor Juhnke.

Juhnke opened the box's lid and turned it so Hitler could see all the dials and knobs, and most importantly, the typewriter-like keyboard.

Hitler's eyebrows went up. "Why that resembles our Enigma machine."

Juhnke smiled, for the first time since his arrival, thought Marston. "Yes, *Mein Führer*. But it is an American SIGABA machine. It is used by the United States Army for all of their encoded message traffic. It was captured recently and sent immediately to the Berlin *Abwehr* office. I have been tasked with breaking the machine down and determining how we can begin to use it to read the Americans' messages as soon as they are sent."

Hitler jumped to his feet. He raised an outstretched hand heavenward, as if receiving a gift from the gods. "Do you all understand the importance of tonight? In my own perceptive manner, I have promoted to field marshal our greatest living general, Field Marshal Glockner, who will lead our troops in the west to victory. This marvelous gift from the *Abwehr* will provide additional advantages to our field marshal and other generals."

Hitler's eye seemed to take on a demonic glare. "We are invincible. We have always been invincible and this night proves it once again!" He pounded his fist on the table, rattling the glasses still standing there.

The table erupted in repeated *Heil* Hitler, *Sieg Heil*, and salutes that went on for a couple of minutes.

Marston was able to surreptitiously check his watch again. He hoped Saunders would arrive on time. The attack was more important than ever with this new revelation, a captured American cipher machine. Who knew what terrible ramifications it might have on the western front?

RONN MUNSTERMAN

Chapter 24

Cave
Somewhere on west coast of Greece
1 October, 2225 Hours, Athens time

Dunn shook hands with Colonel Doukas. "How'd you know we were in trouble and how did you find us?"

The two men were seated at the table, which had been set upright again, along with the two chairs. The lantern had shattered, but Doukas had it quickly replaced. The bodies of the other resistance colonel, Manos, and his man impersonating Georgoulakos had been removed from the cave. Dunn's men reacquired all of their individual weapons, including Jonesy, who grabbed hold of his Springfield like a lost treasure. Dunn thought Jonesy was hugging it, but decided it might just be a trick of the lighting.

The men were busy chowing down on several K-rations each and drinking a lot of water. Doukas's men, three dozen, were split, half inside and half outside. Those outside had set up a perimeter of fifty yards, while those inside were seated or lying down. Some were eating food they'd pulled from their own packs.

"When Stavros didn't return on time, I sent a party out to find him right away. They came back and reported the fishing vessel tied up on the pier. They checked the ground at the end of the pier and spotted truck tire tracks and boot prints around the tracks that didn't match any we've seen here. We assumed they were American and that you'd been abducted.

"The tire tracks were not from a German vehicle, so we knew it was someone who was Greek. We've been having trouble with Manos over the past month. You're familiar with the two main resistance groups?"

"I am."

Doukas nodded. "He's been trying to take over in this part of the country, where communism is less popular than in the more populous areas, like Athens and Thessaloniki. We can only guess that he had been spying on us," he shrugged, "as do we on him, and followed Stavros this morning. He must have surprised him and forced the information from him." Doukas's face became a mask of pain and sadness that Dunn had seen all too often during the war. "Stavros has a pregnant wife, and two children. It would have been easy for Manos to threaten their lives. Any man would have done anything to protect his family. I hope you understand."

Dunn was thinking about Pamela and the baby. "I do understand. I hold no ill thoughts against your man. I offer my condolences to you and his family."

Doukas nodded. "Thank you. The family will be cared for, of course."

"Good to hear."

"We found you by process of elimination. We knew he would hide you. I think he wanted to horn in," Doukas glanced at Dunn, "is that the right term?"

"Yep."

"Horn in on what we have planned. He assumed, correctly, it was a big event and that it must have value. He wanted whatever that value was, in this case, any weapons we can take during the attack."

"You think it's wise to continue the attack?"

"Yes, he didn't know what it was. Even though Stavros knew, Manos was too stupid to ask the right question. I know this because none of his other troops in the area have moved anywhere, let alone near the target."

"He did ask me what we were doing here, so I think you're right and he didn't know anything. Are his troops going to be a problem?"

Doukas shook his head. "They will wait for him to return. When he doesn't, they'll assume the worst. Since their leader and second in command are dead, the third in command will attempt to assert his authority. They'll have some infighting for possibly a week or more. So, no, they won't be a problem."

"We're still on for the attack tonight then?"

"We are if you are."

Dunn nodded. "That's what we're here for. Care to show me your plan?"

Doukas pulled a map from his shirt pocket, unfolded it, and spread it out on the table.

Dunn held up a finger. "One second, please."

Doukas nodded.

Dunn turned in his seat. "Cross?"

Cross looked up at hearing his name, saw Dunn looking his way, and waved a hand. He set down his K-ration and canteen, and joined Dunn and the Greek commander.

Doukas carefully laid out his plan of attack using the map, which had pencil markings on it. He gave Dunn and Cross the strength for both the Greek and German troops. He indicated on the map where his three platoons would start and when and where the fourth would join. He said what he expected Dunn's men to do. When he was done, he sat back and asked, "Do you see areas where we can improve the attack?"

Dunn had been making mental notes while the colonel talked.

Dunn said, "A couple of suggestions, if I may, sir." Dunn pointed to a couple of spots on the map. "If your heavy machine guns are set up on the roof of the buildings here and here, you'll have a strong crossfire as well as a depressed firing angle. You'll be able to cover much more ground and have a very good killing zone."

The colonel made a couple of marks on the map where Dunn had pointed.

The men discussed the attack for a little longer, and Dunn said, "My sniper can add a lot to the attack, and he'll need to be on this building. He could for instance, target and take down any guards walking around. He always has a man with him as a spotter and to help protect him."

Doukas nodded.

"Are you intending to target any vehicles, sir?"

"I hadn't planned on that. We have limited explosives."

"How about gasoline and bottles? And of course, cloth, matches or lighters."

"Of course. Good idea."

"Those would work wonders on the vehicles." Cross said.

"So they would." Doukas said.

Near German supply depot
Kastrosikia, Greece
2240 Hours

Doukas had the foresight to get his men in position prior to taking his reserve platoon to go search for the Americans. He'd found them rather quickly because he knew the EAM's late commander, Colonel Manos, was a creature of habit and had a love affair with caves, thinking, incorrectly it turned out, they were impregnable. The fact that the cave was just minutes from Kastrosikia had been a blessing as far as time consumption was concerned.

The full moon was a quarter of the way up in the eastern sky, shedding light on the city of Kastrosikia laid out below them. The air was cool, perhaps forty-five degrees, but a light breeze from the south made it feel a little colder than that. Doukas was on top of one of the buildings Dunn identified as a perfect place for a heavy machine gun. The weapon had already been moved into place as had the other one on a building a block away. Panzerfausts were stationed on three sides of the depot to stop any reinforcement by the Germans from the outside. The fourth side was where the assault on the depot would take place, from the south. The main warehouse was of medium size about thirty yards square and two stories tall, with lots and lots of windows, which could make access easier.

Dunn's men would join Doukas's first platoon, strengthening the main attack on the barracks. Dunn's sniper, Jonesy, was on top of the same building as the first machinegun with his partner, Lindstrom. His Springfield had a long suppressor screwed onto the barrel. He already had his first three targets in view, three guards walking a repetitive pattern along the front fence facing the main assault group. Another pair of guards was positioned at the main gate to the depot.

The German barracks, large enough for a platoon strength unit, was to the west of the warehouse. There were no lights on anywhere in either building. A number of trucks were lined up in typical German neat order along the south fence. The distance from the fence to the warehouse was about twenty yards, so the assault group wouldn't have much ground to cover.

Doukas checked his watch in the moonlight. He nodded to himself, and almost spoke aloud to his dead second in command. He was already missing his big friend Stavros. They'd been through much together and Stavros would have enjoyed seeing the German war supplies destroyed or captured.

He ran in a crouch over to Jonesy and Lindstrom, patting Jonesy on the helmet.

"Fire when ready, Mr. Jonesy." When Dunn had introduced Jonesy to Doukas in the cave, the Greek had grinned and repeated Jonesy's name several times, as if he just loved the way it rolled off his tongue. He had immediately started calling him 'Mr. Jonesy.' Jonesy, for his part, just grinned each time.

He lined up the scope's crosshairs on the guard the farthest distance from the main gate. Jonesy's shot would amount to only a hundred yards. He squeezed the trigger gently until the weapon spit out its .30-06 round at 2,800 feet per second. The bullet slammed into the guard's chest, seemingly instantaneously, but in reality a tenth of a second had passed. Jonesy smoothly racked the bolt and shifted his aim. He picked off the other two guards walking the perimeter. Next, he sighted on one of the Germans at the gate and squeezed the trigger once more. As he activated the bolt again, the remaining guard turned at the wet slapping noise made by the supersonic bullet piercing his companion's face. Jonesy sighted on the man as he started to move toward the other guard to see what had happened. Another squeeze. Another enemy solider down.

Doukas lifted a small radio to his mouth and spoke into it.

Three platoons of Greek Resistance fighters plus a small American squad rushed across the street and poured through the main gate.

Chapter 25

Colonel Jenkins' office
Camp Barton Stacey
1 October, 2045 Hours, London time

Mark Kenton had taken a phone call from Colonel Jenkins only fifteen minutes ago. The colonel had seemed unusually subdued, but had declined to explain why he needed to see Kenton at such a late hour other than to say it was urgent. He had added 'please.' If Kenton hadn't already been worried, the 'please' sealed it. He'd called Lieutenant Adams and told him to meet him at Jenkins' office. Adams had asked what was up, but Kenton had to say he had no idea, but that it was likely bad.

Adams arrived first, but had waited outside for his boss. The two Americans stepped into the office. Jenkins and Lieutenant Mallory were sitting at a table.

The world outside the window behind the colonel's desk was black. A single light was suspended from the center of the ceiling by a chain. Both Mallory and Jenkins were smoking cigarettes and their smoke trailed toward the heat of the overhead light.

Kenton and Adams sat down, Kenton opposite Jenkins. Jenkins wore an expression of such dejected shock, Kenton knew for certain something horrible had occurred.

"What happened, sir?" Kenton asked.

"Saunders' lost half of his men before they even left the plane."

Both Kenton and Adams blinked in disbelief. They knew Saunders and his men well.

"How?"

"Saunders thinks it was a German night fighter. It must have been over fast. They are near their mission target, which is fortunate because they're in Austria."

Kenton raised an eyebrow, but said nothing. This was a first. "Who made it?"

"Barltrop. Evidently he was at the door when the attack began. The jumpmaster forced him to jump and helped as many get out as possible before the plane rolled over and exploded. Kopp, Chadwick, and Dickinson."

"Jesus Christ. That's just . . . horrible."

Jenkins nodded glumly.

"He's asked for help from us," Jenkins motioned to indicate Mallory and himself. "But we've no one available. He specifically requested Dunn's squad. Is that in any way possible?"

Jenkins' expression was as close to forlorn as Kenton imagined it could ever be. Kenton understood completely. Dunn had lost three men at one time in Italy, plus one who lost a leg and was sent home. Kenton recalled how he'd felt at the news.

"Dunn is in Greece right now." Kenton tried to think of a way to meet Jenkins' request. "The soonest he would be available to fly into Austria would be tomorrow afternoon, assuming his mission goes off with no hitches."

Jenkins looked at Mallory, who shrugged. "That's too late for the primary targets, sir. He's supposed to leave in the morning."

Kenton watched the exchange between the British officers, and then asked, "Who are the primary targets, Colonel?"

"Hitler and Himmler."

Kenton just stared at Jenkins for a long moment. "I know you're not kidding, but how high up does that order come from?"

"All the way."

Kenton shook his head. Churchill approved it. "Where is the hit supposed to take place?"

Jenkins sighed. "It's a castle in western Austria, south of Salzburg about fifteen miles. It's a big meeting place for the SS."

"Oh, for . . ." Kenton stopped himself. He was about to complain about the Nazis and their weird ways. "Go ahead, please."

"We have an agent there who is helping coordinate the attack. Saunders and his men rehearsed a castle breach several times at Arundel Castle and solved it after the third attempt."

"You say he lost half? Five men?" Kenton asked.

"Tragically, yes."

"Dunn and his men total eight because they lost two on the last mission." Kenton didn't go on to explain that one of the two had been killed by Dunn because he was a traitor and had murdered one of Dunn's men. "So now we're talking about thirteen men for your attack. But I have to ask: if Hitler and Himmler will already be gone tomorrow morning, what's the point of continuing?"

"That's a fair question. The answer is simply that Hitler's plans might change and he could still be present. He's famous for changing plans at the last moment because he's so afraid of another assassination attempt. Another consideration is that Hitler went there for a specific reason. We don't know what that is, but if it's important enough for him to leave Germany, maybe another high value target will still be there tomorrow night. We haven't heard from our agent tonight, and might not, so we don't know anything for sure. But it seems a logical conclusion."

"I can't disagree with you, sir. If I commit Dunn, what's the extraction plan?"

"We had a previous plan that we had to toss because of the night fighter's possible presence. So a C-47 to land nearby for a quick pick up. I think we should have the one taking Dunn stay on station nearby."

"Given that Saunders' plane *was* shot down, I'd want a radar equipped fighter or two to go with that aircraft."

"Lieutenant Mallory can arrange that," Jenkins said, his voice rising a bit in hope.

"Dunn will check in after his current mission. I believe that will occur after he gets back on a sub headed for Italy." He checked his watch. "I'll alert the signals group to call me right away."

He turned to Adams. "We need to requisition the C-47. Coordinate with Lieutenant Mallory for the Mosquito night fighters. You find the airstrip closest to where they'll land in Italy. Also find the best airborne bunch over there and get them to deliver enough parachutes for Dunn."

"Yes, sir," Adams said as he pulled out a notepad. He began writing.

To Jenkins, Kenton said, "Dunn's got Thompsons and M1s. I imagine it's safe to say he's going to need suppressed Stens. Can you arrange that for us?"

Mallory spoke up for the first time, "I'll handle that, sir."

Jenkins stood up and the other men did, too. "I don't think there's a need for us to reconvene, do you, sir?"

"No, Colonel. I'll call you when I hear from Dunn. If you'll call me when everything else is arranged?"

"I will."

Kenton turned to Jenkins' aide. "Lieutenant Mallory, would you give Lieutenant Adams the particulars on the location, plus a rundown on the castle that we can pass on to Dunn? At least a version for an encoded message?"

"Yes, sir."

The men all shook hands, saluted and Kenton departed, leaving Adams to gather information from Mallory.

When Kenton stepped outside, the cold air seemed to slap him in the face. He shivered. As he walked toward his Willys jeep, he wondered if it was really the cold making him shiver.

Chapter 26

German supply depot
Kastrosikia, Greece
1 October, 2255 Hours, Athens time

Dunn led his men toward the barracks. He and his men were on the left flank of the EDES first platoon. The second and third platoons peeled off to the right, angling for the warehouse with their explosives. The fourth platoon carried the panzerfausts and spread out around three sides of the facility's perimeter.

On the way through the gate, Dunn bent over to check on the two guards there, to make sure they were dead. And they were. He set his men up in a line facing the barracks from the south side of the building, the narrower side, with windows, but no doors. Dunn was on the far left with Schneider and they had a clear view of the back door. Prior to the assault, the young Greek platoon leader had wanted Dunn to go around the back and guard the door from there. The kid, as Dunn thought of him, spoke English, but barely. However it was good enough that, with a few hand gestures added, the point had been made. Dunn promptly shook his head and explained about the danger of friendly crossfire, using his own gestures. The kid's eyes had widened and his face darkened in embarrassment. Dunn patted him on the shoulder, and told him it was okay.

A Greek took position to the side of the front door. He grabbed the door handle and yanked the door open. In seconds, an entire EDES squad was inside yelling and screaming at the German soldiers. Dunn heard one shot fired and assumed one of the Germans had made a play for a weapon. *Not smart*, he thought. He figured it was fifty-fifty as to whether any Germans would bolt through the back door, or through one of the three windows he could see.

A second ticked by and the back door burst open, nearly thrown off its hinges by two unarmed soldiers at a full run. They ran a few steps and spotted Dunn and Schneider with their Thompson .45s aimed at them. One stopped and raised his hands. The other turned tail and ran in the other direction.

Dunn fired off a three-round burst over the man's head, who stopped in his tracks. He turned around and raised his hands. Dunn motioned for them to walk forward. When the men reached Dunn and Schneider, the big man commanded in German, "On your knees."

The men complied.

No more shots came from inside the barracks, which Dunn thought was good news. Less likely to attract reinforcements. Even though the panzerfausts were ready, it was better not to have to deal with it.

A moment later, some Greeks popped out of the barracks, leading a string of Germans with their hands up. Other Greeks followed. Dunn estimated there were thirty German soldiers, counting the two on their knees in front of him. When Doukas had told him he wanted to capture as many Germans as possible, Dunn had been surprised. The Greek colonel had explained that he would use the prisoners as trades for Greeks, EDES members, who had been captured by the Nazis.

Watching the men traipse by, Dunn hoped the colonel got his money's worth.

The young Greek first platoon leader broke free from the line and headed toward Dunn when he saw the two Germans. He grabbed each one by the collar and tugged them to their feet. The two men ran over to join their dejected comrades. He offered his hand to Dunn, who shook it. Then the young man was off to join his men.

Dunn looked past the line of prisoners headed toward the gate. Greeks were running out of the warehouse in two different lines. One made a beeline toward the trucks so precisely arranged by the south fence. The other group of about fifty men, was moving in pairs, with each pair carrying various sized crates between them. Dunn smiled. Spoils of war.

He turned to his men, "Time to get out of here. Back to the fallback point."

Cross took the lead and the men ran after him. They squeezed through the gate with the flood of Greeks, and German prisoners. The Greeks were yelling at the Germans, prodding them along.

The first of the Molotov cocktails flew into the back of a truck. Soon, many flaming bottles arced through the air and all of the trucks were on fire. The Greeks ran toward the gate.

Once through the gate, Cross turned west, following the street. The squad ran two blocks and took up a position behind a chest-high stone wall that surrounded a large house located on the northeast corner of the intersection.

Several explosions broke the night silence. By the size of them, Dunn guessed some of the trucks' fuel tanks had gone up. They were too small for the warehouse explosives. The thing was, there was no mistaking the sound. German troops in the city would have heard and would be on the way in minutes.

Across the street from them, standing guard in an alleyway, were four Greeks with panzerfausts. Dunn waved at the men, who lifted their free hands.

Dunn knew Doukas was organizing his men so they could climb aboard their own trucks. Escaping was always the trouble with sneak attacks.

Dunn checked his watch. Four minutes had passed since the trucks exploded.

"Should be any time, men," he said.

The men nodded.

At that moment, Jonesy ran up behind Dunn. "I'm here, Sarge." Jonesy's Springfield was strapped over his back and he was carrying his Thompson in his hands.

Before Dunn could answer, rumbling clanking sounds came from the north.

Dunn looked over at the Greeks. All four had clearly heard the sounds because two of them stepped out of the alley and ran along the edge of the one-story building toward the intersection.

An enormous explosion sent shockwaves through the air and ground. Several more followed. Dunn glanced over his shoulder. A gigantic fireball broiled skyward and the night shadows gave way to the bright light.

Suddenly, the rumbling sounds of the vehicles were closer. Dunn saw both of the Greeks at the intersection raise their weapons. A second later, the rocket powered warheads streaked across the intersection. The Greeks ran back toward the alley. Dunn and his men stayed put, and ducked down behind the wall. Both warheads hit their targets and the German halftracks exploded, sending metal and humans into the air. Shrapnel slammed into the stone wall and ricocheted off, sizzling through the night air. When the shrapnel stopped, Dunn raised his head to peek. The two halftracks were burning furiously, their black smoke adding to that of the warehouse behind him. There were no other vehicles in sight.

Dunn checked his watch. Time to go. He waved at the four Greeks and pointed to his watch. They nodded and took off to the south down the alley.

"Time to go, guys. Jonesy, lead the way."

Jonesy stood up and ran across the street, the rest of the squad following down the alley.

They ran two blocks south, and a couple to the east. They found a truck waiting for them and climbed aboard. The Greeks who had been across the street were already seated on the floor, wide grins across their faces. Blowing up Germans was exhilarating.

One of them pounded on the back of the truck's cab and the driver put it in gear and the truck started moving.

Dunn went over and sat down by the two who had killed the halftracks. He patted them on their backs and gave them a thumbs up. Dunn had recovered his cigarettes and Zippo from the cave. He offered his package of Lucky Strikes and each Greek fighter took it and passed it on until all four were ready for a light. One of them had a lighter, which he passed around. The last one to get the package tried to hand it back to Dunn, who pointed at him. The Resistance fighter smiled and pocketed the cigarettes.

Dunn felt the truck making all kinds of turns, and it seemed to get on a straightaway. A few minutes later, it swayed from side to side as it maneuvered through a series of four curves. Another straight road followed and about five minutes later, it slowed down and made a sharp right turn. A minute later, it stopped.

Dunn crawled over his men and climbed down. He discovered they were at the beach already. The jetty where the EAM fighters had captured him was off in the distance.

A second truck pulled in. Dunn could make out that Doukas was in the passenger seat.

"Out of the truck, fellas. We're here."

The squad clambered down onto the beach and spread out, facing the road. Just in case.

Doukas got out and walked over to Dunn, his hand extended. The men shook hands. Doukas had a large paper bag in his other hand. He lifted it toward Dunn.

Dunn took the bag. "What's this, sir?"

"Cypriot Flaouna for you and your men. It's like a very sweet raisin bread."

"You didn't have to do this."

"We wanted to. One of my men's mother."

"Tell them both thank you."

"I will. And thank you for all of your help."

Dunn shrugged. "I don't really think you needed our help. Your men are well trained and disciplined. Your attack was very good."

Doukas smiled. "Well, your Mr. Jonesy helped out considerably. The Molotov cocktails allowed us to destroy the trucks. And there's the matter of the friendly crossfire problem, no?"

"Ah. You heard about that."

"My platoon leader told me himself."

"Well, that took courage. That's a credit to him."

Doukas nodded. "It is." He looked out at the sea. "What time does your boat come?"

"Midnight to four a.m."

"Not too long to wait."

"No, sir. Feel free to take off."

"No, we'll wait with you. It's not long."

"Aren't you concerned about the Germans heading this way?"

Doukas grinned. "Not at all. We left breadcrumbs, is that right, breadcrumbs?"

Dunn nodded.

"So they will be following the breadcrumbs north. Sadly they will go quite some distance before they realize they've been tricked."

"Nice move."

"Thank you."

"Thanks again for getting us out of hot water in the cave."

"Our pleasure. We can't afford to have our guests mistreated."

Dunn grinned. "What's next for you?"

Doukas's face grew grim. "I'm afraid I have some housecleaning duties ahead. A trusted man betrayed me by giving me false information. It cost me the lives of many men."

"Ah. Sorry to hear that."

Doukas shrugged, and he looked out at the black waters of the Ionian Sea.

Aboard the HMS *Torbay*
2 October, 0019 Hours

The black rubber assault boat was hauled aboard the HMS *Torbay*, and quickly deflated while Dunn and his men went below through the forward hatch.

Dunn got his men settled back into their temporary quarters and headed aft with Cross. They arrived at the control room.

The boat captain, Lieutenant Commander Reynolds, had kept the watch for himself, wanting to be available when the pickup took place.

"Glad to see you made it okay."

"Thank you, sir. Had a bit of a rough go at first." Dunn explained what had happened.

"Thank God for that other Greek commander, right?"

"Yes, sir." Dunn glanced around and found the radioman's position, where a young sailor sat reading something on his tiny table. "If I may sir? I'd like to report in."

"Permission granted. Mr. Evans?"

The radioman looked up. "Sir?"

"Assist the sergeant."

"Yes, sir."

Dunn pulled Cross along with him to the radioman. "Got a pad?" Dunn asked.

"Yes, Sergeant." Evans slid a five by eight inch pad of paper over to Dunn and a stubby pencil.

Dunn tore off a piece of paper and wrote his message quickly, sticking to the salient points, leaving out the cave episode with the EAM. That would be better discussed in person with the colonel. When he finished, he handed Evans the paper. "How long?"

Evans would have to encode the message before sending it. "Five minutes."

"Mind if we hang out here?"

Evans shrugged. "Not at all."

Evans finished encoding on time and sent the message.

Ten minutes passed and Evans began writing the response, which was a long one. It took him almost ten minutes and two pieces of paper to decode. When he was done he gave it to Dunn, keeping his face impassive.

Dunn read both pages quickly. Normally he would have handed the first one to Cross when he'd finished it, but this time he kept them. He reread them. Dunn looked at Cross.

Cross noted that the color had drained from Dunn's face. "What is it, Tom?"

"Some terrible news about Saunders' men."

Chapter 27

1 mile south of Hohenstein Castle
1 October, 2330 Hours, Salzburg time

Saunders raised a hand and the squad stopped. He turned around and motioned for them to gather close to him. When they did, he whispered, "I'm going to step out and take a look, see how much farther."

They were walking through pine forest, staying just inside the tree line just to make sure they would pass unnoticed. It was a bit challenging, as some of the trees were very close to each other and sometimes Saunders would have to lead the squad around a cluster of trees before getting back on their northerly path.

Saunders edged himself close to the open space. He examined the land in front of him for several moments. Satisfied no one was moving around, and hoping no one was watching from a hidden place, he stepped past the tree hiding him. He knelt and looked north. And up.

There, not more than a mile away sat the white castle. It practically gleamed in the moonlight. He studied it. The book Lieutenant Mallory had found from Oxford was a real help. He spotted portions of the three rings of walls surrounding the castle, and the keep on his side. He couldn't see any lights anywhere, but that didn't necessarily mean anything; they might have just drawn the drapes. If anyone was still up, that is. The eastern slope was easy to see. It looked pretty steep from his vantage point. He wondered whether it would prove to be a more difficult ascent than was first thought. Would they require the ropes, the only climbing gear to survive the attack on their plane? On top of that would be the fatigue of climbing after marching three miles with all their gear.

Without rising, he scooted back through the tree line and rejoined the men.

"A mile to go. It's a monster of a castle. It looks just like the photos and drawings we saw."

"See anything going on?" Barltrop asked.

"Quiet. No lights, but they could still be up. Hitler's a night owl."

"Our insider said they would probably be in the great dining hall," Barltrop said.

"Correct. They're probably having to listen to Hitler ramble for hours and hours."

"Oi."

"Right, lads. Off we go."

Saunders retook point and the men advanced. Saunders wanted to get to the eastern slope by midnight. He wondered whether his request for Dunn had been successful. He knew Dunn himself would never say 'no,' but it wasn't his decision to make.

As he walked, he mentally updated the original breach assault plan to include thirteen men instead of ten. That would be a lot moving parts and Dunn and his men wouldn't have the benefit of the rehearsals and the Oxford book. Bloody hell. *What was I thinking*, he thought, not for the first time on this awful night.

Chapter 28

Yet another hour of the unbearably tedious evening had passed for Marston. He'd had to carefully stifle yawns a number of times. He spotted a few SS officers around the table suffering from the same problem, which gave him some measure of comfort.

Speeches had rotated between Hitler, Himmler, and even Glockner had given a short one. At the moment, Colonel Neubart was thanking everyone for coming and saying how proud he was to serve the *Führer* in the capacity of castle commandant. Hitler waved a hand as some sort of acknowledgement.

Hitler abruptly rose to his feet and everyone jumped up. He let his gaze travel around the table, appearing to make eye contact with each man. When he did that to Marston, the spy felt the power of the man, and the moment passed. When he was done, Hitler gave a stiff-armed salute and the men returned it, clicking their heels together.

Hitler spun around and walked out of the room, Himmler and Bormann having to hurry to catch up.

Caught by surprise, Marston had time to glance at Colonel Neubart, who seemed transfixed by Hitler's sudden exit. Marston lowered his arm and left his place at the table. He walked as fast as possible without giving the appearance of running and exited the dining hall. He spotted Hitler's group nearing the front door.

Bloody hell, he thought. Is Hitler leaving? Had they missed their one chance to get him?

Marston sped up to catch up with the top men of the Third Reich just as they entered the main hall. Their heels clicked on the stone floor.

Marston maneuvered himself so he could speak, not to Hitler, but to Hitler's secretary. "*Herr* Bormann, is everything all right?"

Without breaking stride, Bormann looked at Marston. "The *Führer* has changed his plans. We are departing."

Marston knew of Hitler's proclivity for changing his movements suddenly. It was the one thing that kept him unpredictable and, as Marston had just learned firsthand, made it impossible to assassinate him. He knew there was no way he, a simple major, could change Hitler's mind.

"May I be of assistance in any way?"

Bormann shook his head as they reached the double doors leading outside. "*Nein*, but thank you for a fine evening. Please pass along the *Führer's* gratitude to the colonel."

"Yes, sir. I will be sure to do that."

Marston stopped and watched the men go through the doors into the night. *Ah, bugger, now what?* Things were starting to pile up. He had no idea where Saunders and his men were or why they had missed the opportunity.

The castle doors slammed shut, the sound echoing across the main hall. Marston turned away and headed back to the dining hall. When he arrived there, the men were milling about. From the snippets of conversation he could hear, they were apparently as surprised, and disappointed—even if for different reasons—as he, at Hitler's sudden departure. He spotted Colonel Neubart standing near the kitchen doors, talking with a couple of the waiters.

Field Marshal Glockner and his aide were standing at their places at the table chatting with a couple of SS captains. Marston continued sweeping his gaze around the room and found the *Abwehr* agent, Juhnke, sitting by himself. Juhnke was watching Glockner in much the same way as Marston, appearing to not be actually interested, but in reality, he seemed to be very interested. This intrigued Marston and he continued to watch him obliquely.

Juhnke suddenly stood up, picking up the SIGABA machine by its handle. He walked slowly around his end of the table and Marston wondered where he was going. Marston started down the table to follow. His curiosity was soon answered when Juhnke stopped beside the field marshal.

Marston rounded the end of the table and took a path that would allow him to pass close by the men. They exchanged handshakes and moved off a few feet from the table so they could speak privately. Glockner had pointedly made his aide stay put. Marston altered his direction, aiming for a pair of SS officers he'd come to know fairly well during his month at the castle.

"Good evening, gentlemen," Marston said.

The two officers stopped their conversation and smiled at Marston.

"Major Seiler," said the one who was a major himself.

"Did you enjoy the time tonight with the *Führer*?" Marston repositioned himself so he was a few feet from the officers and perhaps five feet from Juhnke. Marston had his back to Juhnke.

Both men replied that they did indeed enjoy the evening. *What the bloody hell else could they say?* Marston thought.

While the two SS officers continued their conversation, unconcerned that Marston just stood there smiling and nodding, he listened to the more important discussion taking place behind him. Both the field marshal and Juhnke were speaking in whispers but Marston was able to focus completely on them, tuning out the two SS officers as well as the hubbub of the room.

Glockner: "You're sure you can figure out how this works?"

Juhnke: "I have no doubts."

Glockner: "How long?"

"Perhaps two months to get it done."

"You'll ensure I receive messages first?"

"I will ensure that, Field Marshal."

"Excellent. I will be in your debt, which of course, has value to your career."

"Thank you, Field Marshal. I'm honored by your trust."

Marston kept his attention focused on the two SS officers in front of him. A moment later, Juhnke came into his peripheral vision on the right and moved off toward the exit. Marston excused himself from the conversation and followed, keeping a safe distance between himself and Juhnke.

Juhnke was already at the base of the spiral staircase when Marston entered the main hall. He started up the stairs and Marston jogged along the hall to catch up. He ran up the stairs.

Marston reached the second floor when Juhnke was part way down the hall, and not too far from his room. Marston backed down the stairs until he was out of sight. He listened and soon heard the light clink of a skeleton key turning in the lock, followed by the creak of the wooden door opening on its old hinges. Next came the sound of the door closing and its being locked from inside.

Marston shook his head, trying to figure out what he'd seen and heard in the past few minutes. He walked down the stairs and wandered along the stone hall. The field marshal and Juhnke had arrived together. What machinations could they have worked up during their trip? Was Glockner attempting to ensure his prominence on the western front?

The field marshal and Juhnke were both staying an extra night at the castle, leaving on Tuesday morning. Marston stopped walking and stared absently at a sword and shield decorating the wall next to him. He turned over an idea that had suddenly popped up. Would it serve a valuable purpose, he wondered.

Chapter 29

Eastern base of Hohenstein Castle's mountain
Monday, 2 October, 0005 Hours

Saunders led his four men into an opening amongst the pine trees. The valley spread out below them and the east slope of the castle's mountain towered above them. It seemed to be very steep, but they wouldn't need the ropes to make the ascent after all. A minor victory for a mission that had gone to shambles.

"Have a sit down, lads," he said. "Kopp, here by me."

The men didn't argue.

Kopp sat down next to Saunders and got the radio ready. He looked at Saunders, who nodded. While setting the frequency, he picked up the handset and put it to his ear.

Saunders checked his watch. Just after midnight.

Kopp spoke into the mouthpiece, giving the squad's codename, Oxford, for the books Mallory borrowed, and waited. A reply came almost immediately.

"Hold one," he said, giving the handset to Saunders.

"Oxford here," he said.

"You may expect your friends for breakfast. Meet them on the western shore."

"Roger. Understood. Oxford out."

He held out the handset to Kopp, who took it and put it away.

Saunders frowned. Breakfast did not mean breakfast, and west meant east. "Some good news and bad news. Dunn's coming, but not until after dinner time tomorrow night. Er, I guess that's tonight. We're to meet them here on the eastern slope."

"Bugger, Sarge. We have to wait here all day?" Dickinson asked, exasperation in his voice.

"Aye. We should work our way part way up this bloody mountain and find a place to sleep. We'll take it in shifts of four hours. Two will take watch at a time. I'll go first, who else?"

Chadwick spoke up first, "Me."

Saunders nodded. He started to say something, but a sound he recognized from off in the distance stopped him. He got up quickly and made his way to the tree line. Barltrop jumped up and followed.

The sound became clearer. An aircraft, very low. Taking off from the flat land of the valley.

Saunders followed the sound and found a glint of moonlight off metal. A half mile away, a trimotor plane was climbing into the cold Austrian night air.

Saunders thought the plane was a Junkers 52, the same kind that carried Hitler. "Fook. I bet that there is our targets."

Barltrop shook his head.

"Now what, Mac?"

"Don't know, Steve. I think I need to make another call. Find out if our insider has any news."

Saunders and Barltrop pushed through the tree branches and rejoined the other three men.

Saunders filled them in quickly and Kopp made a second call. Saunders reported the possibility that the targets had moved on. The response was simple: will verify and get back to you. Stay put. Saunders ended the call and Kopp put the radio away.

"Back to the plan, lads. Uphill and some sleep."

The men rose and Barltrop took point while Saunders took the last position.

On the way up the steep slope Saunders had trouble getting the image of the fireball out of his head. It had killed his five men, the aircraft's crew, plus the two extra pilots who were to fly Hitler's now departed plane to freedom. Ten men had died in that instant.

He raised his gaze from the ground to the four men in front of him. At least they were alive.

With that thought, he looked back down at the ground and kept putting one foot in front of the other.

Chapter 30

Stelios Pavlou's house
Preveza, Greece
2 October, 0139 Hours, Athens time

Stelios Pavlou sat in his small living room with the lights out. His hands dangled from the cushioned armrests of his favorite chair. One held a half smoked cigarette, the other, his revolver. His wife and three daughters were sound asleep in their bedrooms. Tears ran down his cheeks. He debated for the sixth time in five minutes whether he should just raise the gun and end it all. He'd betrayed Colonel Doukas, who was far from a stupid man. It wasn't going to end well at all. The lie the SS officer, Captain Deichmann, had suggested, that he say his source had been wrong would last as long as it would take for Doukas to hear it. Then Doukas would order him killed. To make an example of him. Even if the colonel didn't kill him, Deichmann intended to use him forever. It seemed hopeless.

He took one more drag on the cigarette and stubbed it out in a ceramic ashtray. He didn't want to burn down the house with his family inside.

He thumbed back the hammer and raised the barrel to his temple.

He wondered if he'd hear it go off.

Should he keep his eyes open, to see as long as possible?

These seemed to be logical questions.

Like the endless 'why' questions each of his daughters had asked at the age of four. Why daddy? How come?

Images of his three beautiful, sweet girls flooded him with love.

He lowered the gun and released the hammer gently, and dropped the weapon on the floor. He put his head in his hands and sobbed silently, his shoulders shaking. After some time, he lowered his hands and wiped his eyes with the back of his hand. He took some deep breaths. He was amazed by how exhausted he suddenly felt. He lay his head back on the chair's soft back.

He slept.

Something woke him. What was it? He blinked his blurry eyes and listened.

Tap, tap, tap. Someone was knocking on the door, but very lightly. The softness of the knocking seemed all the more frightening.

He stood up on shaky legs and took a couple of steps, but stopped and retreated. He bent over to pick up the revolver. Once again, he cocked the hammer. He approached the door quietly.

Tap, tap, tap.

He turned an electric knob by the door and the outdoor light came on. Keeping the weapon by his right thigh, he put a hand on the doorknob, He turned it and pulled the door open a few centimeters so he could see out. His heart dropped in his chest.

"Hello, Stelios. May I have a word with you?" Colonel Doukas asked.

Pavlou lowered his head in resignation and opened the door wider. He took a step to go outside, but the colonel held up an empty hand. "Let's just step inside, please."

Pavlou noticed the colonel's sidearm was still in its holster. At least he wasn't going to shoot him in his doorway. That gave him hope. He looked into Doukas's eyes, but couldn't read anything. He stepped back inside and said, "Of course, Colonel. Come in."

A moment later, the men sat down. Pavlou had turned on the lights. He'd also laid the revolver on the side table. Doukas had noticed, but said nothing.

"I apologize for the lateness of my visit," the colonel began, "but we were rather busy tonight."

"It is nothing. I'm glad to see you."

Doukas raised a dark eyebrow. "I think not. Isn't there something you'd like to tell me?"

Pavlou sighed. He might not make it to morning after all. "Will you please take good care of my family, sir?"

Doukas tiled his head in surprise. "Your family? What?" He leaned forward, putting his forearms on his thighs, and clasped his hands. "Pavlou, I have absolutely no intentions of hurting you or your family. Just tell me exactly what happened."

Pavlou's relief was so intense he could hardly believe that only an hour ago he'd almost killed himself. Now that Doukas *wasn't* going to execute him, he realized how much he wanted to live. And how close he'd come to jumping over the precipice.

"Perhaps start at the beginning, no?" Doukas prompted.

Pavlou nodded, now suddenly anxious to get it off his chest. He told Doukas how he'd been picked up by the SS. How the SS captain had threatened his family if he didn't pass on the information he wanted. How they'd taken him home and the same captain told him he was going to work for him forever. If he didn't, well, they were pretty teenaged girls weren't they?

When Pavlou said this about the girls, Doukas's face darkened and he looked away, as he clenched his jaw. Pavlou stopped talking.

After a few seconds, Doukas expression changed to one of resolve.

"This SS captain. His name?"

"Bertram Deichmann. He's staying at the mayor's house."

"Yes. I know this man. He is evil."

Doukas looked away again. He was clearly thinking, so Pavlou sat in silence. He thought about offering the colonel something to eat and drink, but decided it might be best to leave the man alone.

Doukas slid his gaze back to Pavlou and he smiled. It was the same kind of chilling smile the SS captain had given Pavlou after threatening his family. Pavlou swallowed reflexively.

"Are you ready to help me rid ourselves of this cretin?"

"Yes, colonel. I am," Pavlou immediately said.

Chapter 31

Southern base of Hohenstein Castle's mountain
2 October, 0842 Hours, Salzburg time

Marston was forced to break from his evening routine due to the events of the night before. He needed to report in about Hitler, Himmler, and Bormann leaving abruptly from the dinner party. The story he gave the guards was that he needed to go into the village for some personal items. They'd accepted it at face value. Why not? He was Colonel Neubart's aide.

He drove down the winding driveway this time, instead of 'going on a walk.' A bright October sun bore down on the landscape. The air was cool and fresh and Marston rolled down the window to breathe it in.

At the last gate, the guards waved him through and Marston continued on down the last length of the private road. To maintain his cover he drove the mile to the village and parked the car in front of the general store. There were no other vehicles on the street. He marched into the store, which was long and narrow. The store owners, an older couple, smiled at him, although he thought they might be forcing it. Not all Austrians were Nazi fans. Of course they were smart enough to know to keep those thoughts to themselves.

"Good morning, Major," the man said, from behind the counter. He wore turtle shell glasses and a white mustache. He seemed to take pride in the fact that he recognized Marston's rank.

"Good morning. I'm looking for a new straight razor." He smiled and brushed a hand along his jawline. "Not quite as close as I prefer."

The woman, who was on Marston's side of the counter, said, "This way, sir." She was tall and thin, and wore her white hair in braids wrapped into circles on her head in the way favored by Germanic women and girls.

She led him down the next aisle over and pointed out some packaged razors in three prices hanging from the rack. Next to the razors were other items a man would need, the cup and pestle to mix the shaving cream, which came in a box, also available. He grabbed the most expensive razor and a new cup-pestle combination.

Back at the counter, he spotted a jar full of licorice sticks.

"How much for the whole jar?"

The man told him and Marston said, "I'll take them all."

He paid and left with his purchases in a brown paper sack.

He tossed the sack on the passenger seat and got in the car. Just after leaving the village, he passed a boy of about twelve, who was leading a cow down the road toward town. As Marston was about to pass by, the boy stopped walking and gave him a Nazi salute. Marston cringed at the sight, but returned it as best as he could from inside the car.

As he approached the road that led up the mountain, he turned off on the narrow farmer's access road and traveled a few hundred yards. He drove the car off the road and into an opening surrounded by pine trees, and stopped. He turned off the car and got out. Two minutes later he knelt and retrieved his radio from under the downed birch tree.

He made contact and gave his report, and requested permission to alter the mission goals. Then he received a response that shocked him.

"Your friends ran into a problem and only half of them can make it. Assistance is being sent and will arrive in time for breakfast tomorrow." This translated to after dinner tonight.

"Understood," Marston said.

"Stand by."

Marston wasn't happy about that. It meant someone was making a decision, and taking too long. He needed to get going.

Just as he was about to push them along, he heard, "Your dinner plans are approved. Make the best meal possible."

"Understood."

He turned off the radio and recovered it with leaves.

He rose to his feet and looked around the forest. Somewhere north of him, Saunders and his men should be waiting for night as well as reinforcements. He thought about heading their way and making contact, but decided against it because he'd be unacceptably late returning from the village and that might raise questions and get people's attention focused on him. He could not risk that.

So instead, he was soon back on the road to the castle. He gave each guard at the seven gates two licorice sticks and received grateful grins from all of them. He parked the car in the area designated for the castle vehicles. Eight other cars and a couple of trucks were parked there, too. The cars Hitler and his entourage used had been returned to their spots.

Portrait Room
Hohenstein Castle
2 October, 1545 Hours, 7 hours later

Marston found himself in the Portrait Room again. Something had drawn him back and he knew very well what it was. Or who it was. His fascination was too great. The woman in the painting gazed at him again from her seat in front of the tree. The room's lighting was different from the first time he'd seen her. It was early afternoon and it had been nighttime when he'd first met her. Due to the light change, he noticed a tiny brass plate just below the ornate wooden frame. In intricately scrolled engraved lettering he read: Lady Adelaide Bierschbach, 1490, age 28. She would be related to the elderly couple he'd chatted with about the castle, perhaps a great-to-the-nth grandmother. She had a small smile, a curled lip, not as subtle as Mona Lisa's, which would be painted thirteen years later, but one that made you realize she knew something funny that you didn't. Marston liked her even more for that and he silently thanked the painter for capturing that impish expression. She was a member of the family he'd connected to Aryan ancestry while in Berlin before coming to the castle. Here she was in living color.

Sighing deeply, surprised by how this painting, this long dead woman, affected him, he finally started to move away again, but something else caught his eye. To the left of the painting on the stone wall, he spotted a slight indentation in the seam between two stones. If it hadn't been for the light positioned over the painting spilling outward onto the wall's surface, he would have never seen it. He put a hand on the wall and rubbed his fingers over the indentation. It felt . . . loose, the way a bolt wiggles when the nut is not tightened completely.

Frowning with concentration, he applied pressure with his forefinger and the loose piece sank into the wall. It stopped after sliding an inch. Marston's finger's was buried in the seam up to the first knuckle. A sudden *clunking* sound came through the wall. He partially heard it and partially felt it. He yanked his hand back and the touchstone returned to its original position.

The wall began to move. A section of three stones, about a yard wide, retreated into the wall and rotated to his right, behind Lady Adelaide's picture.

A musty smell immediately assailed his nostrils, not unpleasant, but . . . old. He pulled out his torch, which he always carried these days, and he turned it on. The beam revealed an opening about six feet in depth and about six wide, He pointed the beam at the floor where he saw steps leading downward into the darkness. He glanced quickly back at the room, in the direction he'd come from. No one. He stepped into the opening and turned around immediately. The question was how to close the door behind him. He played his torch along the edges of the door, and found a short lever angled upward at a forty-five degree angle in the wall on the right side.

Part of him wanted to try the lever and another wanted to run away. He pulled the lever. The same *clunking* noise sounded, but louder in the small enclosed space, and the door began to close. He didn't even have to step out of the way. The stone wall slid past him, silently settling back into its original position.

A literary recollection he could have done without came forward, making his heart jump: Edgar Allen Poe's terrifying "The Cask of Amontillado" and its unfortunate victim of revenge, Fortunato, who was bricked up alive behind a wall in Montresor's catacombs. He shuddered and looked at the lever again. It was pointing downward at a forty-five degree angle. He grabbed it and pushed up.

Nothing.

Bloody hell.

Then the welcome *clunking* sound. He let out the breath he hadn't realized he was holding. As soon as the door was open all the way, he checked the Portrait Room again to make sure it was still clear. Finding it empty he closed the door again, satisfied he could get out and not meet Fortunato's fate.

He was ready to find out where this secret passageway led. Aiming the torch down the stairs, he drew himself up as if in preparation for a fight, and took the first step. When he had traveled a distance that seemed to be the equivalent of one story, he arrived on a landing and the stairs turned right. On the left wall was an empty steel bracket designed to hold a burning torch. He paused a moment to relate his position to the castle above. The Portrait Room ran north-south and the first set of stairs ran in parallel to the north. Now they were turning east, back under the center of the castle.

He descended another floor and came upon a second landing, and the stairs turned right again, to the south. Another torch bracket was on the wall. As he went down farther, the stone walls changed from smooth to the rough cut edges common in the foundations of ancient homes back in England. The air was cooler and it began to feel damp. He touched a wall and it, too, felt damp.

After reaching a third level, he was three stories below the castle. To the left, east, he was met with a dark tunnel and no more stairs. Glancing at his torch, he wondered if the batteries would last for the whole adventure, wherever that led. He considered retreating and locating a spare torch, but decided to go ahead another five minutes and take stock of his situation. Checking his watch, he strode off into the darkness, the torch beam bouncing on the floor as he walked.

At the moment he decided it was time to check his watch, the light caught something solid straight ahead. He took a few more steps and found a solid stone wall. Aiming the torch at the right side of the wall, he found another lever sticking out at a forty-five degree down angle.

Smiling to himself, he raised the lever. The familiar *clunk* sounded deep inside the stone. To his left, as he expected, a stone door swung open. Fresh, cold air seeped into the tunnel. When the door stopped moving, he stuck the torch into the opening. Unsurprisingly, he discovered a cave about the size of a living room. Of course, he thought. What better outlet for an escape tunnel?

He walked across the dry, rocky cave floor quickly. The way forward curved left, changed course after a few feet back to the right, and straightened. He walked a few more steps and stopped. He turned around and played the light around. If he didn't already know better, it looked like the cave ended right there, a nice deceptive illusion.

He turned back around and the cave's entrance was just a few yards ahead. Clicking off his torch, he exited the cave where he met sunshine through the heavy outlines of many pine trees.

As he had expected, he'd come out of the castle on the east side, which had a slope heavily covered by the evergreen trees. Stepping farther outside, he turned around and looked up and over the cave entrance. Easily visible was the first, and lowermost castle wall. He was completely outside the castle grounds.

He turned around and examined his surroundings. It looked just like what it was, a mountainside forest through which paths downward were available. Marston felt a charge of excitement. This must be what it felt like to discover something, a thing no one else knew about. A thing about which legends were written, like pirate treasure. It was obvious that this discovery could drastically change the plans for entering the castle.

The question was where were Saunders and his men? He was supposed to meet them lower on this same slope. Should he try to connect with Saunders now? Would it do any good? He would have some risk when he got back to the Portrait Room, and perhaps it would be better to wait and confirm his discovery was still a secret. Glancing around once more, he decided to wait to make contact until later, after dark. Caution was often a prudent choice for a spy.

He reentered the cave and retraced his steps. Once he was back inside the tunnel, he pulled on the lever and the door swung shut. By the time he reached the castle floor where his adventure had started, his legs burned and his brow was soaked in sweat from the exertion of climbing three stories. Soon he was back in the Portrait Room with an open stone door behind him. Unsure of how to close it from this side, he wondered if he might have made a mistake. But he realized the engineers would have thought of this problem and created a simple method. He found the depression in the stone's seam again and put his finger on it. Instead of feeling wobbly, it was solid. He pushed. It gave way easily and the door swung shut.

Marston stood in front of Lady Adelaide's portrait for a moment, then turned right and headed back to the door. He declared his evening exploration a rousing success because he had discovered a better way for the castle breach than climbing over the walls. They might be able to make the mission viable again. All was not lost as it had appeared last night.

Hohenstein Castle
2 October, 1930 Hours, about 3 hours later

After dinner, Marston headed toward the Portrait Room. He passed an SS guard, a corporal, patrolling the interior and nodded to him. The man waved.

The room was dimly lit, as it typically was in the evenings, the only light coming from the lamps over the individual paintings. When he stood in front of Lady Adelaide, he checked the room behind him. It was empty, so he depressed the secret passageway's device. Once inside, he pushed on the lever. As soon as the door swung back closed, he took off down the steps, his torchlight bouncing along the stairwell with every movement.

At the cave entrance he stopped and listened carefully to the outside world. Satisfied no one was moving around, he stepped outside. The sun had set almost an hour ago. The full moon was up, rising just over the peaks to the east, looking enormous like a Harvest Moon. A few long, stringy clouds were present and one moved across the lower part of the moon's face. He looked away, but glanced back right away. What he saw made him laugh soundlessly. The moon had a temporary mustache.

With only had a rough idea of where Saunders would be, he headed in that direction hoping they wouldn't end up playing blind man's bluff. Going downhill seemed rather treacherous, because sometimes it was difficult to see where his feet were going to land with each step, but he made progress for about five minutes. He found an opening amongst the pine trees. He knelt and looked at it. No one was there, but he knew from experience that crossing an open area was not safe. He curled around the clearing and was about half way to the other side.

From the darkness came a Cockney accented voice, "The King wears roller skates."

Marston stopped walking and replied in English, "The Queen dances with polar bears."

A bear stepped out from the dark shadows and resolved into a big Commando. Marston recalled the man had a red handlebar mustache and hair, but in the moonlight couldn't discern any color.

The men shook hands.

"This way, Mr. Marston, isn't it?"

"Yes, and you're Saunders?"

"I am."

The two had met briefly at the post-mission thank you party held after Dunn had blown up the Nazi Atomic Bomb Laboratory. Saunders and his men, who with the help of a P-51 Mustang pilot, stole a brand new jet bomber, the first of its kind, from the Horten brother's hangar in Germany.

The spy followed Saunders through the trees and into more shadowy darkness. They walked a short distance parallel to the mountain, not downhill, which gave them both apparent limps with one foot higher than the other. They broke into another, smaller opening and Marston spotted four men kneeling, their weapons at the ready.

"All okay, lads. Lookit who we have as a guest." He pulled Marston forward.

The men rose to their feet and came over to greet Marston.

Saunders said, "Let's sit down and talk."

The men found places to sit and Marston plopped down next to Saunders and Barltrop.

"So how'd you recognize me?"

"Well, first I wondered what idiot spy would dress up in an SS uniform." He leaned forward to look at Marston's epaulets. "A major at that."

"Oh, right. You remembered me as an SS colonel."

Saunders grinned. "Not really. I saw your face in the moonlight when you looked up way back there."

Marston was dumbstruck. When he'd looked up at the moon's mustache. "You followed me for quite a while. Why wait so long?"

"Just seeing if you were heading in the right direction. Impressive navigation skills, Mr. Marston."

"Thanks. Uhm, look, I heard something went wrong and I see you're only five."

Saunders nodded glumly. "Aye. We lost five men, plus five air crew. Plane was attacked by a night fighter. We're all that got out."

"I am so truly sorry."

Saunders nodded, but was silent.

Marston waited a moment, giving time to Saunders, who seemed, naturally, quite upset. Even his humor had been nothing but a way to stop the pain he had to be feeling. Marston looked around at the other men. Their faces were mostly in shadows, but he could make out the same shocked expressions.

"I understand some help is coming?"

Saunders nodded. "I asked for Dunn and his bunch."

"Oh, sure. That's great." Marston knew Dunn well. It had been Marston who'd actually located the atomic bomb facility and taken Dunn to it. Last August, Marston had been working in

Paris with the French Resistance, and had run into Dunn again. They'd stopped the Nazis from dropping a deadly biological weapon on the city. Another day at the office.

"It will give us a total of thirteen." Saunders thought, but did not say, 'Is that bad luck?'

"Plus me."

Saunders grinned. That solved the thirteen problem. "Yes, Major, plus you."

"I heard some time after dinner tonight. Do you know when?"

"No more precise than that, sir. Same info."

Marston nodded.

"Sir, did we lose our targets?"

"We did. Hitler, Himmler, and Bormann left close to midnight."

Saunders said to Barltrop. "I was right." He looked back at Marston. "We saw the plane take off and guessed it was them."

"All is not lost."

"What do you mean? Are they coming back?"

"What? Oh, no, not that." He waved a hand as if the loss of the top most Nazis was no big deal. He went on, his voice rising in excitement, "We have another opportunity. Two, actually. At the dinner, Hitler appointed a general to permanently take over for Rommel. You've heard he was injured when a Spitfire attacked his staff car?"

"Aye."

"He promoted the bloke to field marshal. He'll be heading to the western front tomorrow, Army Group B."

"So we're going to kill him?"

"Capture, if possible. He seems to be Hitler's newest fair-haired boy. Two things, he's intimately knowledgeable of plans on the western front, and it would strike a blow to Hitler's command structure in the west at a time when they are in dire need of someone strong."

"Hm," Saunders said, apparently still disappointed by missing Hitler.

"And I said there were two things. A man from the German *Abwehr*, their Military Intelligence, presented a stolen American cipher machine. It's called the SIGABA, whatever that stands for. It's used by the American Army, in particular. The man is headed back to Berlin to begin work on decoding how it works. Then the Germans will be able to read message traffic to all American commands."

"Bloody hell," Barltrop said.

"So you want to steal it back and return it to the Americans," Saunders said.

Marston nodded vigorously. "Yes. We must get it. It's actually a higher priority than capturing Field Marshal Glockner."

Saunders thought over what Marston had just said. The machine couldn't stay in German hands, that was for sure. As for the new field marshal, if making him disappear disrupted the German High Command, so much the better.

"We should work on our attack plan. We still need to breach the castle, starting with those three massive walls."

Marston grinned. "About that."

"What?"

"I have a better way."

"You do?"

"Yes. Care to enter through a nice neat tunnel?"

"Huh. I assumed you had climbed up above us and thinking you missed us, were on the way back down the mountain for another pass."

"Nope. Popped out not far from where you first saw me."

"That would simplify things for everyone. How you'd find the tunnel?"

"The usual way of those things, I think. By complete accident."

"To answer your question, yes, we would love a tunnel." Saunders checked his watch: 1940 hours. "Dunn should be arriving soon."

As if in answer, the men heard the faint, unmistakable sound of airplane engines, far in the distance to the south. Multiple aircraft.

Chapter 32

3 miles south of Hohenstein Castle
2 October, 1948 Hours

As the sound of the airplanes overhead diminished, Dunn and his men gathered up their parachutes. Dunn wondered what the C-47 pilots really thought about having to fly in circles twenty miles to the south so they could return for a quick pick up. As long as their pair of British Mosquitos, which were equipped with radar, stayed with them, they'd probably be less worried.

Dunn got his bearings, like Saunders had done, using the North Star and quickly determined the right direction. He led his men to the tree line, as had Saunders, and they took off to the north.

Eastern base of Hohenstein Castle's mountain
2 October, 2048 Hours, 1 hour later

Dunn halted the squad. He was sure he was in the right area. The compass reading to the castle's keep, which gleamed white in the moonlight, matched the very precise directions he'd received from Saunders by way of the communications center in Italy.

Upon arrival at San Cataldo, Italy, the men had debarked from the HMS *Torbay* giving their thanks to the captain and crew. A truck was waiting for them at the navy docks and drove them to the British airbase about ten miles north. Once there, they contacted Colonel Kenton and got the details needed for the mission. Following that, they tracked down their parachutes. Each man immediately unpacked and examined his new parachute, looking for any tears. Next they painstakingly checked the lines to make sure they weren't frayed. No one discovered any problems, and they carefully and methodically repacked the chutes. Next stop was the armory, where they stored their Thompsons and M1s, and Jonesy's Springfield. Jonesy wasn't happy about leaving his baby behind, especially after having it taken for a short while by the Greeks. They picked up suppressed Stens and plenty of ammunition for them, and some plastic explosives, detonators and timers. They had an all-day wait for the take off at 1630 hours.

Dunn looked out on the valley to the east. It seemed so peaceful it was hard to believe a terrible war was taking place just two hundred fifty miles away to the northwest. He was wondering how he was going to find Saunders, and kind of wished he had one of the cricket clickers the men used on D-Day to identify themselves to other Americans. He figured Saunders would track *him* down.

Sure enough, a minute later he heard a gruff voice coming from the darkness. "How's Pamela getting along?"

Saunders bearlike shadow came into view and Dunn walked over to meet him. The men shared a handshake, and Dunn pulled Saunders into a hug, patting his back.

"Sorry about your men. Really sorry."

Saunders patted Dunn on the back in return.

"Aye. A bad one. Very bad. Worst ever." He let go and stepped back.

The two men examined each other's faces. They'd both lost a lot of men over the past five months. It looked to each of them as though it was starting it take its toll. They both knew that with the failure of General Montgomery's *Operation Market Garden*, all hope for an early, by Christmas, end to the war was out of the picture. How much longer, though, no one knew, but certainly not until the next year. How many more men would they lose before the end?

"Let's see what we can do tonight," Dunn offered.

"Aye. Follow me. Got one of your old friends up the hill."

"Oh, yeah? Who?"

"Wait and see," was all Saunders would give him.

Dunn signaled to his men and everyone took off up the mountain slope. It was a ten minute climb, and although Dunn felt they hadn't really covered that much distance, he was breathing hard by the time Saunders came to a stop in a clearing.

Dunn spotted the SS officer immediately and he was able to make out a face. He broke into a grin and said, "Mr. Marston!"

The men met in the middle of the clearing and shook hands.

"Really good to see you, Sergeant Dunn."

"You, too, Neil."

"As much as I'd love to catch up, we'd better get our heads together and work out the plan."

"By all means."

While Marston and Dunn were saying hello, Dunn's men greeted Saunders' four men, expressing quiet sympathy for the loss of their friends.

Soon, the men were in a tight circle, all fourteen of them.

"Here's what we have in front of us," Marston began when he had everyone's attention. He looked at Dunn. "I've already told Sergeant Saunders and his men the news. Several things, actually. Hitler and Himmler have already left the castle."

A few groans of disappointment interrupted him. He held up a hand. "But I have two new targets for us. There's a newly promoted field marshal, named Glockner, and a man from the

Abwehr, German Military Intelligence, is here and with a captured SIGABA machine. That's a high level cipher machine used by the U.S. Army." Marston stopped talking to let that sink in. The expressions on the Rangers' faces matched the seriousness of the situation.

"The good news is I found a tunnel earlier today." He paused as an excited murmur went through the new arrivals. "It brings us up to the castle in a room that's very close to the armory's location, so you'll be able to secure it quickly and prevent them from getting their weapons.

"From here, it's another ten minute climb to the cave that conceals the entrance to the tunnel. From there, another ten minutes through the tunnel and up three flights of stairs to that room I mentioned. It has a secret door we'll use to exit the tunnel into the room. The two targets are staying in separate rooms toward the front, or south side, of the castle on the second floor. Easy access for you. I'm thinking you could exit the castle the same way and make your way to your pickup zone."

Dunn glanced at Saunders, who nodded. "Dave, Steve, any thoughts? Any problems?"

Cross shook his head. Barltrop said, "Can't think of any."

"Sounds like it beats crawling over three castle walls and breaching the door," Dunn said.

"Aye, that's my thinking, too."

"The tunnel is in incredible condition, considering it's likely five hundred years old," Marston said.

"Good to know. Don't want to have to worry about a collapse," Dunn replied. "If we get separated, let's make this location a checkpoint on the way back to the pickup zone. All gather here first?"

"Aye, good idea. Everyone got that?"

Everyone answered, "Yes, Sarge."

"A suggestion, if I may." Saunders stood up and rubbed his hands together. "What say we go into the tunnel so we can get out of this cold air? We've been outside for a long time and would welcome a little warmth."

Dunn nodded. "We haven't been here that long, but that's a great idea."

The men rose to their feet and stretched out the cobwebs. Marston took point and they made their way to the cave entrance. The men all marveled at the illusion hiding the tunnel door from the front of the cave. They marveled again at how smoothly the door opened. And they marveled at the craftsmanship of the tunnel, the walls and flooring.

Saunders poked Dunn in the ribs.

"I think we can leave our climbing gear behind inside the tunnel, since we don't need it anymore."

"Good point."

The sergeants told the men to stash their gear and the Commandos and Rangers happily shrugged off their secondary packs, glad to be rid of the extra weight. They were only carrying their typical primary packs with extra ammo and some explosives.

Barltrop decided to keep his coil of rope.

Saunders asked, "You're taking the rope?"

"Never know."

Saunders nodded.

Marston waited impatiently and was happy when the men finally appeared to be ready. "All set?" he asked hopefully.

"Aye," Saunders said.

"Yep," replied Dunn.

Marston set out, shining his torch along the floor ahead of him.

As Saunders walked he turned on his torch and played its beam on the rough stone wall.

"How old did you say this tunnel is, Mr. Marston?"

"It's old as the castle itself, which is five hundred."

"Bloody hell, they were some engineers."

"Wait until you see the door at the top."

"Can't wait."

Soon, they were at the bottom of the stairs that would come out three floors above, next to Marston's latest new friend, Lady Adelaide's portrait.

Chapter 33

In the Hohenstein Castle tunnel
2 October, 2125 Hours

The men sprawled out in the relative comfort of the much warmer tunnel. Lindstrom got out a pack of cigarettes and was about to light up, but Marston stopped him.

"Better not. We don't know where the air might go from here. Could give us away."

"Oh, sorry," Lindstrom said, and put the cigarette back in the pack.

"Okay, let's pick up where we left off. Mac, what are the precise orders on the field marshal?"

Saunders looked at Dunn. "Capture first, if possible, otherwise kill and take a photo. Steve's got the camera. For the *Abwehr* guy, whatever the circumstances dictate."

"Okay, shall we go over responsibilities for once we're up there?"

Dunn and Saunders led the discussion, laying out who would do what and when. They asked Marston several questions about guards and people who might have some reason to be up and about in the middle of the night.

They spent about thirty minutes planning. When they were done, Saunders checked his watch. It was almost 2200 hours.

"Shall we say oh one hundred hours?"

"Yes." Dunn looked at Marston. "Does that work?"

"Yes, it would work. The majority of the officers will be asleep, or at least in their quarters. The staff will be sound asleep for a four-thirty a.m. wake up for the day's work."

"Neil, anyone going to miss you if you don't return until one a.m.?" Dunn asked.

"No, I have free run of the castle as I'm the commandant's aide. I asked for the night off for my research project and he agreed."

Saunders asked if there were any more questions and no one said anything.

The men settled in for the three hour wait.

0100 Hours

The men rested quietly, saving as much energy as possible. Dunn, who had not dozed off, checked his watch. Time. He roused Saunders, and woke up his own men. Marston had stayed awake the whole time, too.

Marston rose to his feet and walked over to where Dunn and Saunders were standing together.

"Gentlemen, you ready?"

"Aye."

"Yep."

Marston turned and started up the first flight of stone steps. Saunders and his men followed first.

At the landing closest to the hidden door, the last one, Marston stopped. He turned and faced Saunders. He waved at Dunn to join them and when the Ranger climbed up to the landing, Marston said, "I think I should go up alone from here. Check things out."

"Good idea," Dunn said, and Saunders nodded.

"Right. I'll be right back."

"Okay," Dunn said.

Marston walked up the last set of stairs and when he reached the space behind the closed hidden door, he took a moment to get his breath back. *Getting a little too old for this,* he thought.

He pushed on the lever and watched, still amazed by it, as the door swung open smoothly and quietly. He turned off his torch and stepped through the door and turned left.

"Hello, Major Seiler. What have you found there?" Colonel Neubart asked, a shiny, black Luger aimed at Marston's chest. Standing behind the castle commandant were five SS guards armed with MP40 submachine guns. All pointed at Marston's midsection.

Chapter 34

St. Louis Insurance Company Building
St. Louis, Missouri
2 October, 6:03 P.M. U.S. Central time

Gertrude Dunn had indeed been smiling when she got off the train at the fifty-three-year-old St. Louis Union Station, which was a mile west of downtown and the Mississippi River. A handsome man in his early thirties met her, calling her name softly. She turned to face him and he handed her his identification card, which looked just like Thompson's and that of his recruiting partner, Johnson. The young man's name was, ironically, she thought, John Smith. He also showed her the two pictures Johnson had taken.

Smith dug into his pocket and handed her a quarter.

She raised an eyebrow. "What's this?"

"Mr. Johnson said to give it to you if you were smiling when I first saw you."

"Oh, right. The bet." She took the coin and dropped it into her small purse.

That had been almost an hour ago. Smith had escorted her, carrying her suitcase in spite of her protests, as they walked two blocks north and entered the St. Louis Insurance Company's brick, six-story building. In the small foyer a receptionist smiled at them as they walked past to the elevator. They got out on the fifth floor and Smith led the way to an office half way down on the right. He opened the door and stepped back so she could go first.

The room was spacious, apparently actually a couple of offices with a wall knocked out. There were a dozen desks, in three rows of four, facing a black chalkboard. The windows were all closed and their white venetian blinds pulled closed. Ten other people were in the room, nine sitting in the student desks, five females and four males. The other person sat behind the teacher's desk. Gertrude felt like she'd time warped back to her senior year. She eyed the desks and selected the only one left on the front row, which was on the far side of the room. She'd never sat in the back row a day in her life, and she wasn't about to start.

Mr. Smith placed her suitcase along a wall where nine others sat in a row. He waved goodbye and disappeared through the door, closing it behind him. The instructor introduced himself as Mr. Jones, which garnered a few chuckles from the group. He instructed the class to introduce themselves, name, where they were from, and their age, starting with the young man nearest the door.

After the introductions, Gertrude learned that, at eighteen, she was the youngest one there while the eldest was a twenty-three-year-old male. A few eyebrows went up when she stated her age, especially among the other women. Gertrude noticed and idly wondered if they were going to be a problem.

Mr. Jones checked off their names on a piece of paper, or at least that's what Gertrude thought he was doing. She was wrong. He stood up, or perhaps unfolded was more apt because it turned out he was quite tall, much taller than her brother, Tom, possibly six-six. He told everyone to line up in front of the windows. He paired them up, which was what he had been actually doing on the paper, by calling their names. He told them to arrange themselves so they sat next to their partner.

After some bustling and jostling, Gertrude and the rest of the students found their seats. Gertrude offered her hand to her partner, a thin man in his early twenties with wispy blond hair.

"I'm Gertrude."

He looked at her hand and for a split second she thought he wasn't going to take it. But he did, giving her a limp fish handshake. "So you said."

Mistake. Her eyes narrowed. "And you're Ralph Emerson."

"Whoo hoo! You remembered my name. I'm impressed. Bet it's because it's like the poet." He smirked at her.

A bigger mistake. She gave him a wide smile and scooted her desk over until it touched his. She leaned closer. "Ralph. Just so you know, I came here from a place where I made army rifles. I worked with men ten times as tough as you are. So spare me your attitude."

He gave her a pleasant smile, and laugh lines appeared at the corner of his blue eyes. "Take it easy. I was just testing you." He leaned closer, but she pulled away. "When I heard you say you were eighteen, I wondered what the recruiter's had seen in you. I figured you must have done pretty darn well on the tests, but I bet you gave them the same attitude you just gave me, too."

Without missing a beat, she said, "I knew you were testing me."

"Did not."

"Did, too."

They stared at each other for a moment, and burst into laughter.

He offered his hand and she took it. This time it was a firm handshake with a smile.

He pointed at the paper the instructor had given each pair. "Shall we solve this?"

"Yes."

Chapter 35

Portrait Room, in front of Lady Adelaide
Hohenstein Castle
2 October, 0105 Hours, Salzburg time

Marston was armed, as he always was, with his own 9mm Luger, but it was in his holster, which had a cumbersome and regrettably snapped-closed flap over the weapon. Besides, there six of them. He'd never stand a chance.

"Colonel, you'll never guess what I found!" Marston said in a loud voice, praying that the sound would carry down the stairs to Dunn and Saunders, and to Schneider, who would understand the language.

Neubart looked nonplussed for a moment and his pistol lowered fractionally. "What are you talking about?" He raised the pistol again. "What are you doing anyway?"

The colonel tilted his head in the direction of one of the guards. Marston recognized him as the one he'd nodded to earlier. "The corporal noticed you come into this room and when you didn't come out for a long time, he checked this room only to find it empty!"

"Remember when I first arrived here, I asked to explore the castle for anything that might connect it or the families to Aryan heritage?"

Neubart nodded, although to Marston it seemed rather reluctant.

"You gave me explicit permission to go anywhere." Marston gave the colonel a sheepish smile. "I'm sorry, sir. Perhaps I should have told you before I went any farther. Would you have preferred that?"

The colonel still seemed confused, which was definitely a good thing.

"I do recall giving you permission. What have you found?" The colonel suddenly remembered he was pointing a gun at his aide and slid it back in the holster, snapping the flap closed. He waved a hand at the SS guards and they lowered their MP40s.

So far so good, Marston thought. But he still needed to separate the good colonel from his guards. Marston took on a conspiratorial demeanor, looking sideways at the SS guards, but speaking softly to the colonel. "Begging your pardon, sir, it may be best if I show you my sample, em, alone." Marston looked at the colonel and raised one eyebrow.

The colonel said to the guards, "Return to your posts."

The men nodded and turned around ready to march off.

Neubart said, "Wait."

The guards turned back around.

He raised one finger. "Not a word of this to anyone." He pointed to the still open door next to Lady Adelaide. "Understood?"

"Jawohl, Standartenführer!"

"Dismissed."

The men marched off toward the exit.

Marston played the timing well, not saying anything at all to the colonel, who was growing more curious and impatient by the second. As soon as the door closed behind the guards, Marston said, "Look at this, sir." He pulled a gold coin from his pocket and held it out to Neubart. The coin had been a present for himself, purchased weeks ago in a Salzburg shop.

The colonel snatched the coin from Marston's fingers. His eyes widened, just as Marston had hoped.

Marston leaned closer and pointed at the coin. "See the date, sir?

"Seventeen eighty-seven . . ." Neubart looked at Marston, his eyes shiny. "Are there very many of these?"

"Many, many, sir. And other artifacts, swords, shields. This could be the find of the century. And while the castle was under your excellent command . . ." Marston let that thought hang in the air a long moment. He said excitedly, "I just wish we could have found it before the *Führer* arrived, so we could have shared the fantastic news with him!"

"Yes, that would have been wonderful."

"Shall we go take a look, Colonel?"

Neubart nodded enthusiastically. "Yes, right now."

Marston stepped through the door and waited until the colonel followed.

"How do you close the door?"

Marston thought hands on experience might be a good thing and said, "Push that lever down, sir." He pointed.

Neubart pushed, and grinned at the way the door slid shut. "Amazing engineering."

"Yes, sir."

"How old do you suspect it to be?"

"It has to date back to the original castle based on what I've seen below, so the mid-fourteen hundreds."

"Gott in Himmel." God in Heaven.

Marston started down the stairs, walking on the right side on purpose. The colonel walked alongside him since there was plenty of room. He played his light on the steps. "It's not far, sir. Just down a few flights of steps." Marston said this loudly, hoping again that the men below would hear and take appropriate action.

When they reached the first landing, he was relieved to find that the Dunn and Saunders had moved the men. "Just two more flights sir."

Just before the pair reached the point where the tunnel turned left to go east, Marston came to a stop, allowing the colonel to get ahead a couple of steps. Marston followed the colonel as the man turned the corner, catching up to him.

Two torches flashed bright beams aimed at the colonel's face. He instinctively raised his left arm to block the light.

A voice in the dark behind the lights said, "Halt!"

"Was ist los?"

Marston deftly snapped the flap open on the colonel's holster and drew out the Luger.

"My apologies, colonel. All is not as it seems. Hands up, please." Marston said in German as he poked the man in the back with his own gun.

Barltrop stepped out of the shadows. He had several lengths of rope in his hand, just cut from his larger coil. Turning the colonel around roughly, he brought the hands down where he could tie them together. He pulled a handkerchief from his pocket and after spinning the man around, forced it into his mouth. He tied a rope around the man's head, sealing the cloth in his mouth.

Barltrop leaned close to the man's ear and said, "Do you understand English?"

He got no reaction from the colonel, so he asked Marston, "Do you know if he speaks English?"

When Marston answered 'no, he doesn't' in his British accent, the colonel started making angry grunting noises and tried to advance on Marston in his fury. Barltrop swatted the man in the back of the head with his fist, which caused him to flinch and stop moving.

Marston merely gave the man a condescending smile and a wink. This seemed to infuriate the colonel even more as the grunting sounds increased, but Barltrop whacked him again. The sounds stopped.

Barltrop said to Marston, "Tell him this: you may be a prisoner, but you make any more noise and I will shoot you myself." Barltrop held up his suppressed Sten so the man could see it.

Marston translated the message, and asked, "Do you understand?"

The colonel glared at Marston, but nodded.

Saunders and Dunn came forward, walking past Marston. Saunders tugged him by the sleeve of his jacket and Marston followed. They walked around the corner onto the landing.

"What do you think, Mac?" Dunn said. "Do we hog tie him and leave him for later, or leave a man with him?"

"I'd rather leave someone with him, but if we have to change our plans and can't come back this way, that's a big problem."

"So hog tie him it is."

"Aye."

The men went back around the corner and Saunders told Barltrop what needed to be done.

"Gladly," Barltrop responded. Soon the colonel's ankles were tied together, and he was flipped over onto his stomach. Barltrop tied another length of rope to the ropes binding the hands and the feet, so the man's legs were bent toward his back. Barltrop tugged on the ropes to double check that they were secure and stepped back. A tiny measure of compassion struck Barltrop and he placed his torch in a nearby old fashioned combustion torch holder and switched it on. The light reflected off the cut stone ceiling.

"Tell him that's so he doesn't go crazy."

Marston translated, but the prisoner said nothing.

Saunders asked, "We all ready?"

"Yep," Dunn said.

"Yes," Marston said.

"Anyone have any questions on what they're supposed to do?"

"Does the field marshal speak English?" Barltrop wanted to know.

"Yes, his service record indicated so," Marston replied.

No one else said anything.

Saunders nodded to Marston, who took the lead.

Soon the men were lined up in pairs on the stairs just below the exit by Lady Adelaide. Marston had tucked the colonel's Luger into his wide leather belt. He pulled it out and then activated the door's lever. The door swung back and open. Marston stuck his head through the opening, his Luger at the ready. The room was empty. He stepped through and the Commandos and Rangers followed.

RONN MUNSTERMAN

Chapter 36

SS Guard Armory
Hohenstein Castle
2 October, 0121 Hours

Hauptscharführer, Master Sergeant, Rolf Biermann lifted the sling of his MP40 over his head and then released the weapon's magazine. He pulled back the charging bolt and ejected the live round in the chamber and inserted it into the magazine. The other four SS guards who had answered the colonel's sudden call for help were doing the same thing. Biermann was thirty-five years old and had been a member of the SS since 1935. Prior to that, he'd been a young beat policeman in Munich.

The man next to Biermann was the first to speak since they'd left the portrait room. "What do you think is going on?"

Biermann glanced at his guard. He shrugged. "Who knows? That Seiler seems to be all right. He knows what he's doing around the castle and the dinner with the *Führer* went off without a hitch in large part because of him."

Biermann thought back to the short interaction in the portrait room. Did it seem that the man had been nervous? Or maybe it was just being overly excited. Everyone knew he was searching the castle for Aryan information. Biermann's police officer instincts kicked in as he replayed the event in his head again. It was obvious the man had found a hidden room or something like that. Biermann hadn't been able to see inside the opening. A particular movement by Marston suddenly appeared in his memory. He'd given the guards a sidelong glance while talking to the colonel. He'd had seen that same glance among Munich street crooks when they were hiding something, and or lying to him or a partner police officer.

What was Seiler really trying to do? His eyes narrowed.

"Get your weapons."

The men looked at him in surprise and the man next to him asked, "What? Why?"

"We're going back to the Portrait Room. Something's not right with that Seiler after all."

"Not right? What do you mean?"

"No time to explain. Get your weapons ready. Now."

"But the colonel—"

"The colonel isn't here. I am."

"Jawohl, Hauptscharführer."

The men quickly reloaded their MP40s and seated a round into the chamber.

"Let's go," Biermann said.

He led the men out of the armory, making sure the last one out closed and locked the door. They ran up the stairs toward the main hall. Biermann held out an arm to stop them when they reached the first floor. He held a finger to his lips and the men nodded, suddenly on combat alert.

The men ran across the stone floor toward the Portrait Room's door.

Biermann put his left hand on the doorknob and turned it.

Chapter 37

Portrait Room
Hohenstein Castle
2 October, 0126 Hours

Barltrop had point and he saw the gold-plated doorknob on his side of the door rotate. The door opened to its own right, so luckily he would be hidden briefly until whoever it was on the other side stepped all the way into the room. He waved his arm at the men behind him.

The immediate problem was there was absolutely no place to hide. No furniture close enough, no little rooms off to the side, except for the secret stairwell, which was at the far end of the room.

Saunders was right behind Barltrop and he darted to the left to stand right up against the wall. The Commandos and Rangers behind *him*, did the same thing, weapons at the ready. Chadwick was next behind the big redheaded sergeant.

Saunders pulled his combat knife.

The door began to swing open.

Barltrop slid backward, following the arc. He was initially worried that the gap between the door at the hinges and the door frame would increase enough for someone to see him, but the door was hinged in much the same way a piano keys lid is, with no gap.

The front metal bill of a black SS helmet appeared. The guard was getting ready to peek around the door. The helmet began to rotate, which would bring the face into view. An MP40 snout appeared, the barrel level.

Barltrop grabbed the barrel with his right hand and pivoted, yanking as hard as possible.

The guard flew into the room, tumbling to the floor right in front of Saunders, landing on his back. The guard's weapon slipped from his fingers and bounced off the floor, the sling keeping it nearby.

Saunders punched the guard in the chest with the knife and the man died silently.

Chadwick hopped over the dead SS guard and knelt behind the open door, and leaned out. In a split second he took in the sight of four enemy soldiers, who were temporarily frozen, perhaps still expecting their leader to come back into view.

He squeezed the trigger and the suppressed Sten bucked.

Before any of the guards could return fire, they'd all been hit and were down. Barltrop ran through the door, checking the main hall for other targets.

It was empty. He checked each of the guards and confirmed that Chadwick had killed them all. The guards had fallen on a dark burgundy carpet that ran along the wall.

Barltrop ran back into the room and held up four fingers. The Commandos all ran out into the main hall. While Barltrop stood guard, each of the four grabbed a man by the arms and dragged him into the Portrait Room, settling them along the right hand wall, the same one that held the door.

While the British soldiers were handling the guards, Dunn led his men to the door. He peeked into the main hall. Dim lights were on, and visibility was good. Marston joined Dunn, who pointed toward a door beside the spiral staircase.

"The door to the armory?" he whispered.

"Yes."

Dunn beckoned Goerdt and Schneider. They came forward and Dunn pointed at the door. Goerdt patted Dunn's arm and nodded. The two men ran across the hall, opened the door to the downstairs and disappeared through it, closing it behind them.

Dunn pointed at Jonesy and Lindstrom, and to the right, toward the main entrance. The two men took off and settled in place behind a support column. They knelt, weapons up, Jonesy facing the door, Lindstrom, the hall.

Dunn looked at Marston and whispered, "Ready?"

"Yes."

He looked at Saunders, who nodded.

Dunn ran toward the staircase, Marston behind him. Dunn's three remaining men followed, then Saunders and his men.

Dunn ran up the spiral staircase stone steps staying close to the curved wall on the right. When he was almost able to see the second floor, he stopped. He moved up one more step. The long hallway was empty. A few wooden tables were situated along both walls. Small busts adorned each one. Several low wattage electric lights were spaced along the right hand wall providing more than adequate nighttime lighting.

Marston had already told Dunn and Saunders which room General Glockner was in, as well as the *Abwehr* man, Juhnke.

Dunn positioned Wickham at the top of the stairs.

Marston tapped Dunn on the shoulder and held out a skeleton key. *Herr* Juhnke was about to receive a very rude awakening. Of course Marston had lied about there being just the one key to the man's room.

Dunn, Cross, and Martelli ran down the hallway toward Juhnke's room on the right, two down from the general's. Marston joined them.

Saunders led his men to the general's door. He already had the spare key in his hand. Dunn and his men reached the *Abwehr* man's door and stopped. Dunn looked back at Saunders who nodded. Each man bent over slightly and slid his key into the keyhole.

Saunders turned the lock as slowly as possible. With a light snicking sound, the pins fell into the right position. He put a hand on the knob.

Dunn's key met resistance right away and he couldn't get it to go more than an eighth of an inch. He removed his key and realized what had happened. The man had locked the door and left the key in the lock, twisting it so it couldn't be pushed back out.

Two floors below, Schneider and Goerdt were inside the armory. Picking the lock had been child's play for Goerdt. While Schneider laid a lump of plastic explosive behind a 9mm ammunition box sitting on the floor, Goerdt guarded the partially closed door and watched the dungeon-like hallway. Schneider set the timer for ten minutes, as Dunn had asked. Next he inserted the detonator into the plastic. All was set. The men left and Goerdt picked the lock back into a closed position. They ran down the hallway and started up the stairs.

Saunders turned the knob and pushed gently on the door, standing to the side of the opening. Chadwick was on the other side.

Dunn motioned to Marston and pointed at the key that wouldn't go in. Marston's face fell. So much for the spare key. He held up his hands in the universal sign for 'now what?'

Dunn thought for a moment, and then scratched the key along the surface of the door, making a slight scraping sound. He repeated it for a few seconds and then tapped the business end of the key against the wood three times. He put his ear to the door. Nothing. He started all over.

Barltrop stepped between Saunders and Chadwick, and entered first. His gaze swept the room in the ghostly light from the hallway. The general was on the bed to the left, lying on his side, facing away from the door. Barltrop kept his eyes on the still form and beckoned with his left hand. Kopp entered. The two men advanced, Barltrop going to the far side of the bed.

Through the door, Dunn heard rustling sounds, a groan, and a thump. The flapping sounds of slippered feet came next.

"Was ist es?"

Although Dunn couldn't understand the words, the angry tone came through the door quite clear. He nodded at Marston.

"Herr Juhnke, it is I, *Sturmbannführer* Obert Seiler. You have an urgent phone call from Berlin," Marston said, trying to keep his voice low.

"What? At this time of night. Take a message!"

"My apologies, *Herr* Juhnke, it comes from the *Führer's* office."

"Mein Gott!"

The key on the other side rattled in the door.

Goerdt and Schneider entered the main hall. Goerdt waved at Jonesy and Lindstrom near the front door and got acknowledging waves back. Goerdt led the way down the main hall, running along the left hand wall. When they reached the end of the main hall, they took up kneeling positions so they could see down a hallway running off to the right. Marston had said the majority of the guards were billeted there. The two settled in to wait.

Barltrop waited until Kopp was in position to the sleeping general's left and nodded.

Kopp grabbed the general's shoulder and slammed him onto his back. He pinned him down with his right hand and jammed the Sten's cold suppressor in his ear.

Glockner's eyes flew open just as Barltrop's hand covered his mouth.

"I know you speak English, General, so listen carefully. We know exactly who you are and you're coming with us. My friend here is going to gag you and tie your hands behind your back. If you cry out or struggle, I will shoot you and no one will hear the shot. Nod if you understand."

Glockner moved his head slightly.

"Right, that's very good. Okay, Geoffrey, go to it."

Dunn stepped back and got into a firing position, his Sten at eye level and aimed at the center of the door.

The door opened inward to the right and Juhnke stood there in his striped pajamas, a pistol in his right hand, which dangled by his thigh. He saw Dunn and his eyes focused on the black hole of the Sten aimed at his face. It took a split second to register that something was wrong, terribly wrong.

Dunn jumped forward, his left hand aiming for the gun in Juhnke's hand.

Startled into action, Juhnke raised his gun hand intending to shoot Dunn. Dunn got a grip on the man's wrist and pushed the barrel to the side.

Juhnke's weapon went off, the shot terribly loud in the castle's nighttime silence.

Dunn had time to think, *Oh shit!*

Chapter 38

St. Louis Insurance Company Building
St. Louis, Missouri
2 October, 6:31 P.M. U.S. Central time

Gertrude and her partner, Emerson, solved the problem in fifteen minutes, but it had been a rocky time. They'd argued first about what the problem actually was, then debated which method to use to attack it. When they'd finally agreed, they'd used up over five minutes. Gertrude noticed that none of the other pairs seemed to be having the same kind of trouble, which frustrated her. The class had been instructed to stand up when they solved the problem. In spite of their initial difficulties, Gertrude and Emerson were the only ones standing when Mr. Jones said, "Time."

"Be seated," Mr. Jones said. He turned to the chalkboard and wrote the problem there. His handwriting was actually very good. He faced the class.

"What kind of code is this?"

Everyone raised a hand.

Jones scanned the room and his gaze settled on Gertrude. He'd heard their arguments and unknown to them, had moved slightly closer to hear better. Both had solid points of view and he knew either would have worked, but Gertrude had convinced her partner that her method would be faster, and it proved to be so.

"Miss Dunn?"

Gertrude rose to her feet. "It's a simple substitution cipher."

Jones nodded, as did some in the class. A few of them appeared to be disappointed that they hadn't been called upon. "How did you determine what the cipher key is? I noticed you and Mr. Emerson had a lengthy discussion on that topic."

Gertrude's cheeks turned pink. She had been so focused on the problem she'd forgotten others could hear her, too.

"Yes, we did. We ended up choosing a method where we determined the frequency of the appearance of each letter. We applied the known English letter usage frequency to find the decoded letters that appeared most often."

Jones held up his hand and she stopped.

"Show me your letter usage information. I did not give you a paper with one on it."

"Er, we don't have one on paper, sir. It's in here." She tapped her temple.

Jones blinked. Of the class he asked, "Who else has the letter usage frequency table memorized?"

Everyone looked away, at their shoes or at another person nearby.

"Miss Dunn? Would you be willing to come up here and write that down for us?" He held out his piece of chalk.

Gertrude nodded. "Sure." She stepped forward and took the chalk. She glanced over her shoulder at Ralph. He smiled and winked at her. She began to write and behind her, Mr. Jones opened a desk drawer. He rummaged around and found the paper he wanted.

Gertrude finished and turned around. Jones took the chalk from her and motioned for her to stay right there.

Jones held up his paper and compared his list to hers. He raised his gaze to look over the top of the paper at his student. He said in a low voice, "You have eidetic memory."

Gertrude glanced at the class, who were all leaning forward. She wasn't sure whether they'd heard him.

"Yes, sir."

"Excellent. Please be seated, Miss Dunn, and continue explaining how you and Mr. Emerson solved the puzzle."

Gertrude explained by saying after finding the most likely candidates, they applied logic in the form of deductive reasoning as to which letter was the key. They whittled it down to three possibilities and by actually performing a few substitutions, were able to eliminate two.

When she finished, the class spontaneously clapped their hands.

After it died down, Mr. Jones asked, "I assume no one else attempted the letter usage frequency?"

Everyone shook their heads.

"Each partner write your name on your papers and pass them up to me."

There was a flurry of activity as the students did that. Jones neatened up the stack of papers and slipped them into the bottom desk drawer, which he then locked. He picked up the phone and dialed a two-digit number. Someone evidently answered immediately because he said something the class couldn't hear.

A moment later the door opened and Mr. Smith entered. He was followed by a young woman, possibly in her mid-twenties.

"Anyone hungry?" Smith asked. He received vigorous nods from everyone in the room.

"All right. First we'll take you to your quarters, up one flight for the men, down one for the women. You'll have ten minutes to unpack. Everyone meet downstairs in the lobby. Anyone who is late, misses dinner."

Mr. Jones spoke up next. "A couple of rules that you are to abide by at all times while you are here for training. You heard earlier that all of you are close to the same age. You are all unmarried and available. However," he leaned forward putting both hands on the desk, "rule one is that while at this facility there will be no fraternization between sexes. I don't have time to put up with shenanigans, and you'll discover you don't have time to dilly-dally around with each other. That's why men and women are on different floors. If a member of the opposite sex is discovered on the wrong floor, he or she will be sent home immediately. If one of you entertains a member of the opposite sex in your room, no matter how innocent your intentions are, you will *both* go home. There is no appeal. No 'I'll do better from now on.' There will be no 'from now on.' Have I made the ramifications of breaking the no fraternization rules crystal clear?"

Everyone replied, "Yes, sir."

"Rule two is related to consuming alcohol. Remember who the hell you are working for. The U.S. Government. You will, eventually, if you survive this training, be handling material that is classified. If you have a problem with alcohol and it shows up here, you are gone. We understand the need to unwind, but being even less than a bleary-eyed drunk can cause you to talk about things you shouldn't. Therefore, every time, *every* time, you leave this building you will be escorted by a chaperone."

Jones straightened back up, towering his full six and a half feet. "Any questions?"

No one moved.

Jones said, "Class, may I introduce the female's chaperone, Miss Brown? You've all met Mr. Smith, who will be the chaperone for the males. I want to be clear: they are not your friends. They will be constantly assessing you as a candidate. Your behaviors, good and bad, will be reported to me. I have the final say on everything including who stays and who goes home."

Jones sat down and nodded to Smith and Brown.

"Ladies, come grab your suitcases and we'll head downstairs to your quarters," Brown said.

The six women got to their feet and grabbed their suitcases. Gertrude was in the middle of the group.

Brown nodded at Jones and Smith, and led the women out the door.

They walked down the hall toward the elevator, but passed it, instead going all the way to end of the hall. There, Brown pushed open a wooden door with a window in the top half. As the women's line bunched up, Gertrude inadvertently bumped the suit case of the woman in front of her, who had stopped suddenly.

"Oh, sorry," she said.

The woman, a few years older than Gertrude, turned around and said, "Watch where you're going, kid."

She turned around and started down the stairs.

"I said I was sorry."

The woman stopped, causing Gertrude and everyone behind her to stop again. The woman turned around again and looked up at Gertrude, who was a couple of steps higher.

"You're just a damn showoff. Little Miss Eidetic Memory. More like Little Miss Teacher's Pet." She started to turn away, but Gertrude bent over and grasped her right trapezius muscle and gave it a twist.

"Ow! That hurt."

Brown had stopped walking at the sounds from above and started back up the stairs to see what was happening.

Gertrude let go of the woman's shoulder, but leaned closer. "People who are showoffs never have the skills to back it up. I have the skills. You know what you are, though?"

The woman just stared at Gertrude.

"You're a bully. I despise bullies because they think they can run around scaring people all the time. I'm not taking your damn shit. Do you understand me?"

Brown reached the two women. "What's going on here?"

Gertrude smiled at her. "Just having a discussion about different personalities."

"She hurt my neck. She pinched it somehow."

Brown looked at Gertrude.

"I thought she missed her footing and reached out to help. I'm so sorry I hurt you. A complete accident."

The woman's mouth dropped open at the blatant lie. "That's not true. Ask anyone."

Brown nodded. "Anyone see what happened?"

The woman behind Gertrude said, "It's like she said. The lady seemed to lose her footing and this girl tried to help. That's all it was." She smiled sweetly.

Brown looked at all three women, and said, "Hm, hmm. Well, let's go. Can't miss dinner."

She went back to the front of the line, which started moving again. The woman behind Gertrude sped up to walk beside her.

"I despise bullies, too." She raised her voice, "Did you hear that, bully?"

"Leave me alone," the woman replied without looking back.

"Will do," Gertrude replied, smiling at her new friend. She stuck out her hand. "Gertrude."

"Yes, I know that. Barbara."

The women shook hands as they continued down the stairs.

"Were the d-word and s-word too much?" Gertrude asked.

"She cursed first, so no."

"Oh, yeah, that's right."

"So where'd you'd learn that pinch thing?"

"My brother's an Army Ranger," Gertrude said, pride heavy in her voice. "He taught me."

Chapter 39

The gunshot surprised the German, but he began to struggle harder. Dunn had to let go of his Sten to get a two-handed grip on the man's gun. He rotated left and shoulder butted the much heavier man, who took a floundering step backwards, but not fast enough to keep up with his momentum. As he was going down, Dunn gave a vicious twist and yanked the pistol from the man's hand just as the German fell on his ass.

"Grab the machine," Dunn said to Marston as he stuck the German's pistol in his belt behind his back. He grasped his Sten and aimed it at the man's face. "You be quiet." Just in case the man spoke no English, he held a finger to his lips and said, "Shh."

The man nodded, but turned his head to discover Marston with the SIGABA machine in his hand.

The German drew a deep breath to yell for help.

Dunn dropped to a knee and short-punched the man in the solar plexus. All the air he'd just sucked in gushed out and he rolled over on his side, holding his chest. Unable to take a breath because his diaphragm was temporarily frozen, he began to claw at his throat.

Marston stepped around the fallen man.

Dunn said, "Tell him to relax. The air will come in a few seconds."

Marston told the man that, but the German continued his frantic clawing.

"Ah, fuck. We've got to go. Leave him. He'll be all right."

Marston stepped into the hallway.

Dunn looked at the keyhole. Ah, some good luck finally, the key was still there. He snatched it out of the lock and walked into the hallway, closing the door behind him. He locked the door and dropped the key in his pocket.

On the main floor, a hand slammed down on a red button. A ringing alarm went off.

Saunders heard the shot and tapped Dickinson on the arm, and pointed to the end of the hallway. Marston had said there was another set of stairs, a normal kind, there. Dickinson nodded and started down the hallway. Just then, the general's aide burst out of his room, a pistol in his hand. He turned toward Dickinson and raised his weapon.

Dickinson fired three shots on the run and the man collapsed, dead. Dickinson pulled him back into his room and closed the door. He ran to the end of the hall and took up his position there.

Everyone in the general's room heard Juhnke's shot. The general's expression turned hopeful. Barltrop and Kopp got him out of the bed and into a pair of shoes. They moved to the door. Barltrop stuck his head out.

"Where to, Sarge?"

"Waiting for Dunn. Hang on a minute."

Jonesy heard the shot from upstairs and got ready.

An alarm went off.

He fired a three-round burst at the first SS guard through the just opened door, dropping the enemy soldier. A second form appeared and he fired again, but the man jumped back just in time. He ducked behind the heavy wooden door. Jonesy fired again at the door, but the wood was so thick it simply absorbed the 9mm rounds.

Goerdt and Schneider heard heavy boots coming their way and raised their Stens, aiming down the hallway. They waited until six guards were completely in view, and opened fire. The first three guards fell and the others behind them spun around to go another way. Another burst killed them. The six bodies cluttered up the hallway. Anyone else coming would have to hurdle their own men.

Lindstrom pivoted and leaned around the support column's right side. He had a clear view through the door. A helmet appeared on the right side. Lindstrom waited and was rewarded when a shoulder and chest appeared along with a face. He aimed and fired, striking the man in the upper right chest. The man's useless right hand dropped his weapon. He crawled away outside.

"Get him?"

"Yeah, but he got away."

"Don't worry about it. You cover the door now, I'll cover the main hall."

"Okay."

Jonesy moved around the column and set up aiming into the main hall.

Dunn, Cross, Martelli, and Marston ran to Saunders.

"Time to go!" Dunn said. "We've poked the hornet's nest!"

Saunders gave a short whistle and when Dickinson looked his way, waved his arm. Barltrop and Kopp, like two London Bobbies, frog marched Glockner, who was pinned between them, as they guided him down the hallway to the stairs. Soon, all the men on the second floor were entering the main hall and running across it to the Portrait Room.

Two more guards appeared at the main entrance door. They had dashed all the way up the driveway from the closest gate and found one guard lying on his back, passed out from blood loss. Upon seeing a guard in the doorway who appeared to be dead, they held back. The door was open about forty-five degrees. One ducked down low and peeked through. He spotted men running across the main hall. Excitement took over caution and he raised his MP40.

Lindstrom popped out from behind the pillar and shot him twice.

On the lower level, underneath the spot at the end of the main hall where Goerdt and Schneider were positioned, two dozen SS guards pounded down a long hallway that would eventually lead to the armory.

Dunn whistled and when Goerdt looked his way, beckoned him, and pointed at the door to the Portrait Room. Goerdt took another look down the hallway. It was clear. So he tapped Schneider. The two men ran toward the Portrait Room.

Commandos and Rangers arrived in mass in the Portrait Room. Dunn entered last, taking a last look at the main hall to make sure no Germans were there. It was empty. But to his left, where Goerdt and Schneider had been, he heard some soft footsteps. Someone being slow and careful. He pushed the door closed and bent to examine the lock. He tried Juhnke's key that he'd taken out of the man's door, but no luck. He tossed the key and looked around. An old winged chair sat across the room, in front of a portrait of really old man and his hunting dog. Dunn shook his head at the picture and wrestled the chair into a tilted position, with the top edge wedged underneath the door's gold-plated knob. It undoubtedly would not last long, but it would slow down a rushing attack.

Dunn told Schneider to request the C-47 pickup and to be quick about it. He wanted to make radio contact while still above ground and not in the tunnel deep under the mountain.

Marston led the way to the escape door. Saunders and his men, and the captured field marshal would be the first to go out. Marston took one last long look at Lady Adelaide, then he pushed the secret button. He was still carrying the SIGABA machine.

Dunn's men gathered around the escape exit.

Schneider touched Dunn's shoulder. "Sarge," Schneider held up his wrist so they could both see the time. "The plastic should go up any moment. The pilot said fifteen minutes and he'd be on the ground."

Dunn nodded, picturing their position relative to the armory. They should be safe. However, it wouldn't hurt to speed things up. Just as he arrived, Marston had just pushed some sort of hidden switch and the door was swinging open. Dunn checked his watch. Fifteen minutes. Good. About right.

"Let's go, guys, the explosives are due to go off any second. Mac, fifteen minutes and the plane'll be here."

Marston went through the door.

Saunders noticed Marston had stared at the portrait, and he looked at it for a few seconds. Beautiful woman, he thought, but not my Sadie. He went through the door first, followed by Barltrop and Kopp who still had Glockner between them. Chadwick and Dickinson went next. Marston stood inside the doorway, out of the way, positioned so he could push the lever to close the door one last time.

Dunn pushed his men ahead of himself and checked the watch again. No explosion. He grabbed Schneider by the arm.

"Bob, you sure on the time?"

Schneider looked at Dunn with a pained expression on his face. "I'm sure I set it right, but something's not right. I'm sorry. Do you want me to go back?"

"No, we need to get out of here. Go on." Dunn said. He took a quick glance down the Portrait Room, then went through the door and down the stairs.

Marston stepped forward and activated the lever. He waited until the door was completely closed, and he, too, ran down the stairs.

Once the armory door was opened, twenty-four SS guards sprinted inside. The sergeant in charge, a man in his middle thirties, Oskar Reinhart, who was wearing a pretty pissed off expression, shouted instructions. Reinhart had been the head of the castle's SS guard unit for almost a year and he enjoyed the assignment very much. To have some sort of breach in castle security was an insult to his professionalism. But as he thought about it, better now than when the *Führer* and his entourage were here.

Reinhart went to a box on the wall and pressed a button, shutting down the mind-numbing alarm.

Reinhart's men were pulling MP40s off the racks on both sides of the long, narrow room.

He shouted another order.

A guard reached down and picked up a box of 9mm ammunition. *"Scheiße!"* Shit! He backpedaled.

Reinhart walked over to see what the hell was wrong, half expecting to see a rat. Instead he saw a block of plastic explosive with a timer on it. He bent over to examine the timer. It was on twelve o'clock and had stopped ticking because the minute hand had struck the little contact pin.

"Out! Everyone out and close the door."

The guards ran out the door. The man with the ammunition box carried it with him.

The sergeant knelt on one knee and looked at the wire from the timer to the detonator. It was intact. The bomb should have exploded, but it hadn't. He placed a hand over the detonator without touching it. He was relieved to note that his hand was steady. This was either going to work and he'd live to laugh about it one day, or there'd be nothing left of him.

He gingerly gripped the detonator between his forefinger and thumb. Grasping the block of explosive with his other hand, and gently, oh so gently, he slowly pulled on the detonator. It was excruciatingly slow. Finally, the thing was free from the explosive.

After pulling the wire from the end of the detonator, he put the device on a shelf, between two small boxes so it wouldn't roll around. He'd dispose of it properly later, although it was obviously defective, otherwise the armory would have been so much history.

He rose on shaking legs and opened the door. He gave what he thought was a smile, but the men saw a grim line. "It's taken care of. Get back in here and finish what you were doing. We have to go find out what's happened."

Chapter 40

Escape tunnel
Hohenstein Castle
2 October, 0137 Hours

Saunders rounded the corner at the tunnel level expecting to find the trussed up colonel. Saunders played his torch up and down the tunnel, but the colonel was gone. What the bloody hell? Did the man break free of his bindings and run away?

He walked slowly toward the spot where the colonel had been left on his stomach. Taking a knee and shining the light around, he saw funny looking marks across the centuries-old dust. "Well, I'll be buggered!"

Barltrop stepped close and asked, "What happened to him?" He was sure he'd tied everything as tight as possible.

"He got onto his side and kind of inch-wormed his way along." Saunders played the light ahead again. The tracks left by the hog-tied colonel were as clear as if they'd been foot prints. "I reckon we'll find him somewhere ahead. How far can you inch-worm yourself in fifteen minutes or so?"

Barltrop shrugged. "Find out soon."

Saunders said to the others, who were piling up behind Barltrop, "Colonel's wandered off a bit. We'll find him eventually."

"Yeah, he'll get to the exit and won't be able to reach the lever to open the door," Marston said. "Probably find him staring at it wishing he could fly, if he makes it that far."

This earned a few chuckles.

"This way, men," Saunders said, waving down the tunnel. "In case there's any doubt."

More laughter echoed off the five-hundred-year-old stone walls.

Barltrop reached up and retrieved the torch he'd left for the colonel's sanity. He flicked it off and put it away.

Saunders took off and the rest of the men trooped along after him.

SS guard commander, Sergeant Reinhart, led his men up the stairs to the main hall. He pushed opened the door with one hand and aimed his MP40 with the other. The hall was empty. Stepping through the door, he immediately spotted a dead body, one of his men. He assumed it was one of the two on duty at the door, but couldn't tell from his position. It was confusing. Only one shot had been heard by the man who sounded the alarm, but did that shot kill this guard? He scanned the rest of main hall. Empty. He signaled the men behind him and they nodded. He ran toward the front door. Behind him, several men fanned out from the stairwell door and covered the main hall.

Reinhart discovered two more bodies, and when he looked out the front door he could see another one. He recognized one who had come up from the nearest gate. Rising, he examined the main hall. Where had the attackers gone?

His first thought was the guests. He ran over to his men who had made their way into the main hall. Selecting two, he sent them up the spiral staircase. While he waited for them to return and report, he wandered across the main hall. A dark red or burgundy carpet ran along the wall in front of the door leading to the Portrait Room. He walked across the carpet, but didn't see anything unusual. He turned around and walked toward his men, stepping off the carpet and onto the stone floor. When he lifted his boot that was first to hit the stone floor, it felt funny, as though he'd stepped in gum. He looked down. Below him was a perfect imprint of his boot print . . . in red, very dark red.

Spinning around, he went back to the carpet. He couldn't really see much of anything, but when he tapped the toe of one boot around, it squished. He didn't bother sticking his finger in it. Something had happened here and he was standing right outside a closed door.

He heard pounding footsteps on the spiral staircase. The two men ran over to him and one said, "Sergeant, the field marshal is not in his room. His uniform is still there. *Herr* Juhnke is locked in his room and screaming his head off about his machine being stolen by the Americans! And Colonel Neubart's room is empty, also. We found the field marshal's aide in his room, dead. Shot."

Reinhart directed his men to join him as he turned to the Portrait Room door.

He turned the gold-plated doorknob and pushed. The door refused to budge. Wondering whether it was locked, he pulled out his master skeleton key. A few seconds later, he learned the door was unlocked, therefore something was blocking the way. He pictured the room he'd walked through hundreds of times and determined that a chair across from the door must have been jammed under the doorknob. Only one solution left.

He ordered everyone out of the way and raised his MP40. *There's going to be hell to pay for this*, he thought. Standing back two meters, he fired a couple of three-round bursts into the doorknob. The knob shattered and fell off the door, taking with it the metal rod that connected the knobs through the door. Ramming his shoulder against the door, it opened a few inches. The heavy chair was slowing things down. He pointed at another guard and the two of them shouldered the door open wide enough for them to get through.

Reinhart peeked around the door. No one. Well, except for the dead guards lying next to the wall. Who the hell did this? "Get in here!" he shouted, his anger rising.

His men ran into the room and past him. Each man looked down at the dead men, their friends.

"See what we're up against?" He shouted again.

"Yes, Sergeant!"

A one-hundred-year-old carpet runner ran along the wall, a dark blue in color. He pulled his flashlight out and turned it on. He ran along the wall. Even though the lights over the paintings were on, he aimed his flashlight at the carpet. He raised an eyebrow. Dusty footprints? Dropping to one knee, he rubbed a finger across the clear marking of a combat boot. It was not German, which he hadn't expected it to be. He followed the prints in the direction they had come from, toward the end of the room. There could only be one explanation. Running along the wall, he followed the boot prints. He stopped next to Lady Adelaide's picture. The prints had come through the wall?

He faced the stone wall and stared at the section next to the Lady where there had to be a door of some kind. The light shining on the portrait bled over to the wall.

What's this? He stepped closer. He raised his hand and touched the seam between two stones about chest high. A part of it felt loose, like it might fall out. He pushed it.

Saunders kept a fast pace through the tunnel, shining his torch ahead about ten yards. Finally, there on the tunnel floor, inching along, was the colonel. Saunders ran up beside the man and knelt down. He put a hand on the man's shoulder and said. "That's quite a feat, there, sir."

The colonel looked at Saunders, his expression defeated.

Marston ran up to join Saunders.

Saunders pulled his knife.

The colonel's eyes widened.

"Don't worry," Saunders said. Marston translated.

The Commando rolled the man over onto his stomach and sliced the rope connecting the hands and feet. Next he cut through the bindings around the ankles.

"Let's get you up."

Marston repeated it in German.

Saunders sheathed his knife and grabbed the man by an elbow and got him into a sitting position.

"Can you stand?"

A shrug after Marston's translation.

"Steve."

Barltrop went around the colonel and grabbed the other elbow. The Commandos lifted together and got the man on his feet. He wobbled a little, but stayed upright, leaning against the wall.

"You'll have to come with us. Might as well, since you were trying to go that way anyhow," Saunders said.

Marston translated.

Neubart nodded.

Saunders took off again, but at a slower pace. Marston was right behind him and Saunders asked over his shoulder, "How much farther to the cave?"

"Should be a couple of minutes."

"Right."

Reinhart's finger sank into the depression as Marston's had. He heard the same *clunking* sound in the wall and the door swung open. He turned and grinned at his men.

"Found it!" He pointed at one of his best men, Corporal Hans Lang, and said, "Take half the men. Get a truck and go down the mountain. This must lead to an escape tunnel. There's only one place it can come out: directly east of where we are in the castle on the downslope. Whoever we're chasing must have an escape vehicle somewhere down there. Find it. Go to a point just inside the forest and wait for them to come to you. We'll be the hounds and drive them your way."

"Yes, sergeant," the corporal said. He selected the closest eleven men and led the way out of the Portrait Room at a run.

Reinhart gathered the other eleven men and said, "I have no fucking idea what's ahead. Keep your eyes and ears alert and watch for side tunnels." He turned and ran through the door and down the stairs, his flashlight beam bobbing on the stairs.

Chapter 41

Escape tunnel
Hohenstein Castle
2 October, 0142 Hours

Saunders reached the end of the tunnel and stepped aside for Marston, who went right to the door's lever and pulled. As the door swung open and the cold, but wonderfully fresh, outside air rushed into the tunnel, Neubart stared wide eyed.

Marston noticed and in German said, "Welcome to the outside world."

Dunn joined the group by the exit. "How we doing, Mac?"

"Ready to head for the clearing."

Dunn nodded. "Very good." He looked around at all the climbing equipment they'd left behind. "Shall we take all of this with us?"

Saunders looked around at all the packs filled with ropes and such. A grin crossed his face and his handlebar mustache twitched. "Let's leave them. Mess with future archeologists."

Dunn laughed. "Great idea."

Saunders went through the door and Barltrop pulled the colonel along with him. Chadwick joined Kopp to help with the field marshal. Soon all the men were weaving their way through the cave.

Corporal Lang, who was leading his men down the mountain, chose to drive the truck himself. He rode the razor-thin line between reckless and as fast as humanly and mechanically possible. On one particularly sharp curve the truck swayed so much the driver's side tires almost left the road. Rounding the last curve, he headed along the road running to the village. In his mind's eye he knew where he needed to go. He seemed to recall a farmer's road that ran along the eastern side of the mountain. He slowed down, so as to not outrun his headlights which were just small slits due to the blackout covering. He downshifted to first gear and slowed down some more, to just fifteen kilometers per hour. Creeping along, he kept his eyes on the left side of the road. A moment later, he was rewarded with a gap in the trees.

He turned the truck onto the same farmer's road Marston had used. It was narrow, meant for one vehicle, and he kept his speed at ten kilometers per hour. Driving a short distance, he relied on his internal map, and stopped. Turning off the engine, he doused the headlights, pulled on the parking brake, and jumped out of the truck. Letting his eyes adjust, which didn't take but a few seconds, he looked up at the mountain. If it hadn't been for the light from the full moon, he might not have been able to see the white stone of the outermost wall. It was exactly west of him. He was where he thought he'd be.

Sergeant Reinhart had ordered him to search for an escape vehicle, and to move into a position just inside the forest leading up the slope. Somewhere up there would be an exit from the tunnel. The enemy would be coming out expecting to go free. *We'll stop them*, he thought.

Running to the side of the uncovered truck, he spoke to one of his men, "Drive the truck another half kilometer and come back. You're looking for any vehicles. Take Mauer with you."

"Yes, Sergeant," was the reply.

"The rest of you, get out and follow me."

After all of the men were out and off to the east side of the truck, it started up and drove off into the night.

Lang led his men through a line of deciduous trees on the east side of the road and when they popped out into the open field, he directed them to split up and look for a hidden vehicle on this side of the road. As he ran along the edge of the open field, he heard low thrumming sounds coming from the south. He stopped to listen, turning his head to try and locate the sound.

He realized the sounds were coming from above him. He looked up. Was that a reflection?

Dunn and Saunders, and their men, swapped positions, with Dunn taking point and the Rangers right behind him, followed by the Commandos. Marston stayed with Dunn. Using his built in direction finder, Dunn led the men straight to the clearing. He stopped at its edge, holding up a fist to stop those behind him. Examining the clearing, he determined it was empty. He tapped Jonesy and pointed. Jonesy nodded and disappeared into the forest to the south. Dunn waited patiently and a couple of minutes later, Jonesy reappeared from the north, having made a complete circle around the opening.

"Clear, Sarge."

"Thanks." Dunn said. He motioned with his hand and he and the rest of the men walked into the opening. Under the original attack and escape plan everyone was to gather here, but that seemed a superfluous action. When Saunders sidled up next to him, Dunn said, "I don't see any reason to stay here since were already together."

"Aye. Let's keep on moving."

"Okay." Dunn found Lindstrom nearby and said, "Eugene, you have point. Straightest line to the landing zone."

"Yes, Sarge.

Lindstrom looked around at the men and when everyone seemed ready to move on, stepped out of the clearing into the forest. Dunn was next, then Marston and the rest of the Rangers. Barltrop still had Colonel Neubart by the elbow and was guiding him along. The man had proven to be resilient, his legs recovered from being tied up, and he was able to keep up. Chadwick and Kopp were managing with the field marshal.

Chadwick asked, "Are you doing all right, Field Marshal?"

Glockner gave him a sullen nod.

Chadwick patted him on the arm. "I bet this kind of ruined your weekend."

Saunders had the last spot in the line.

Sergeant Reinhart was running as fast as was safe in the tunnel. He hadn't seen any side tunnels, which was a relief. That could have taken ages to have to check them, too. Suddenly his light picked up a bunch of objects lying on the floor straight ahead. He raised the beam and the stone wall at the end of the tunnel materialized. He slowed to a walk, as did his men. He knelt beside one of the objects and realized it was a military pack. He opened it and pulled out a coiled rope. He nodded. Yes, that had been the original plan. But someone on the inside had located this tunnel. They'd come in and left through it. They had Field Marshal Glockner, Colonel Neubart, and the SIGABA machine. And they'd killed a lot of his men. They were good. Very good. Commandos, almost certainly.

The question staring him in the face was how did they get through this wall? He shone his flashlight on the wall. He spotted the lever immediately. He pulled it and the door swung open, letting the fresh, cold air into the tunnel.

"Let's go, men."

He stepped through the doorway and discovered the cave.

Corporal Lang glanced away, and back where he'd seen the glint of moonlight reflecting off what must be an airplane. He found it again and was able to make out the whole shape; an American C-47, the one used by paratroopers on the day of the 6th June invasion. The plane was descending and appeared to be headed for a landing only half a kilometer away.

Sergeant Reinhart's orders had been clear, to find the escape vehicle. Well, hell, he'd done it!

He kept one eye on the aircraft, which was now banking slightly left to line up its approach, and whistled a low couple of notes. His men responded by running his way. The truck had reached the end of its search path, turned around and was heading back, its little tiny lights streaming weakly ahead of it.

Lang took his eyes off the airplane and checked to make sure all of his men were present, including the two from the truck. He turned back and watched the C-47 land. Its engines were much louder.

He was so focused on the troop plane he didn't hear the two black, British Mosquito night fighters fly over the landing zone. Nor did he see them bank right and go into a racetrack path overhead.

RONN MUNSTERMAN

Chapter 42

Eastern slope of Hohenstein Castle
2 October, 0147 Hours

The pine trees and mountains reminded Lindstrom of the many times he and his family or friends had gone hiking in Oregon's wilderness. A touch of homesickness struck him, but he shook it off. He picked his way carefully through the forest, finding the safest path down the steep incline. On occasion, he had to grab a tree trunk or branch to steady his footing. He made sure Dunn saw what he was doing before moving on. It was slow, but hurrying would have but one result: tumbling downhill and breaking something. As soon as Lindstrom passed one particularly large pine tree, he had an unobstructed view of the valley. He stopped. He heard the droning sounds of aircraft overhead and looked up, but it was impossible to see anything through the trees. Scanning the part of the valley he could see, a dark shape seemed to be trundling across the field from south to north.

"Sarge."

Dunn stepped up beside Lindstrom.

"What?"

Lindstrom pointed. "I think that's our ride home." He pointed upward. "I think we have some air support."

Saunders, who had caught up from the tail end, listened. "Aye. That's got to be a couple of Mosquito night fighters up there. Nice to know we'll have escorts out of here. Wouldn't care for a repeat of our inbound trip."

Dunn eyeballed the distance to the C-47, which was turning around to face south. To the men he said, "Looks like five or six hundred yards from the bottom of this slope. Let's keep our eyes and ears open."

He rejoined Lindstrom and gave him the go ahead and the line of men started downhill again.

Sergeant Reinhart popped into a clearing unexpectedly and stopped. He wanted to turn on his flashlight, but was afraid it would give him away if anyone ahead was watching their rear, and it would destroy his night vision. He left the light in his pocket. Some moonlight filtered through the thick pine trees, but what he really wanted to see was the ground for more foot prints. He frowned. He really needed to know.

Sighing deeply, still worried about giving his position away, he walked into the center of the clearing and knelt down. He pulled his light from his pocket and covered the lens with his hand. He closed his dominant eye to save his night vision. Putting the lens centimeters from the ground, he switched on the light. His fingers glowed red, just like they did when he was a kid back in Cologne playing with his father's flashlight in his bedroom.

He created a gap between his forefinger and middle finger and moved the light around a little. He found the first boot print in seconds. It was pointed east. He immediately turned off the light and opened his eye. That was all he needed, confirmation he was right on their trail.

His men had been traveling in a column formation, but he said to them, "Line formation. Two meter spacing. Only fire if fired upon or if I give the order. Remember, they have two of our own with them."

The men nodded and moved smoothly and quietly into their positions. He gave the order and they started forward.

Corporal Lang was in a tight spot. He knew where the plane was, but he was supposed to go back and lay in wait for the enemy being driven to him by the sergeant. So he made the logical decision to split his force. It might breach a basic tactical premise, but wouldn't capturing or destroying the C-47 serve a greater purpose? He laid out his orders to six men and they formed a skirmish line, five meters apart and began advancing on the C-47.

He took the other five men and they pushed through the trees on the east side of the farmer's road. He also ordered a skirmish line and the men increased the distance between them to a couple of meters. He gave a signal and the men ran across the road and into the forest. After covering five meters, he called a halt. The men each located a good hiding place, and settled in to wait.

They were about fifty yards from the edge of the forest according to Dunn's mental map and clock. Something had been nagging him for the past few minutes. When it finally became clear, he sped up and caught Lindstrom from behind, grasping him by the shoulder and making a shushing sound. Dunn rotated and held up a hand for the men behind him. The line stopped and everyone took a knee, except Saunders who made his way up quietly to Dunn.

In a whisper, he asked, "What's going on."

"Been thinking."

"Don't hurt yourself."

"Ha ha. The guards are going to figure out who we've taken and what Marston is carrying. They'll not take that lying down."

"No."

"How hard was it for you to find that switch that opens the secret door?" Dunn asked Marston.

Marston frowned. "A few seconds. What are you saying? That they're chasing us?"

Dunn nodded. "Yep. Once they get into that room and see the dead guards, they'll figure out where we went and send men into the tunnel after us." He went silent for a moment.

"What else?" Saunders prompted.

"If they find the secret passage, they'll see pretty quick it's got to come out somewhere on this slope. What would you do, Mac?"

"I'd send someone down to the bottom of the mountain and make a beeline to a spot at the bottom of this slope. So that means we're probably in between two of their units."

"Yep. And we need to find the unit between us and the plane fast. They probably saw the aircraft land. They might send some men over to capture it. Eugene, go get Bob."

Lindstrom took off uphill. A moment later Schneider showed up with the radio.

"Call the pilot. Warn him that he may have the wrong kind of company coming."

"Will do, Sarge." Schneider knelt and started the call.

"I think we need two groups, very spread out with a gap of twenty yards between them. We might be able to find the guards ahead of us and get the drop on them. Let's keep the field marshal and the colonel back a ways, make sure their gags are tight. Might not hurt to scare them a bit about making any noise," Dunn said.

Saunders nodded. "Sounds good to me. We'll take the left if you'll give me a lad."

"Yep." Dunn grabbed Goerdt, who was standing nearby. "You're with Saunders for a while."

"Sure thing," Goerdt replied as he joined the British Commandos.

Schneider finished with his call and reported to Dunn, "The pilot thanks you. They've got M1s aboard for hot landing zones, so they're more or less prepared to defend the plane. Plus the Mosquitos are flying around somewhere close."

"Okay, good. Thanks, Bob."

"Sure."

Schneider shrugged the radio onto his back.

The SS guard leading the attack on the C-47 was excited by the opportunity to lead. It showed that the corporal trusted him and saw leadership qualities in him. This would be a chance to prove himself more than he had before. The problem with his thinking was that it'd been quite some time since his last combat experience, and guarding a castle hadn't exactly been a hard job. He halted his men at two hundred meters from the plane. Waving his men into a kneeling position, he watched the plane for any sign of movement, but saw none.

He rose to his feet.

That was that last thing he ever did.

As soon as the pilot got the call from Dunn's radioman, he'd ordered the jumpmaster to get the M1s out of their storage container and load them. Keeping all the lights off, the pilot and jumpmaster, a rather grizzled and grumpy sergeant, climbed down quietly to the ground using the rear door. Since the pilot had already turned the aircraft around to face south, they were on the east side of the plane, opposite from any approaching enemy soldiers. The copilot stayed in the cockpit to coordinate with the leader of the Mosquitos. The jumpmaster and pilot took up prone positions directly beneath the spot in the fuselage where the exit was located. This placed them a safe distance from the main landing gear and the tail wheel, to hopefully prevent punctures by enemy fire.

The bright moonlight made the field in front of the men perfectly clear. The jumpmaster saw a man rise. Even if he hadn't already known that the men were German, the distinctive helmet shape gave him away. He lined up the two hundred yard shot and pulled the trigger. The enemy fell straight down, but he couldn't tell where he'd hit him.

Five Germans returned fire.

The copilot shouted over the radio, "Enemy, two hundred yards west of the aircraft!"

The lead Mosquito pilot banked over left and angled his nose down. He spotted the yellow flashes from the German weapons and aimed for that spot. He pressed the trigger button and his four .303 Browning machineguns lit up the night. He was pretty sure he'd laid his bullets on the targets, but zoomed away and prepared to come around again. Behind him, the second British night fighter fired into the same area, although he didn't see a single muzzle flash.

The jumpmaster waited a few seconds after the two Mosquitos had roared away and fired a couple of shots, spaced a few seconds apart. He was trying to provoke return fire, but none came.

The copilot had watched the entire strafing attack and witnessed all five of the Germans getting cut down. He told the night fighters, "Great job. All targets appear to be down."

"Roger."

Chapter 43

The men heard gunfire coming from the valley, and the scream of the two Mosquito night fighters' engines, and the *brrrtt* of their machineguns, as they dove and soared away.

Dunn glanced at Cross, who gave him a thumbs up. Dunn nodded in reply, but wondered whether everything was all right at the C-47. Only one way to find out: get past the Germans.

Martelli was in the left-most position of Dunn's main group. Saunders and his men, plus Goerdt, were thirty yards farther left. The hope had been to be able to pinch the Germans in front of them between the two units. It didn't quite work out that way.

Martelli took enemy fire first from his left at about forty yards, but as can happen so often in combat, first contact is brief, shocking, and yet everyone survives. Martelli ducked behind a tree and returned fire, spraying the spot where he thought he'd seen the muzzle flash. Sympathetic fire lit up the forest on both sides of the line. Now everyone knew where everyone was, more or less.

Dunn estimated they were facing a half dozen men.

Then as quickly as it had started it stopped. What was happening was each soldier was waiting for the enemy to fire again so he could zero in on an actual target.

Sergeant Reinhart and his men heard the gunfire ahead and started running through the forest, a dangerous proposition on the slope. The firefight was perhaps two hundred yards away, directly ahead.

Dunn redirected his men so they were lined up facing the enemy head on, rather than from the original oblique angle. Saunders and Dunn had planned this maneuver. Saunders and his men would maintain the same angle of fire to prevent friendly crossfire. It was up to Dunn to reinitiate the attack.

He was kneeling near Wickham and motioned for him to aim at a particular area. Dunn estimated the distance to the enemy to be forty yards following the squad's latest realigning movement. Moonlight filtered through the trees fairly well and visibility was superior to five minutes ago when they'd been surrounded by pine trees. Here, the forest tree mix included some deciduous as well, which opened the forest floor a lot.

Dunn raised his fist, and then dropped it.

His men cut loose. Their suppressed Stens' 9mm rounds tore into the forest at 1,000 feet per second. On the north side, Saunders and his men opened up, aiming at the same location. The Germans tried to return fire but the onslaught was too accurate and it seemed to never stop. Tree branches and leaves were shredded and filled the air. It was an odd firefight. Only the muzzle sounds of the Germans' weapons were loud enough to be heard. The Stens' muzzles made a chuffing sound, and you could hear metallic clinks as the bolt was slammed backward by the rounds' gases.

Dunn saw his target slump and slide down the tree trunk he was hiding beside. Another enemy soldier nearby fell.

Suddenly shots came from behind Dunn.

"Behind us!" Wickham shouted. He rotated and began firing uphill.

Dunn glanced over and saw a dark stain spreading on the Texan's shirt around the right bicep. He turned to face uphill and spotted some motion and a few muzzle blasts about seventy yards through the trees.

Suddenly, from the right, Dunn heard a shrill whistle.

Saunders had ceased weapons fire.

"New targets behind us. Fire!" Dunn hollered at his men, who turned around and began firing uphill, a distinct disadvantageous position to be in. Dunn and his men were trapped between two German units and were firing at anything moving above them. Dunn guessed there were a dozen Germans attacking. He still didn't know yet what had happened out on the field where the C-47 was parked and waiting, their only way home.

Saunders' squad's weapons lit up again, and the men were moving fast left to right. The two remaining Germans on the downhill side rotated to meet the sudden charge, but were hit almost at the same time and fell, dropping their MP40s. Corporal Lang realized as he fell that he'd made a mistake by splitting his forces. It was his last thought.

Saunders' men stopped firing at a signal from him. Dunn looked over his shoulder and spotted the big man moving toward a position on Dunn's right flank. Saunders was waving his men into a firing line facing uphill.

Once again the firefight suddenly stopped and the leaders on both sides used the lull in the action. Dunn had the advantage of only needing to make it impossible for the German commander to make progress. Dunn's disadvantage was that a fighting retreat almost always created casualties on the departing unit, and Wickham had already been hit. His other disadvantage was having to bring along the captives. The colonel would be left behind, but not the field marshal. He was a definite target to keep and take home. The two men had wisely dropped to the ground to avoid getting shot by their own men.

Dunn and Saunders were hampered by the distance between them. Saunders and his men were to Dunn's right by about ten yards and neither knew for sure what the other was planning. Dunn decided to just make it obvious. He slid along behind his men, staying low and using trees for cover. As he passed each of the men, he gave instructions. He turned around and ran back to his original place.

He raised his Sten and fired. Wickham joined him and they sprayed the area about fifty yards out. Martelli, Jonesy, and Lindstrom darted left and started uphill. It was the standard fire and advance tactic.

Saunders assumed Dunn was flanking the Germans and ordered, "Fire!"

More Stens chuffed in the night air, their lead tearing into the forest uphill.

Reinhart watched another of his men drop. He was down to four counting himself. Four against, what? A dozen perhaps? And where was Corporal Lang and his eleven men? He was wishing at the moment for a radio, but at the time of the alarm, his expectation was that he was meeting a threat inside the castle. He hadn't thought at all that he'd be leaving the castle grounds. His men didn't even have grenades. He shook his head at his stupidity. Nevertheless, he was committed to fighting to the last man because of his SS oath to the *Führer*.

"Keep firing, men. Any targets."

He and his men began firing again, which only sealed their doom.

Martelli, Jonesy, and Lindstrom each found a tree to kneel behind. They were only twenty yards from the four Germans who seemed to be firing blindly downhill. Jonesy was in the lead of the trio and he lined up a shot on an SS guard who seemed to be the leader. He had been giving commands as the Rangers made their way up to a flanking position.

Jonesy fired a three-round burst. Martelli and Lindstrom fired at their targets.

Reinhart felt the impacts of the American's bullets striking his torso. Amazingly, he didn't die that instant, but he lost control of his body, which suddenly seemed overly tired, sort of like after a rigorous workout and a ten kilometer run. He sat down abruptly and fell back. The cold mountain air seemed odd. It was becoming colder, but he also felt as though he was being embraced by something loving and warm. Was there a God after all? Was that what this was? Above him, the trees swayed in the breeze and he saw the stars above. The heavens. Heaven . . .

Dunn found the SS sergeant lying on his back, his eyes open and staring at the heavens. His face seemed . . . peaceful. Dunn leaned down and closed the man's eyes.

Aboard the C-47, the men were all seated on the benches along each wall of the fuselage. The jumpmaster closed the door and waved to the copilot who was watching from up front. The pilot goosed the engines and the plane lumbered down the open field and when it reached take off speed, rose into the cold Austrian night. The two Mosquitos took up positions on either wing.

Dunn glanced at the field marshal sitting across from him. The man stared at Dunn, his expression unreadable. The plane leveled off and Dunn got up. He grabbed a blanket from the seat beside him and held it out toward the German officer. The man nodded; his hands were still tied together. Dunn wrapped the blanket around the man's shoulders and over his front.

"We'll get you somewhere warm soon, sir. I'm sorry we don't have any coffee aboard."

Glockner shrugged. "No matter." He examined Dunn's face, and then his gaze took in the American flag on the right shoulder and the Rangers patch on the left. He looked at Saunders, who was leaning against the far bulkhead, his feet crossed and stuck out into the aisle. He seemed to be asleep.

"Rangers and Commandos."

"Yes, sir."

"You appear to be excellent soldiers."

Dunn didn't say anything for a long moment. They *were* excellent soldiers. They'd broken into a Nazi castle and stolen a field marshal and recaptured an American cipher machine.

They'd brought along the castle commandant who'd they untied and let go outside the C-47. Not a valuable enough catch. They'd wiped out the SS garrison guarding the castle. And had suffered only one casualty, Wickham's right bicep. The slug had torn a hole through and through. Martelli had bandaged it already, but it was going to be awhile before Wickham had full use of it again.

"Just doing our job, sir." Dunn got up and returned to his seat.

He stretched out like Saunders, thinking of Pamela, as he tended to do when he'd finished, survived, yet another mission. He was looking forward to seeing her, touching her, kissing her. Thoughts of the baby made him smile. He opened his eyes and looked at Glockner, who he guessed to be in his late forties. Curious, he got up again and sat down next to the field marshal.

"Are you married, sir?"

"I am."

"Your wife, she is safe?"

"Yes, thank you."

"Any kids?"

Glockner looked away and said, "Just a girl now."

Dunn touched the man on the shoulder. "Sorry."

"Me, too."

Dunn changed seats again. If he had a son, would he want him to follow in his army footsteps, liked Colonel Kenton's boy was doing at West Point? What would the world be like in eighteen years when his son would be old enough to decide on his own? Dunn shook his head. The year 1963 seemed so far away.

Chapter 44

SS Headquarters
Former residence of the Mayor
Preveza, Greece
2 October, 0742 Hours, Athens time

SS Captain Bertram Deichmann finished his morning coffee and admired the sun from his kitchen, the mayor's kitchen. It had been a particularly glorious sunrise, a beautiful red. If he'd been a member of the German Navy he would have known the saying, 'red sun at morning, sailor take warning.' Whether that knowledge would have saved his life is a question for the ages. As it was, he heard a commotion at the front of the large house.

Unconcerned, he set his coffee cup down, got up and walked toward the living room and the front door, where the noise originated. His first clue that something was amiss appeared in the form of his personal SS bodyguard falling backward through the open front door, the back of his black uniform shiny, as if it were wet. The second clue arrived when a tall, slender Greek stepped into view with a huge handgun with a suppressor on the end of it. He fired into the face of the downed guard. He immediately changed aim.

Deichmann recognized the Greek man as Colonel Doukas, whose picture he'd seen often. He stared down the barrel of the gun for a split second and then pivoted and ran back toward the kitchen. He didn't quite make it.

Another Greek who he had indeed seen before and in this very house, Stelios Pavlou, barred his way. He also held a large suppressed handgun. It was aimed at his face.

Deichmann grabbed for his own gun.

Pavlou shot him in the shoulder.

Deichmann screamed and grabbed his shoulder with his left hand, his face a mask of pain.

"You can't do this!" he shouted in Greek. "I am an SS captain. You'll die for this."

By this time, Doukas had moved up behind Deichmann. He rammed his gun into the man's kidney.

"Into the kitchen," Doukas said.

Deichmann walked into the kitchen, having to pass by Pavlou who refused to move out of the way.

"Be seated."

Deichmann sat down at the same chair from which he'd admired the sunrise. It suddenly didn't seem as beautiful.

Pavlou stepped in front of the captain, and sat down across the table from him, his gun aimed at the captain's chest.

"Get me something for this wound. You will pay for this,"

"No. And no. You deserve nothing," Pavlou said. "You threatened to ruin my family, my daughters and my wife, and then kill them all. You deserve to die."

Deichmann thought fast. "I wouldn't have done anything to your family. I just needed to give you some incentive to work with me. Perhaps we could strike a deal?"

Pavlou smiled a shark's smile. "What kind of deal?"

"A nice house to start. You can have this one."

Doukas, who was still standing behind Deichmann, lowered his gun and laughed out loud. Pavlou joined in.

"You make a good joke," Pavlou said.

"No, no, not a joke. You can have this house. And I have money."

Pavlou stopped laughing. "Money?" He glanced up at Colonel Doukas. "Money?" He looked back into Deichmann's blue eyes. "Money you've stolen like you've stolen this house?"

Deichmann said nothing.

"I tell you what," Pavlou began. "I'll take this house."

Deichmann's expression turned hopeful. Maybe he'd get out of this.

"And I'll give it back to the mayor and his family."

Deichmann's face turned red. "You can't do this."

"We are doing it, you piece of shit," Doukas spat. "You cost me twenty men!"

Deichmann's expression switched to defiant. "If you kill me, my men will hunt you down. They'll do to both of your families exactly what I told you before. They'll kill you both and a hundred more Greek mongrels just like you. They'll wipe out this city."

Doukas walked around the table so Deichmann could see his face. "Big threats from a man facing two guns." He looked at Pavlou. "Perhaps we should continue this elsewhere."

"Where do you have in mind, Colonel?" Pavlou asked.

"One of our larger, deeper caves." He stared at Deichmann.

"You're going to torture me? You can't do that. That's against the Geneva Convention."

Doukas laughed. "You're seriously claiming rights under a convention you yourself have shown no inclination of following while you've been in Greece? You are disgusting. As for torturing you, no. We are not barbarians like you."

"You can't kill me. Someone will find out and everything I said will come true."

Doukas stepped close to the captain and patted him on the head, like a child.

"Oh, Captain, that presupposes that they find your body. Remember the cave I mentioned?"

Urine trickled onto the floor beneath the captain.

Pavlou laughed.

Chapter 45

The Berghof
Berchtesgaden, Bavaria, Germany
2 October, 1605 Hours, Berlin time

Eva Braun, a lithe, athletic blonde, sat on the patio overlooking the Bavarian Alps reading a romantic novel. Her black Scottish Terriers, Negus and Stasi, lay beside her legs that were crossed and stretched out on the chaise lounge. She wore tan slacks and a waist length coat to battle the cool mountain air. She held a cigarette in her right hand. The patio was the only place Hitler allowed anyone to smoke because he despised it.

Hitler was seated nearby reading reports on the army's condition on both fronts. He was frowning. His beloved German Shephard, Blondi, lay on all fours next to him, her chin on her front paws. Hitler's left hand dangled and he absentmindedly stroked her fur.

Stasi suddenly jumped up, staring off in the distance, and wagging her tail. She barked a couple of times at some real or imagined threat, perhaps a bird flying too close.

Hitler glanced at his mistress. "Calm your *handfeger*, my dear."

He always referred to them as hand brushes, which annoyed Eva each and every time.

Braun didn't reply, but said something softly to Stasi, who lay back down.

Hitler had left Hohenstein Castle abruptly, but not for the reasons most people believed, which was to simply change up his plans to reduce the dangers of another assassination attempt. Instead, his reason was that he wanted to see Eva. Berchtesgaden was only seven miles from the castle across the German-Austrian border and the flight had taken mere minutes. He'd been able to spend the rest of the wee hours of the morning with her before retiring to his own bed at five a.m. She'd been delighted to see him and spent her time with him making jokes and laughing at his.

Hitler loved the Berghof. He'd designed and decorated it himself, and why not, he was a great architect! Playing host to many guests, he'd personally greeted a select few on the steps, including Benito Mussolini and infamously, Neville Chamberlain. In July 1940, the Berghof Conference took place. This was where he first brought up the "Russian Problem," which, of course, led to the sneak attack on 22 June 1941, *Operation Barbarossa*. It also led to the humiliation of the German Army at the hands of the Russians, a supposedly inferior race.

Heinrich Himmler and Martin Bormann were somewhere inside the house working on things under their realm.

Hitler stopped reading long enough to lift his gaze to the mountains in the distance. He adored the view and congratulated himself on selecting such a perfect place for vacations and pleasant times.

Martin Bormann suddenly appeared on the patio, his face wearing an expression of shock. He scurried over to Hitler's chair and said, *"Mein Führer."*

Hitler looked up. "What is it, Bormann, that has you in such disarray?"

"I bring bad news from Colonel Neubart at Castle Hohenstein." Hitler said nothing, so he continued, "Your newest field marshal, Glockner, has been kidnapped by British and Americans Commandos. Most of the castle's SS guards were killed in the cowardly attack. The SIGABA machine was stolen from us, as well."

Hitler stared at his secretary in silence, but his mind was a turmoil of thoughts: who to blame, who to punish, what to do next without the brilliant Glockner, what to do without the cipher machine. That would have made such a difference! Why can no one excel at their job?

"The commandant made the report?" he asked, finally.

"Yes, he was kidnapped, but left behind when the Commandos escaped in an airplane."

"Left behind?"

"Yes. His aide, an SS Major Seiler, has also disappeared. We believe he was a spy."

"Have someone from the Berlin Gestapo office arrest the commandant, interrogate him to the fullest. Then shoot him."

"*Jawohl, Mein Führer.* What of the *Abwehr* man, Juhnke?"

"He allowed the most important find of the intelligence war to slip from his hands. Same as the commandant. I want them both dead by this time tomorrow."

"*Jawohl, Mein Führer.*" Bormann hesitated.

"What is it, Bormann?"

"What of the SS failure? They allowed a spy to be in the same room as you, *Mein Führer!* You may have been the original target!"

"I will speak with Himmler, you may sure. As for the other, I had a feeling something was not right at dinner, thus the reason we left early."

Bormann didn't even bat an eye at the obvious lie. *"Jawohl, Mein Führer."* Bormann left to make the necessary phone call to Heinrich Müller, the head of the Gestapo.

Hitler again gazed out at the beautiful vista before him.

Eva, who had overheard the conversation because it interrupted her precious reading time, asked, "Is everything all right?"

Without taking his eyes of the mountains, he replied, "No, my dear. Nothing is all right. It seems I must singlehandedly solve every problem the Fatherland faces. No one else is capable of getting things done." He looked down at his German Shephard. "Blondi is the only living creature I can depend on."

Braun immediately pouted, and said, "And me."

"And you, of course, my dear."

Chapter 46

St. Louis Insurance Company Building
St. Louis, Missouri
3 October, 12:15 P.M. U.S. Central time

Gertrude's instructor, Mr. Jones, said, "That's all for our morning session. Let's break for lunch and be back here at one o'clock."

The class rose and Jones left the classroom, leaving the door open. Gertrude hadn't even realized how much time had passed since seven thirty a.m. when class had started. The window blinds remained closed the whole time and there was no clock in the room. Jones had sent word to everyone the night before to leave their watches in their rooms. The morning session began with an overview of the Office of Strategic Services, its two-year-old history, who its boss was, Colonel "Wild" Bill Donovan, and their place in the organization.

Jones gave exactly zero information on himself, or on Mr. Smith and Miss Brown. He did explain that the St. Louis Insurance Company building was indeed owned by that company, which was listed with the insurance commission of the state of Missouri, and that people could buy insurance if they came into the building. However, everyone in the building actually worked for the OSS.

The rest of the morning had been devoted to learning new skills, which included Morse code. That had turned out to be fun for Gertrude and she memorized all of it very quickly.

When Gertrude walked through the door, the woman she had dealt with by pinching her shoulder muscle was waiting for her. However, the woman had a smile of contrition on her face.

"Could I please talk to you?"

Gertrude examined the woman. She was shorter than herself by several inches. Her hair was light brown and she had an upturned nose that gave her a permanent snobbish look. Gertrude wondered if that was another reason she had taken such a dislike to the woman. Not to mention her mean comments on the stairs.

"I suppose so."

"I wanted to apologize for my behavior last night. That's not really the kind of person I am. I was just under too much pressure. I'm so very sorry for calling you names. Would you please forgive me?"

She held out her hand and it looked as if she had tears in her eyes.

In early life, Gertrude had the tendency to take people at face value and to be trusting of them, believing that most people were good at heart. High school had changed that completely. Duplicity seemed to run rampant there, and she'd been hurt, like many others, by the lies of people she'd trusted. So she learned to force people to prove themselves. As she would have to do with this woman.

She shook hands and smiled. "Of course. I understand. It was a tough day." She offered her arm. "Let's go get lunch and we can get to know each other."

The woman said, "Thank you for your kindness. If you don't mind, I'm skipping lunch." She touched her stomach. "Tummy upset today."

Gertrude touched her on the shoulder. "I'm so sorry.

The woman shrugged. "It'll pass."

Gertrude went on to the elevator and when it arrived pressed the button for the third floor where the small cafeteria was located. She entered the cafeteria and got in line behind her classmates. Barbara, the young lady who'd been impressed by her handling of the bully, was last in line. She turned and waved at Gertrude, who smiled. They made it through the line and found seats at a table occupied by Ralph Emerson, her partner from the day before, and another man by the name of Jim Hooper.

"Isn't this exciting?" asked Barbara. "We're going to work in Washington, D.C."

"Well, that's what they say now. It could change, I bet you," Gertrude said.

"Really? Do you think that?" Barbara asked, disappointment heavy in her voice.

"I do. I don't believe everything I hear anymore."

"You're quite the cynic, aren't you," Emerson said.

"Afraid so. Guess who wanted to apologize to me?"

"The bully," they all said in unison.

Gertrude laughed. "How did you know?"

"We are code breakers, you know. Logic and all that stuff. Besides, she's the only one who acted weird yesterday."

"Yes, about that," Gertrude started.

They all glanced at her in surprise.

"What?" asked Barbara.

"It might be best to be careful what you say around her."

"Why?" Emerson wanted to know.

"She came across as sincere just a bit ago, but something wasn't quite right. Not sure what it was." She had a perplexed expression. "So just a word of warning and to repeat: be careful what you say around her."

The three classmates nodded and Barbara said, "Okay. We'll be careful, right guys?"

"Yes," replied both men.

The woman entered Mr. Smith's office on the fifth floor and sat down in front of his Spartan desk.

"How'd it go with Miss Dunn?" he asked.

The woman spoke in her normal voice, which was with a cultured British accent. "She accepted the apology pretty quickly. I think your assessment is probably on target. She didn't trust me, but went along with it just the same. I think she thinks I'm up to something."

Smith chuckled. "Well you *are* up to something."

The woman grinned. "So I am. I know it's early days, but I think she would make a terrific candidate to come for training at Bermuda Station, rather than complete all of her training here. She wouldn't take anything from anyone, and she's smart enough to do the work. I say we should challenge her more and more each day with puzzle problems and difficult personal interactions. We can reassess after one week. I want to find her limits."

"Without getting pinched, I'd say."

"Or punched, which is probably more likely."

"Well, you're the boss in this case, Ma'am."

She rose to her feet and said in perfect Midwestern American English, "Yeah, you betcha, I'm the boss!"

Chapter 47

Colonel Kenton's office
Camp Barton Stacey
3 October, 1830 Hours, London time

The meeting was late in the day because Colonel Jenkins had unexpectedly been called to London for a day-long meeting. Two colonels, two lieutenants, and two sergeants were gathered in Colonel Kenton's office for the post-mission debriefing. Colonel Jenkins sat to Kenton's left while Lieutenant Mallory, Saunders, Dunn, and Lieutenant Adams formed a semicircle around Kenton's desk. Everyone had a lit cigarette either in their mouth or hand, and it wouldn't be much longer before a bluish haze filled the room.

Dunn and Saunders had arrived at the camp during late evening the day before, the same long, long day of the attack on the castle. The flights from Austria to Italy—where Dunn and his men recovered their original weapons, and Dunn thought Jonesy hugged his rifle again—and Italy to Hampstead Airbase were long and exhausting, even though the men all tried sleeping. After getting their men situated in the barracks, they'd both reported in to their commanders, and then sacked out themselves for twelve hours. Dunn and Cross met with Kenton earlier in the day. Their assessment report was that the Greeks really hadn't needed their help. Kenton had made a note of it and said he and Lieutenant Adams would vet the missions more carefully in the future. He apologized, but Dunn and Cross both said there was no way to know. Besides someday they could tell their grandkids they'd been to Greece!

Dunn had called Pamela to tell her he was back safe and that he'd probably be home late the next night.

Saunders had called Sadie, who had moved from her parents' home in Cheshunt to a small, but nice flat a few blocks south of the Star & Garter in Andover. When he'd said he was okay, she'd detected something in his voice in the way only a spouse can.

"What's wrong, Mac?"

"Nothing."

"Best tell me."

Saunders hemmed and hawed around a full minute and she'd said sternly, "You better tell me what happened you bloody Cockney!"

Seeing as how she'd never used the word 'bloody' before gave Mac a new view into her anger.

"I lost five men. Five good men."

"Oh, Mac. That's awful. I knew something had happened. You simply must learn to tell me these things. It'll be better for you if you do. What happened?"

"Could I . . . could we wait until I can see you?"

"Yes, darling, yes, of course. When?"

He'd replied the same as Dunn saying it would be the next evening.

"I'll start, gentlemen, as I have an update on Field Marshal Glockner. He's been sent to Trent Park for interrogation and long term custody." Colonel Rupert Jenkins looked tired from the day, his eyes were bloodshot from the fatigue.

Trent Park was a monstrous brick house in North London, about ten miles from the center of the capital. In 1939 the British War Office requisitioned Trent Park for MI6. Starting in May, 1942, the house was used solely for captured German high ranking officers, especially generals. The entire house and grounds were bugged with listening devices. The generals had no idea and loosened their tongues in the company of their countrymen. It seemed the generals were actually enjoying their time there. MI6 learned plenty of valuable secrets.

"Did Marston make it back to wherever he was supposed to be?" Jenkins asked Saunders.

"Aye. As far I know. A car picked him up at Hampstead and drove him away. He seemed pleased with how things turned out. We were pretty surprised to run into him there, I have to say. We ended up entering the castle through a secret passageway he'd accidentally discovered. Made things a lot easier."

Jenkins said, "None of us knew who our resource was. He's likely being debriefed by his own people. May already be finished." Jenkins' face brightened. "Capturing Rommel's replacement is an intelligence and military coup, I must say. Happiness in your success goes to the highest level. Our boss, General Smythe, is having a citation typed up for commendations for all involved. I expect it to be approved all the way up."

Saunders started to say something, but Jenkins held up a hand. "I know, Saunders. I took care of it." His face turned serious as he spoke to Saunders. "I insisted that we include the five men we lost: Arthur Garner, Francis Handford, George Mills, Edward Redington, and Bernard Thurston."

The silence in the room after he stopped talking was like a drape, smothering everything under it. Everyone seemed to need a long moment of quiet to remember the fallen men. Each man bowed his head without being told to. Saunders said a prayer in a low voice, and when he finished, the other five soldiers said, "Amen," and raised their heads.

Jenkins cleared his throat to indicate it was time to move on. "As happy as the higher ups are about the field marshal, they are equally unhappy about missing Hitler, Himmler, and Bormann. I explained what they already know, that Hitler is a paranoid little bugger, who often changes his travel arrangements at the last second. We did our best and he got away, but it's to be no reflection on us. In the end, they agreed, and said they'd write up their end of things that way. I said wasn't that mighty keen of them considering it's going to be the exact same thing that Secret

Services will conclude. So, all in all, we did really well. That's all I have."

Kenton went next. "I handed off the cipher machine that Marston rescued and gave to Dunn. The Signal Corps officer was beside himself at getting it back. So a 'well done' goes out for that.

"There's discussion concerning bombing Hohenstein Castle to prevent it from being used anymore as an SS official meeting place." He looked at the men around him one by one, then asked, "Any reason not to?"

No one said anything, but Saunders was thinking of the construction of the castle, the age, the secrets it might someday yield to a group of persistent historians. He recalled Marston's favorite portrait, that of a Lady Adelaide. When Marston had stared at her for a long moment, Saunders had stopped just long enough to take in her beauty.

"Colonel, I think we might want to rethink that. It's over five hundred years old. It's important historically. But even better, isn't it worth something knowing where the SS are going to be? If they continue having their precious little secret meetings there?" He grinned and his red handlebar mustache twitched. He shrugged. "We could always make an encore entrance."

Kenton and Jenkins chuckled.

"I like your thinking." Kenton said, while Jenkins nodded vigorously. "I'll pass it along."

"What's next for us, Colonel Jenkins?" Saunders asked.

Jenkins eyed Saunders briefly. "Make sure you and your men talk with a chaplain if you feel the need. You and your men take two days off. Go to London together or separately, I don't care. Try to relax."

"Replacements?"

"I'll work on that. Don't you worry about it."

"Yes, sir. We'll take care of the men's belongings and I'll write the letters. Will you want to see them?"

Jenkins held up a hand. "No need. I know you'll do a fine job on them."

Kenton spoke to Dunn. "Same goes for you and your men, take two days, go where it suits you. I do know you're still short two men. Working on it."

"Thank you, sir. Got another mission lined up?"

Kenton shrugged. "Yes, as always, but it can wait until you return."

"Yes, sir."

Everyone stood up at once and they shook hands all around. Eventually, salutes were given and returned, and Dunn and Saunders left the office.

As Dunn and Saunders were about to go their separate ways, Dunn asked, "You guys gonna be in your barracks for a bit?"

"Aye. I'm going to fill the men in on the debriefing. That'll take a while, plus the packing up of the men's belongings."

"We're going to stop by, just for a few minutes. That okay?"

"Yes."

"Fifteen minutes."

"See you then."

Fifteen minutes later on the dot, Dunn and his men entered Saunders' barracks. Each of Dunn's men carried two clinking paper bags, except Wickham, who had his right arm in a sling, and carried only one. The men handed out the bags to the British Commandos who were in the middle of packing up the dead men's stuff. The barracks seemed overly empty.

"We won't take much of your time, gentlemen. Won't you open your bag and your bottles? We'd like to make a toast to your lost men," Dunn said. He stood next to Saunders and Barltrop.

The Brits opened their beer bottles and held them up. Everyone closed in forming a tight circle of thirteen men.

"To our fallen friends: Arthur, Francis, George, Edward, and Bernard!" Dunn said.

Commandos and Rangers clinked their bottles together and drank the toast.

Saunders cleared his throat. "Raise your bottles to our Yank friends who came to help us without so much as blinking their eyes. Thank you, lads."

Dunn and the other Americans nodded solemnly. Bottles clinked and more beer was swallowed.

The men moved around, still carrying their beer. Conversations started up across nationalities as it always did when these men got together.

After a while, Dunn checked his watch. No way he wanted to overstay their welcome. "Gentlemen, time to leave our friends alone."

Everyone said goodbye, and the Americans left.

Saunders watched his four men, his only survivors, as they continued going through their friends' things, keeping an eye out for items that might cause embarrassment or pain to the man's family.

The vision of the C-47 exploding behind him, killing his five men plus the three crewmen, and two extra pilots came to him suddenly. He left the main room and went into his tiny office, closed the door, and sat down in his desk chair. He opened a drawer and pulled out a letter pad. Pulling one sheet from the pad, he grasped his fountain pen and leaned over the paper. In surprisingly neat handwriting for someone with massive hands, he started.

Dear Mr. and Mrs. Garner,

I am so sorry to have to tell you that your son, my friend, Arthur, was killed in action on 1 October 1944. Your son was bravely doing his job, defending others . . .

When he finished the one-page letter he leaned back, putting the pen back in its folder. He took a deep breath to gather himself. He had to swallow hard a couple of times to keep his sorrow in check. He had four more to do. After that, he could let go.

Chapter 48

Green Park, North quadrant
Near Buckingham Palace
4 October, 1118 Hours

Neil Marston, wearing civilian clothes—black slacks, white shirt, and a Burberry coat and a derby hat for the chill—for the first time in over a month, walked down one of the many paved paths that crisscrossed the park near the palace. He walked briskly even though he had no particular place to go. He just needed to unwind after the grueling impersonation of an SS officer. A lot of people were out, but they seemed to move much slower than he and he passed by many.

Eventually, he found himself in front of the Victoria Memorial. It was at the end of The Mall. It had been designed and sculpted by Sir Thomas Brock. It was unveiled in 1911, just a few years before the Great War, although it wasn't completely finished until 1924. He marched up the steps and gazed at the gilded bronze Winged Victory. She stood on a globe with an outstretched right arm. Morning sunlight glinted off the polished bronze.

Marston wondered what memorials there would be after the war was over.

He turned around to leave.

And saw her.

She was gliding up the same steps, her upraised face looking at Winged Victory. Her blond hair flowed behind her in the autumn breeze. Her blue eyes seemed intense . . . and kind. She wore a blue dress and an unbuttoned light tan coat. Around her throat lay a silver necklace. He thought of Lady Adelaide.

She reached the top step, glancing down to be sure of her footing, and then noticed the handsome blond man watching her. She smiled.

Marston was rooted to his spot. He saw the smile and his heart jumped. He managed a smile in return and her eyes flicked away to the sculpture, but back to him immediately.

She was about to pass him.

He suddenly realized this was THE MOMENT.

Taking a step toward her, he said, "Hello. My name's Neil."

She stopped and said, "Hello, Neil. I'm Anne." Her voice was smooth and low. He loved it immediately. She held out her hand.

Neil took her hand and said, "I'm very pleased to meet you. Might I join you?"

Anne smiled again, but this time just a corner of her lips turned up, as if she knew something funny he did not.

"I would really like that."

He offered her his arm and she slipped her hand through.

Chapter 49

Anchor Bankside Pub
On the south bank of the Thames, London
4 October, 1632 Hours

The Anchor Bankside Pub dated back to Shakespearean times and a tavern of some sort had occupied the spot for 800 consecutive years. A brick two-story building, the window and door frames were painted the same red as found on the phone boxes. Six people, good friends, sat around a large table outside with a river view. From there, they could see the dome of St. Paul's Cathedral just a half mile away to the northwest.

Each couple sat together, Tom Dunn and Pamela, Mac Saunders and Sadie, and the unmarried pair, Steve Barltrop and Kathy Rosemond, who was Sadie's cousin. She worked for the Royal Navy's Staff Department in London, and since it was a weeknight, everyone agreed to go to her. They'd taken the train from Andover and a taxi from the station to the pub, where they found her already waiting by the front door.

October twilight was settling in and the last of the sun's rays struck St. Paul's, and the cathedral was in shadow. Everyone wore jackets to stave off the chill in the air. The men nursed a beer each, and the women had glasses of white wine, except for Pamela who stayed with tea again. She had no proof, but the idea of consuming alcohol or smoking while pregnant just struck her as wrong for the baby.

"It's good to get away from things, don't you think?" Sadie asked the group, but she was really talking to Saunders. He glanced at her and nodded.

"It sure is," Dunn said.

They talked a while and the waiter brought dinner. The men had splurged for steaks, which cost a fortune, with chips as trimmings. Saunders asked for the house steak sauce, and everyone else agreed that would suit them. Except for Dunn. He asked for catsup. The waiter, surprised but smooth, just nodded.

When the dinner sauces arrived, everyone watched Dunn. He shook the catsup bottle, after first making sure the lid was screwed on tight, and poured a hefty portion on his plate, between the steak and the chips. He peppered everything, and then cut off a piece of the steak. He dipped it in the catsup, the red sauce forming a large drip that never fell before Dunn shoveled the bite into his mouth.

The others around the table seemed to shudder simultaneously, but they got busy with their own meals. Still looking down at his plate, Dunn smiled to himself. Some things were just too much fun.

In between bites, conversation took place.

"Kathy and I have a small announcement," Barltrop said as he grasped her hand. She smiled at him.

Sadie and Pamela shot Kathy hopeful glances, but Steve said, "No, not that. We've just agreed to go steady."

Sadie and Pamela couldn't hide their disappointment, they were sure marriage was in the works, even if it had only been short time.

"Congratulations, both of you," Saunders said.

"I'm happy for you both," Sadie said.

"We are, too," Pamela said, grasping Dunn by the arm.

"Thank you, all," replied Kathy and Barltrop.

Dunn looked at his British friends, both male and female and a question came to mind. He turned to Pamela, leaning close. "Would you consider living here?"

Pamela frowned. They'd discussed this many times and always came to the same conclusion: they'd live in the States, either Cedar Rapids or Chicago. "What makes you ask that?"

Dunn waved an all-encompassing hand. "I like London. We have good friends, and your family would be close by. It's just a thought."

"Right. Well, let's keep that in the back of our minds." Pamela thought Dunn might be reacting to Saunders' and Barltrop's troubles, the loss of so many men. Perhaps he felt he needed to be here for them. When Tom had told her about the deaths of five men, fear struck at her heart. It could have easily been Tom, or his men. "We'll see where we are in a few months, okay?"

Dunn took another bite of catsup-laden steak, and talked around the food. "Sure. That's fine."

"How are you feeling lately, Pamela?" Sadie asked. Everyone at the table knew of her pregnancy fright while in France working as a nurse.

"I feel good most days. A little morning sickness, but it's really not too bad. Biscuits seem to help."

"Are you hoping for one or the other in particular?" Kathy asked.

"No. Whatever God sees fit to give us is fine with us. However, Tom is convinced it's a boy, so we'll see."

That led to a discussion of names and Pamela said, "If it's a boy, he'll be Thomas Percy Dunn, Jr. Percy after my late brother. The girls' list is a little long right now and we're keeping that to ourselves."

"Can't pry that out of you?" Barltrop asked with a grin.

Pamela smiled and shook her head.

When dinner was over, Dunn snatched the check from Saunders' hand and kept it away from Barltrop's grasping fingers. He laid down enough money to cover it plus a good tip, and put a steak sauce bottle on top to keep the wind from blowing it away. They got up and walked over to the wall separating them from the street running alongside the pub. The river was on the other side of the street. Dunn opened a small metal gate and they walked over to the railing above the river. The couples arranged a space of several yards between them for privacy. Each couple stood close together, arms around each other's waists, and leaned against the rail. Soft conversation was lost in the breeze.

A few boats chugged their way downriver to the east.

Sadie pulled her hand from Saunders' waist and turned him so they faced each other. She put a small hand against his cheek. "Are you okay, Mac?"

Saunders took a deep breath. He glanced out at the river, at the cathedral, and back at Sadie. "I will be, I think." They embraced each other and Saunders said, "When I'm with you, I feel all right."

Sadie squeezed tighter and pressed her head against his massive chest. She could hear his heartbeat. She smiled.

"I think I've fallen for you, Kathy," Barltrop confessed as he looked into her hazel eyes.

Kathy nodded. "I thought as much." She sighed. "Me too. Must be love at first sight, huh?"

Barltrop grinned. "Must be."

Pamela put her head against Dunn's shoulder. "I'm very, very happy, Tom."

Dunn put a finger under her chin and lifted. She met him half way and they kissed.

"I am, too."

Author's Notes

The story idea for this book came from nowhere, when I wasn't looking. For that tiny idea to become a book required help from my wife and my oft-mentioned friend, Steve Barltrop. The idea was simply to plop the guys down and breach a castle. The problem was: why? Enter my wife who suggested a brilliant German general, a new Hitler favorite, that we came to know as Ludwig Glockner. As for Greece, I've been planning on sending Dunn there for several years and finally got the opportunity. Chatting with Steve helped finalize what the book became.

Hohenstein Castle is fictional, but is based loosely on castle pictures I found. The name translates to High Stone. The interior layout is all made up, as is the history attributed to the King of Austria and his fictional cousin. Arundel Castle (http://www.arundelcastle.org/) is real as is the history mentioned about it.

Marston's plot to kill Hitler has basis in fact. The British developed a plan named Operation Foxley (https://en.wikipedia.org/wiki/Operation_Foxley), which called for a sniper to kill Hitler on his daily walk from the Berghof to the *Teehaus*. The arrival of the Abwehr fellow, Juhnke, with a SIGABA machine (http://cryptomuseum.com/crypto/usa/sigaba/index.htm) made for a little extra story tension. The secret tunnel was just too much fun to pass up. How can you have a castle story and not have a secret passageway?

Gertrude's developing and continuing OSS story line is too interesting and fun to leave out. My FIRST READERS, and I, really like her feistiness and strength. The idea of making her a codebreaker seemed a logical thing to do with her math skills, and oh, Steve Barltrop brought it up, as well as Bermuda Station – stay tuned. Here's a letter usage frequency chart (https://www.math.cornell.edu/~mec/2003-2004/cryptography/subs/frequencies.html) like she used to solve the substitution cipher problem. To see a real OSS ID badge (Allen Dulles), go to page 19 of this CIA history document (https://www.cia.gov/library/publications/intelligence-history/oss-catalogue/OSS%20catalogue.pdf). Her training location in St. Louis is totally fiction as is the insurance company. The St. Louis Union Station (https://en.wikipedia.org/wiki/Union_Station (St._Louis)) is a beautiful place, although I'm partial to the Kansas City Union Station (https://en.wikipedia.org/wiki/Kansas_City_Union_Station).

Since our heroes all went through the Commando School at Achnacarry House (http://www.secretscotland.org.uk/index.php/Secrets/Achnacarry House), I thought it was about time to give you a link. Here's one to West Point (http://www.usma.edu/wphistory/SitePages/Home.aspx) as well.

The Greek Resistance (https://en.wikipedia.org/wiki/Greek_Resistance) was made up of several different groups. I selected the two most prominent. The items Pamela read to the patients are real. The 27 September 1944 *Stars & Stripes* article about Arnhem (*Operation Market Garden*) is accurate. Go to (https://starsandstripes.newspaperarchive.com/london-stars-and-stripes/1944-09-27) and scroll to the bottom of the page. You'll find the text in very light font. The St. Louis Cards and Cubs records are accurate, taken right from MLB.com's 1944 standings. The Zane Grey book info is accurate, as is the Agatha Christie Poirot book Dunn's mom is reading at home.

Here's the 1,200 meter high Mount Stavrota (http://www.greece.com/photos/destinations/Ionian_Islands/Lefkada/Village/Agios_Ilias/Greece,_Ionian_Islands,_Lefkas_Is._(Lefkada)_-_The_top_of_Mount_Stavrota_(1182_m.)/38190196) in Greece that Doukas climbed as a youth. Hitler was primarily a vegetarian, but he had one weakness, the liver dumplings. Read more about it here: Hitler's vegetarianism and Liver Dumplings (https://en.wikipedia.org/wiki/Adolf_Hitler_and_vegetarianism). Hitler really was known for changing his schedule at the last second. It saved his life at least once. Hitler's Berghof (https://en.wikipedia.org/wiki/Berghof_(residence)) was located in extreme southeastern Germany and on my fictional map, the castle is only seven miles from it. Eva Braun really did have two Scottish Terriers named Negus and Stasi (http://scottishterriernews.com/2011/03/der-fuhrer-pets-eva-brauns-scottish-terriers.html). Hitler called them *handfeger*, meaning hand brush.

The submarine on which Dunn traveled to and from Greece was real: HMS Torbay (http://uboat.net/allies/warships/ship/3498.html).

Saunders losing half his squad in a split second upset some of my FIRST READERS. I wasn't very happy about it either, but this is war.

Marston's walk around Green Park and eventual arrival at Victoria Memorial (https://en.wikipedia.org/wiki/Victoria_Memorial,_London) was a late add to the story, perhaps after edit three or so. It seemed only fitting that he meet someone as beautiful as Lady Adelaide.

The Anchor Bankside Pub (https://en.wikipedia.org/wiki/Anchor_Bankside) is real and has red (today anyway) window and door frames. The outdoor seating where the three couples had dinner is fictional as is their ability to see St. Paul's Cathedral (https://en.wikipedia.org/wiki/St_Paul's_Cathedral) from there.

My wife discovered a really interesting article in October 2016 that will be the basis for Sgt. Dunn number eight. Think of someplace brutally cold, no, not Antarctica, the other one.

I really would love to hear from you. Please email me at sgtdunnnovel@yahoo.com. You can also sign up for my infrequent newsletters so you'll be among the first to know when something new is coming.

RM
Iowa
February 2017

Please consider following me on my blog and or Twitter to get up-to-date info on what's happening with upcoming books.

www.ronnmunsterman.com
http://ronnonwriting.blogspot.com/
https://twitter.com/RonnMunsterman
@ronnmunsterman

The Sgt. Dunn Photo Gallery for each
book: http://www.pinterest.com/ronn_munsterman/

About The Author

Ronn Munsterman is the author of seven Sgt. Dunn novels. His lifelong fascination with World War II history led to the writing of the Sgt. Dunn novels.

He loves baseball, and as a native of Kansas City, Missouri, has rooted for the Royals since their beginning in 1969. He and his family jumped for joy when the 2015 Royals won the World Series. Other interests include reading, some more or less selective television watching, movies, listening to music, and playing and coaching chess.

Munsterman is a volunteer chess coach each school year for elementary- through high school-aged students, and also provides private lessons. He authored a book on teaching chess: *Chess Handbook for Parents and Coaches*, available on Amazon.com.

Munsterman retired from his "day job" in December 2015. In the latter half of his career he worked as an Information Technology professional. His new "day job" fulfills his dream: to be a full-time writer.

He lives in Iowa with his wife, and enjoys spending time with the family.

Munsterman is currently busy at work on the eighth Sgt. Dunn novel.

RONN MUNSTERMAN